NEITHER

NEITHER: AN UNEMOTIONAL PERSPECTIVE

Copyright © 2023 by Grey Izilein.

ISBN

9 781257 630448

1

IN THE BEGINNING

Corporate wars are not my usual setting; I am an instinct-driven predator; I went for blood. But here there were rules. You had to stab your enemy only in the back and smile and be civil about it. But I don't care. I am the butterfly effect's hybrid, leaning on complex situations to thrive. Today would be it! The day everything starts to play out.

Choosing the driver had not been easy, but I finally found Hakim, and he was thrice what I'd hoped for. He had a twin who had a spotless record. He'd been willing to take the fall if anything came up. I didn't tell him what could come up, and he hadn't asked. The money sent the message.

Hakim arrived with the car, a Bayerische Motoren Werke 2042-TZX whose engine sound told you it wasn't a toy. The car was like hers, seal-black, with the same licence plates.

Hakim had followed the plan accordingly. All events had to seem random. The other part involved getting some minor information, which hadn't been hard. We had hacked her driver's phone. After that, all her calls and routines had been monitored carefully. Nothing was left to chance. Her driver picked her up by 5:00 pm and took her straight home, except on Thursdays when she stopped to get some fruit. Today was a Thursday.

I stared as she walked past. She was admirable, really. It's a pity she would be caught in the crossfire of this spiteful retribution. I looked outside and continued playing *Elevate* on my phone. For someone as rich as her, she was hard-working. And it drove her father mad that she worked in a bank, wearing a skirt and refusing her hijab.

I had sent a text masked as her to her driver, telling him not to worry, that she was going on a date, and hoped he wouldn't tell on her. It was part of the protocol that backed up the stories of those who would suffer the consequences of my actions. Currently, the driver was heavily drugged. He would only be too grateful not to have been the one to disappoint her. It was almost spiritual how I cared for the unfortunate ones who would take the fall for this plan.

She walked toward the door, and the driver waved to the security guard. I didn't understand why her driver did that every day, but I wasn't making the mistake of leaving that detail out. I had drilled Hakim on every single bit.

She took her face mask off as usual before going into the car. The engine started, and the vehicle thundered away. I left the bank immediately, following them closely, giving them about a street's distance, with my GPS showing me where they went.

At our designated spot, Hakim parked the car, and I parked behind him. His mask was still on as a preventive measure. When he opened the back door, she was knocked out. The smell of chloroform still oozed from the AC vent of the car.

"You know what to do."

Hakim nodded, switched the licence plates, and proceeded to flush the smell out while I fumbled with a body bag. He then helped me put an oxygen mask on her face while I rolled her up into the bag. At the same time, the submarine floated to the surface in the distance; perfect timing. I put my mask on and dived with the bag into the water.

***

Jason Levine had stage four cancer and would be dead in three months. He said he was born to do this. No one would miss him except for a two-year-old son whose mother didn't want to see him. All he asked for was for his son to be looked after until he finished college.

We placed her in the room, and I turned to give her one last look. She looked lovely as she slept.

Jason stood behind me, peering over my shoulder at her. I reminded him again to take good care of her and to treat her nicely. The fact that she was in our keep did not mean her rights should be violated. She was not the problem, just the equal sign in the equation.

I swam out of the river and got out of my swimming trunks. We watched the sub sink again and disappear into the toxic water. No one would look for her here. People don't come here anymore.

I dressed up, and Hakim drove away. He would drop the car off at a car wash and thank the company with cakes and drinks for making this car available to his friend on his wedding day.

There had been a wedding, and a similar car with the same licence plates, driven by Hakim's twin, had been there. He had taken lots of pictures too.

I drove into town and took a turn onto the street that led to the high-class people of society. The rest of the plan involved an unreasonably long wait.

***

Nigeria, Year 2057

Harlequin looked down on the slums of Lagos from the glass walls of the presidential office. Who would have thought that things would turn out this way after the second civil war of 2029?

Quaran Jared had saved the country from anarchy by stepping up to be president. He was the one who had devised the new electoral system, and all had been well after he'd stepped down. There had been relative peace for a long time, but now it seemed the peace was exhausted.

Harlequin continued to gaze down at the city. Things weren't as bad as they used to be. But it was starting all over again, and that was how it had begun in the first republic. It had to end, and that could be done only through sacrifice. People were dying out there. And it wasn't a religious war; this was a political campaign.

The knock at the door interrupted him. "Come in."

The door opened, and his secretary poked her head in to tell him that everything was ready.

He thanked her; she blushed and shut the door. He looked at his watch; the time was 11:59:54. He reached into the drawer of his desk and pulled out the gun. Looking at the safety again one last time, he took a deep breath.

His watch beeped. It was 12:00 p.m. on a lovely Saturday afternoon. He must be crazy, but this was the only way. Or was it? He didn't know anymore. He put the gun to his head, closed his eyes, and pulled the trigger.

New Nawari District,

Abu Dis, Palestine.

When he walked into the tent, the atmosphere became quiet. The colourful curtains that had been swaying in sync with the movement of the wind seemed to stop. The beaded door started to clatter and jangle, and everyone turned to look at him.

The woman on the floor stretched her hand. She looked to be in her early forties, but ears don't lie; she was well into her fifties. It was like looking at a human banana. You knew it was ripe, but it still held some blotches of questionable green.

"Come," she said.

He hesitated, and she noticed that he was waiting for the others to leave.

"Shoo! Jal avree! The whole lot of you."

Her voice had a bellow in it, like that of a bullfrog. He sure knew how to land in strange places.

After a lot of shuffling and ruffling, the men left, leaving them in silence. He had not moved.

"Come," she said again. He edged forward.

"Closer," he went close until the tips of his shoes rested on the edge of her mat. He had enough respect not to put his feet on the mat until he was told to.

"Sit."

He sat down on the mat, crossing his legs in front of him. The place was, to say the very least, sinister. Bat wings hung from the top of the tent, and a row of animal heads was on both sides of the leather-based structure. Fox heads, deer heads, rabbit heads, shrew heads, hedgehog heads, lion heads… this was Dexter's lab.

A pot shimmered at the end of the tent. It could be filled with human toes. He curled his feet and pulled them close. Shadows seemed to flit around the room.

She threw a knife behind her, and it landed with a clatter among other metal. He nearly shrieked. She gave him an unabashed gaze, noticing his general hesitance.

"Don't be afraid," she said soothingly and adjusted her frail body. In her gown, she looked like a cigarette. He smiled and looked down at the floor.

She opened her woody palms and stretched them toward him. He laid his palms on hers. When he did, her face, which had been almost welcoming, changed into a mask of horror. Her wistful gaze turned grim.

"What happened to your brother?"

What? "I came to ask about my future," he spoke in light tones, trying not to upset her. Whatever she had seen was not his fault.

"You have no future without him. His shadows are your saviours, and yet he is everyone's darkness."

He wanted to say something, but she sprang from the mat, and he sprang up to face her, mostly out of fear. He didn't want his toes in that pot, whatever it contained.

"He is the greatest of you all, and yet surely, I see unfailingly that he will fall by the hand of God. There is something impure about him. His future is shielded by divine will, masked by the face of a great evil."

He wanted to remind her that she was supposed to be saying things about him and not his brother, whenbrother when a bloodcurdling scream from outside cut him short. He looked at the fortune teller, who walked past him to the door of the tent. She opened it, and he followed.

"Acolo el este." A girl said, pointing at him. "El a ucis-o; i-am vazut facand-o," she yelled in tears.

'This doesn't sound good,' he thought.

"He killed her." An angry man, pointing at him, was saying to another who had just joined.

"Was that what she said?" He laughed. "Be assured, I do not have the guts to kill anyone."

He turned with a laugh to face the ghicitoare so she could help explain to them that they were insane. He turned to see her lying on the ground in a spreading pool of blood, her face twisted in horror. Her throat had been slit, and she looked to the sky with open eyes that did not see. So much for wanting to see into the future.

"I didn't kill her!"

He wanted to raise his hands to explain when he saw that they were covered in blood. This was no time for astonishment. The people were gathering; his heart was pounding, and his mouth was dry. He couldn't understand what had happened. His mind was displaced, so to speak.

The people were coming closer and seemed to be approaching him with caution. These Gipsies would never spare him. They would butcher him and put his toes in that pot.

He felt dizzy, and he was sweating. Who wouldn't? He looked longingly at the road. The people were advancing, and everyone was taking up something to tackle him with. There was no talking it out with these people.

He chose the nobler and life-lengthening option. He turned to the road and ran with all his might.

He had no plan; he just knew that he had to run, and he had to do it fast enough to prevent being lynched by Gipsies. They might curse him, but he was prepared to deal with it. He had come with questions, and now he was running for his life. What a trip! "Christ!"

There was another community up ahead. This part of town belonged to the Arabs. Oh! An estate. He passed the sign without catching his breath. His pursuers were close behind, and he was already getting tired. That was when he saw the school. Its green gate had a Muslim sign on it.

He knew that the Gipsies and Muslims here didn't get along. For him, the symbol represented an escape. The gate was open, and he slowed down so as not to attract any attention, even though no one was watching.

His clothes got caught in the gate, but luckily, no one was there. He heard the chant of students rhyming some poems and the sounds of teachers explaining theories and giving unnecessary information to students. He saw a tap running and proceeded to wash his hands.

His pursuers had passed; it seems they had a blood feud with the Muslims and assumed he knew about it. He was wondering what part of the school he was in when he heard a female voice calling to him.

"Pssttt…"

He turned to see a lady from the window of a classroom signalling him to come. He told himself that this was a bad turn of events.

It was the right of a running man to be a self-imposed pessimist. He went to the door of the classroom, where she was waiting, and gave her a dashing smile.

"Mr, would you be kind enough to stand over here?" She pointed to the front of the board. It was a hall full of giggling girls who seemed to be having a good day.

He complied and tried to stay composed. She put on a spotlight; it seemed to intensify his guilt, guilt that he did not deserve.

"Would you mind taking off your shirt now?" Before he could answer, she started to unbutton his shirt. The class was quiet.

"This is the rib cage." The lady pointed a stick at his body, tapping on his rib cage.

He felt exposed, showing his body off to a class of half-witted high school students. The hell was wrong with this lady?

She finished her practical demonstration and asked the children to thank him. They chorused a satisfying "thank you, sir." He smiled and bowed. He wanted to take his leave, but she whispered that he wait, and so he did.

He sat in the back row of the class in his blue shirt and his brown Chelsea skin boots, an African who didn't look anything like a man with a Black heritage. He was tall and huge, 6 feet 5 to be precise; most people exaggerated his height. He was muscular and looked strong, but didn't have the fighting face that came with a man of his physique. The first impression you got after looking at him was that he got bored easily.

Twenty minutes later, she dismissed the class and wagged her finger at him. He grudgingly followed her up a flight of stairs. He was tired. But it was better than being dead.

When she opened her office, the cold air that blasted his face made him remember that he hadn't eaten anything today. He went in, and she closed the office door, locking it behind her. She looked at him with a withering stare for a while. There was an awkward silence which he did not intend to break. After about a minute of studying him, she picked up the phone that was on her table. He moved swiftly, his first instinct being to stop her from making a call that could put him in danger. She dropped the phone. "I see you have something you need to tell me."

"You should let me go," he said.

She shook her head. "You're my visitor and my specimen."

He forced a smile. "I see that my options are limited."

She moved like a phantom from the other side of the table to stand in front of him. "You can call me Denise."

***

As a child, he had never left the residence in daylight; as an adult, he had no desire to, but they were at war, and he had to fight. The compound was vast, and he roamed freely. No one knew that the Quinns had another son.

The twins were known throughout the country and internationally for their wit and humour. They were the bolts that kept the peace in Taraba State between the various classes. They didn't discriminate, and they didn't show off or demean themselves. But he was different.

The sun shone so hot today that he felt he'd burn. When instinct warned him that trouble was on the way, he was right. Why was he thinking these thoughts again? *'Positive thoughts… think positive thoughts. As if an apology of soliloquies will redeem you.'* His mind was tearing him apart from the inside. *'Just shut up!'* He wanted to scream, but they would say he was going mad.

He stood at the edge of the pool and looked at his reflection. He was supposed to be prepared because life was unpredictable. He wanted to dive in, to drown the voices in his head. The older he got, the more intense they became. Unlike before, he had grown accustomed to their voices. Now he knew their names, and ambition talked the loudest. *'I am the penultimate.'*

"You are nothing! I am your master; you will listen to me," he muttered.

How much self-control did he need to attain? But to what would he attain and to what extent? He had his fears and wished they were normal human fears. He would not allow his mind to rule over him. *'So why am I always right?'* But that wasn't what he wanted to know today.

He unbuttoned the sleeves of his white shirt, took it off, and dropped it on the chair. He knelt to look into its face. The water called to him. He put his hand on the water and touched the surface. The ripple spread, just like the events that would soon take place. He spoke to the water: "You are not me; I am not the one."

His father watched from the window of the library. "The boy will be alright." The doctor told him in consoling tones.

***

Bala Sarki, the Sultan, was not just one of the richest men in Nigeria. He had ranked as the third richest man in Africa twice in a row and the fourth richest Black man in the world, with all his assets still a mystery to prying eyes.

Sarki was ruthless beyond common comprehension. Coming from a wealthy background, he had not fought for his wealth, but it seemed he had paid a huge price to keep it, and that included the loss of his conscience.

He had eight wives and as many concubines as he wished to invite in. The walls of his house were a contemporary representation of the glorious castles of old. His house, built deep into the earth and high into the sky, covered at least 3% of the entirety of Taraba state. While his estate made it a full 10%.

But the truth was in no way exposed. Sarki had his assets underground. Because right under the house was a treasure hold of uranium and diamonds, which was why he didn't reside in Sokoto, the seat of the Caliphate.

Sarki had shares and holdings in all major businesses around the world. He was a corporate germ, owning whatever he touched, except for what the Quinns held. Their estate stretched across the border into Cameroon, and the country didn't mind. They had a separate section under international law that legally and unambiguously bound them to both nations.

The greater part of his reserve was in Quinn territory. They were sitting on a treasure that would last fifty generations. But they refused to use their uranium or sell it to him; yet they were equal in wealth to him, and it made him constipated at night.

Two days ago, he had ordered a hit on one of the Quinn boys. The boy had travelled to the Palestinian region. He had been referred by a friend who told him that the land held the last true seer. He was curious, as the brothers usually are, and had embarked on the journey, meeting another friend on the plane, a strategically placed friend who had slipped some mescaline into the drink he carried in his backpack. He had taken two gulps before the plane landed and another when he came down. They had parted ways, but she had followed him to complete the job. He had been oblivious to the death of the seer and had dragged her body out with him, under the hypnotic suggestion of the voice in his head, all of which he would forget when the drug cleared. When the dread of people coming to kill him became stronger than the drug's control over him, he somehow snapped back to consciousness, and the killer's plan spun out of control.

Harlequin was his next target. He would wipe the whole bloody family out. He had proposed partnerships and terms—anything to get his hands on their land, but the Quinns were a proud family.

He spat and looked down the height of his castle to the other part of the city, where their mansion stood. He found it insulting that the whole town loved them. Not because they were wealthy or philanthropists, but because of who they were.

His thoughts were interrupted by the messenger who came up to meet him. "Kun gama?" He asked.

The messenger knelt, and he felt his heart sink. How was it that these people couldn't plan the death of a mere boy? He raised his hand, but the messenger wasn't quite done.

"Harlequin ya rasu."

He was taken aback. This made everything better. "Sun che wai assassination ne. Wasu kuma wai ya dauka rai da hannun shi."

It didn't matter. Sarki felt immense happiness flood his soul. "By Allah, it is a blessed day indeed," he was still feeling grateful when the second messenger found him and, with panting breath, delivered his message.

In a rage, Sarki flung the messenger over the rail, down the tower. He turned to the other messenger, who was trying to sneak away. "Who has my daughter? Who would dare to kidnap my daughter?" The dogari didn't reply. No one knew.

Sarki stared across town at the Quinns' estate. A convoy was going into the estate. Their sadness made his pain a lot less hurtful. He smacked his lips and rushed into the house. The people who took his daughter… What effrontery! They would surely pay.

***

When Nadia awoke, she had a slight headache. She couldn't remember anything, except that she had become drowsy sometime after the car started moving. She looked around her room. Everything was in place, but where was Maryam?

"Maryam," she called.

Jason came over and slid open the slit on the door. That was when she saw that the door had bars in it and the wood was a cover. He smiled and looked at her. She wondered what a man was doing opening her door to look in on her without her permission. He must be another ill-mannered worker.

"Fetch my maid," she hissed. "And did my father change the doors again? So typical."

He smiled at her. The sheer arrogance of royalty.

"Are you mute, deaf or just stupid?" she asked, standing up.

"No," he said. "I can't fetch your maid, and your dad didn't change the door. But I hope you find your stay convenient, princess. You have been kidnapped."

He was surprised at her reaction. She kept silent and sat back on the bed, folding her hands. Then, after a moment, she asked in the politest tone, "Can I have some water, please?"

2

THE MASTERMIND

"Stop! Stop it! Stop it right now! I said, "STOP!" He shot out of bed, drawing deep breaths. He had been drowning in his sleep and was now drenched in sweat despite the chilly weather. He had been sleeping with his face toward the ceiling, which always led to a nightmare; there had been no exceptions.

The room looked unfamiliar as he touched the wet bedsheets, drenched in sweat. He knew he wouldn't be able to sleep anymore tonight, not after this. It was another night where he would have to stay awake and listen to his thoughts. He hated these thoughts that were slowly becoming him. He didn't bother checking the time; it was always 2 a.m., the time of nightmares.

The nightmares were not ordinary, but he always said he was fine to avoid therapy. What good would that do him? The night was calm and serene, yet there was something diabolical about the scenery, as if something was trying to speak to him. He wished he were strong enough to listen.

The dream was like the rest: a wrecked car beside the road, a river running red with blood, full of voices calling his name, beckoning him to come in and help. He had jumped in, only to drown. Even in his nightmares, he was compulsive.

He looked outside the window. A rabbit scurried out of a bush, and he watched it for a moment. It looked happy, as if it had no worries, and then it ran off. He strained his neck to see; the darkness didn't bother him, as he was used to waking up in low light. He saw a fox sniffing in the bushes and smiled as another one came out with the rabbit in its jaws. He loved predators. Tomorrow, everyone would wake up oblivious to all of this.

He sat in the bed with his back against the wall. It felt safer; that was where he fought everything off best. He wondered if he should pray; for a sceptic, he was convinced that God existed, some might say out of personal experience. He pondered on things until he finally fell asleep, curled up like a cat with his back against the wall.

He woke up at 5 a.m., wondering what would have happened if he had fallen into the hole he was slipping into.

Dr Kendrick kept telling him that they were just nightmares, so then why had he never had a good dream? He said a prayer in his mind as he got out of bed.

He always slept in the clothes he had on; pyjamas were for children. His palms were shaking as he went to stand in front of the mirror. He believed that self-reflection involved real self-reflection. Only a lost cause would stand in front of the mirror, look into their eyes, and lie to their soul. Staring in the mirror also helped him master his composure; he could see the deceit in his own eyes when he practised the machinations he had planned.

He made sure that even he couldn't read his emotions, so his face or looks would never betray him. "Today I will smile, and everything will be alright."

When he went down to the dining hall at 7, he flashed his brightest smile and sat opposite his parents and the good doctor.

"Good morning, Father, Mother, Dr."

***

Merceides and Denise waited with watchful expectancy for nightfall before leaving the school. She was now a murderer's accomplice. Merceides had told her everything, but that didn't mean he was yet exonerated by the law.

Her old pickup van was helpful transport; thank God it was only rusty in the back where he was crouching. When the car finally came to a stop, he unpacked himself with licentious caution, thinking they would be in front of a small house on the side of an open street. He was in awe when he beheld an estate that stretched far beyond his sight.

He asked with stunned curiosity if it was her place. She nodded and wagged him on.

They went in through the main door. There were no guards, butlers, or maids—just the two of them in an echoing mansion. It felt like home, except that his house was modestly full. They went up, taking the stairs, and at the third storey, she opened a door. From the decor, he need not ask if it was her room. What he wanted to ask was why she drove a beat-up, broken-down van instead of something classier, like one of the Bentleys parked outside.

"Where are all the guards?"

"You want to make sure no one is watching when you murder me?" She giggled.

He settled into the moment and stood in the middle of the room. She laughed and pointed to a camera hidden so cleverly in the ceiling you wouldn't notice it. She told him to feel comfortable; it was switched off.

He sat on the sofa and observed the room. It was girly, but anything was better than a gipsy tent. "Who are you, really?"

"You're in my room, and that's what you want to know?"

"Before anything else."

"I knew you were Bae."

He told her to quit the show for a stage and be forward. She sat on the bed and took her shoes off. "I know who you are, Merceides. Almost everyone knows of your family, especially you two, the twin brothers who went into the presidential games and came out in a tie, the first of its kind. And then you stepped down for your brother to be president," she looked at him. "People may be cowed, but I know a good plan when I see one."

"By that sequitur, you're convinced you are clever."

"If I am right."

"So who are you? Seeing I have to query you again before you answer me."

"I'm Denise," she said and laughed. "I'm Denise Emerson, Omar."

Mercedes' eyes cleared, as with the utmost respect, he told her that he knew her father.

"Everyone does," she said nonchalantly.

"But he doesn't have a child."

"He didn't want anyone to know."

They talked for a while before she switched the topic back to him and asked what he intended to do now. He told her that he would return home to Nigeria in disguise. She was immediately enthusiastic, asking him if she could come. She had never been to her father's country. He asked if her father would agree, but she laughed and told him that her father didn't care. He had no objections; she had saved his life. If she wanted to visit Nigeria, so be it.

***

Emerson was a powerful man. He was almost as powerful as the brother who had taken his birthright, but he held no grudge, and it was the truth. He detested power, but that was a lie. It had been almost 12 years since he was last seen in the country. He had watched his brother grow powerful under his guidance. Behind every powerful man was a Luca Brasi, or, in his Sarki's case, an Einstein. No one knew that he was the brains behind his brother's success. Outwardly, they appeared distant, but it was a ploy. They were a most deadly alliance that only a few people knew about. A few did not include the Quinns, which was all that was necessary.

Years ago, in high school, four friends, Emerson, Quinn, Sarki, and Aaira, had formed a pact to look out for each other and to rise to power with the sole aim of making their country a better place. But the cookie had crumbled.

In the university, Sarki had become obsessed with obtaining power. Emerson had fallen in love with Aaira, and so had Quinn. And while Quinn was from the middle class without any rich family legacy to help him hold up, Aaira was the daughter of a rich industrialist, and his lowly status was not her concern. She had declined Emerson's proposal and married Quinn with her father's blessing. With his brains and his wife's encouragement, Quinn had built the most envious empire out of nothing. It was why the poor referred to him as *Aladdin* because they believed that he had a genie. But the truth was that Quinn was always more intelligent than he ever let on, and not even his wife knew the true extent of his intelligence.

After their marriage, the couple had a blessing of twins, and then Aaira was unable to conceive anymore. This she had made public, so no one knew when the family's other child was born.

When their last son was born, the first peculiarity they noticed was that his eyes were greenish-blue. It was discovered quite early, luckily, that he suffered from osteogenesis imperfecta. But something else sealed his fate for the worse. Their son had the most unique of all blood types: the

RH null. Fearing for his sake, they never let him outside the gates, making him a ghost to society. He did not exist, even to his brothers at times.

Emerson, on his part, had taken Aaira's rejection well. He had forfeited his position to his brother and had left the country for Palestine, where he had built his wealth and become his god. He had been enjoying a cool evening breeze some months ago when his brother had asked if he would like to pay back some wrong that had been done to him. He had declined, but with the right pictures of Aaira sent to his phone and how she looked more beautiful after all these years, his desire to bring pain to Quinn had grown intensely, and he had agreed.

He had travelled down to Nigeria, where they had plotted a scheme. Killing the family's heirs was the only move they needed to make. It was a joy to hear that one had died, but now his brother's daughter had been kidnapped. He didn't care for children anyway. God would have given him a son if he wanted to bring him back to the faith.

***

When they flew into the country, Denise was captivated by the beauty of Lagos. She had heard that it was now the most beautiful city in the world, but she didn't believe that an African city could be the site of such developments and that its civilisation would beat that of the Western and Eastern states, or even Dubai.

Merceides saw the bedazzled look on her face and smiled in his pretend sleep. She peered through the window of the plane like a child seeing an elephant for the first time. She had a very lovely face and generous lips. If only…

"Your brother is a genius," she said.

He opened his eyes and glared at her. Of course, everything was about his famous brother. All hail Harlequin!

"No offence, but it'll take a lot of convincing to agree that you were the one who came up with these innovations for him," she mocked.

"No offence taken; that was why I stepped down anyway."

But that was far from the truth. None of them was that smart. Their parents, yes, and they tried their best to keep up with their parents' minds, but they could only stretch their minds to an extent.

They were both eight years older than their youngest brother, the brother they hardly ever saw. It wasn't like he was eager to see any of them. He was cold and hostile and had no emotional expression at all. Like, what was up with him? He was a blank slate with nothing on him to read. Anyone who walked his brother's mind would come out scarred for life. Sometimes he wished the poor thing had died. He used to be so fragile and sick, but as usual, he had not accepted his fate. One limb at a time, he had worked until his fragile bones were used to pressure. No one seeing him would believe that he had any form of illness. Physical, or, as Merceides inferred sometimes, mental.

Eleven years ago, when their family was on the verge of one of the most serious financial crises they had come across, it was his ideas that had pulled them through, as crazy as they had sounded.

Recently, he had told him not to travel far, but as usual, he had scorned the idea, saying it was ridiculous to depend on intuition. Now he was only thankful to be alive. He wondered how high his brother's IQ was. But like a parrot, his brother could only imitate human relations; he could bet that deep down he wasn't as human as the rest of them.

***

"Why have I been kidnapped?"

Levine was ready. He pushed the tray to her; she dropped it on the table, folded her hands and waited for him to reply.

"Your father has been a horrible nuisance to a lot of people in this country."

"And you assume I have been on his good side?"

"That is none of my concern, but I'm sure that he is fond of you, which is all I need to hurt him."

She asked how he had gotten into her room to know how to make a replica. He didn't answer but instead told her that nothing stayed hidden and that the time would come when those whom her father had cheated would be avenged. She tried to explain that she had no idea what her father did, and if she did, there was no way she could dissuade him. He wasn't interested in listening.

"So, how do you intend to kill me? You haven't asked for a ransom, which means you have no interest in money. You look pale, and you have coughed more than twice since we started talking. You're sick, something fatal, like a tumour, cancer… You worked for my father, and you have lung cancer from being in the mines, don't you?"

"How smart! You should have been able to escape by now, or at least figure out the logic behind your kidnapping."

"I don't intend on keeping you entertained."

"You silly, rich, spoilt kids; you come out into the world thinking that you're better than everyone else. You lack manners, even in the simple art of etiquette. And instead of learning how to be nice and kind in society, no. What do you do? You take all your crap, mumble-jumble it into a holistic bunch of nonsense, and dump it on the suffering masses, treating us like bees whose sole purpose on the planet is to do your bidding. You think you're invincible, but you're not. You'll see. The whole lot of you. And damn right, I'm dying of stage-four cancer, not from working in your goddamn mines but because your father wouldn't pay the health insurance that is a part of the contract we signed before we started working for him. He's a corrupt liar. We make carpets for him to walk on and mine gold so that you can have ceramic shoes to put your feet on—or whatever the hell you iPod kids put on your feet these days—you fucking selfie generation! I am not the first or last to suffer this, and it's become a trend for those in power. I might not be able to stop it, but I surely would drag you to hell along with me. After all, I'm going to die soon anyway; what have I got to lose?"

Elzaiya lay on his bed with his hand on his chin, watching the scene from his laptop. Nadia had been there for a day and had made no attempts to escape. She ate when she was given food and bathed when she wanted. The whole room had no windows, so she couldn't see outside.

She had the air of someone born into wealth but also the humility of someone who didn't allow it to get into her head.

It was 9:30 on the second night of her kidnapping. He had told Levine not to bother checking up on her. As he watched her through the day, he noticed that she had not prayed — not on the first day and not today either. Could it be that she didn't believe in God?

After Levine closed the slide, she was composed for a moment. When his steps had receded, she burst into tears. He had been waiting for that to happen. It was normal, but he figured she would have cried on the first day and would be hysterical by now. She was an oddly uncommon personality.

There was a box of clothes in the wardrobe he had made, the type a girl like her never wore; she was supposed to be an example to other women. There was a pink gown among the clothes scattered in the box, along with a pair of black high heels. She picked them up and laid them on the bed for a moment, then turned to stare at the mirror. Her skirt was far below her knees, and her long-sleeved top was a turtleneck. She felt stifled in the clothes that she wore.

For a while, she was undecided, and then she turned on the TV and switched channels, settling on a music channel. They were playing the 'Chainsmokers' *Something Just Like This*. She took the clothes to the dressing room and pulled out the sheets. It might be a habit, or she might have been shy, sceptical or just known that she wasn't alone. For about four minutes, she was out of sight. When she came out into the light, pulling the sheets apart, he sat up, surprised. She didn't look like the girl he had kidnapped. The gown clung like skin to her body as if its survival depended on her wearing it. The pink laced material was perfect for the tone of her skin, and the shoes on her feet were the most beautiful kind of marvellous there could be. Her hair, too, he noticed, was not as black as he thought it should be. But his own eyes were odd; who was he to judge?

She ran her fingers through her chestnut brown hair that lightened at the ends and adored herself in the mirror. There was a set of lipsticks on the table. She was consternated for a while until she finally settled on nude. After applying the lipstick, she went to where the refrigerator stood, smiling when she opened it. There was a can of alcoholic beverages among other drinks. She pulled it out and psssttted it open.

After the first passing of gas, she smelt it and coughed. He smiled. She clamped her nose with her fingers and took a gulp. "So this is your last night on earth thing," he leaned back on the wall and observed her closely.

When the can was finished, the music in sync switched to 'Bastille's' *Quarter Past Midnight*. She dropped the can on the table and started swaying to the music, raising the volume to the highest and dancing to the song.

And so she danced, from one song to the next, until she collapsed exhausted on her bed. And then, crying, half drunk, and fatigued, she fell asleep under his scrutinising eyes.

3

EMERSON, THE VILLAIN

There was no one smarter than Emerson. That was what he told himself, and it was what he sincerely believed. The extent of his messiah complex was beyond outrageous. His favourite book was Ralph W. Emerson's *"Self-Reliance and Other Essays"*. He believed that he was chosen by God to show mankind the right way to live; he was God's elect, the highway sign to man's ascension. So, when Aaira turned him down, he took it to be a divine test, and after a bout of depression and advice from an endearing gang of empty bottles, the lord spoke to him in a vision, telling him that he could be his own lord and saviour if he willed it, because he was born to be divine, and he shouldn't deviate from his path. He had accepted this new self, along with an independence that liberated him from all societal obligations and civil behaviour.

During that period, Emerson had spawned a generation of children, all of whom had died from one illness or another; others had been miscarriages. "Tests", he had called them, after which he had ceased procreating and focused on the gathering of all knowledge.

When Denise, a four-year-old girl with a backpack, came to his house and told him she was his daughter, he didn't ask any questions; he simply found her a room while he waited for her to die. It had occurred to him since then that he was not cut out to father a child.

Emerson was impeccably handsome. His beard was rumoured to sometimes turn bluish-black when he was angry, and his brown eyes complemented his dark brown hair. His mother was an Arabian princess whom his father had fallen in love with and, after much ado, had finally won in a duel, as her intended didn't want to give her up easily. She had come to love him dearly over time. When her first six children, all girls, had died, the sultan had given up hope of his favourite wife giving him a son, so he married another woman, and that same year, both wives gave birth to a son each. Emerson came a month after his brother. This did not change the Sultan's mind about whose son would be his heir.

The two brothers and Quinn had grown up on the same street in Sokoto and had met in school. Quinn and Emerson were the most intelligent students in their class until another girl joined in the second term, stealing their tied position as well as their hearts. Quinn had experienced love at first sight with Aaira, and that had been the discontent Emerson spitefully held against him till today.

Whenever Emerson left the house, he wore a navy-blue suit, even to funerals. "What do they care? Their brains are rotting," he would say.

Aside from his flaws, Emerson was a genius, and it showed in all that he did. His only fault was that he loved to dance. Dancing, in a man, was as effeminate as it gets, and his father had sworn that he would not allow his son to disgrace him with that haram.

So, one night when Emerson had returned from the dancing class he snuck out to, he had been abducted by his father's guards, who under his father's orders had tied him upside down, naked, in a glass cubicle and smeared him with blood. And then in the darkness, they had released a horde of flies that seemed to have been bred for that particular purpose.

He had felt like a corpse. Having a fly buzz in your ear was irritating enough, but having them cover your body, buzzing their way into your nose, ears, and mouth, was more than he could bear.

He was turned over and chained in a cross-like position after the blood and smeared with cow dung. He couldn't remember the rest because he passed out, but when he awoke, he hated dancing with more passion than he had loved it. Or so it seemed, but that was not all. In the horror of that night, his fragile mind had snapped.

It was later discovered that he suffered from depersonalisation and derealisation disorder, along with bipolar tendencies. He never told anyone what his father had done to him, nor was his mother ever aware. And when the sultan had died from a sudden illness, no one took note of the fly on the single splash of blood at the head of the bed.

His mother died shortly after, and with her death, Emerson abdicated the throne to his power-hungry elder brother and left, hoping never to return.

***

The room was soundproof, so Aaira screamed all she wanted. She had married Quinn because she loved him; the sex was an excessive bonus. He laughed and moved up to kiss her lips. She slapped him and tried to push him away, but he held her down. They usually spent hours playing, and play involved a lot of sex.

"I hate you."

He laughed again and proceeded to make her change her opinion. When he kissed her again, she was panting. He ran his fingers through her tresses and kissed her neck.

"I still hate you," she pushed him away and jumped out of the bed.

He pursued her to the end of the room, where she threw a shoe at him.

"Really? You must throw shoes, too? I thought you said you loved that one."

"I hate the person who bought it for me."

He burst out laughing. "Merceides got you that one for Christmas."

"Oh!" She looked at the one in her hand.

He ducked and dived. Caught unawares, they went crashing down onto the wooden floor. The sheet she used to cover her body entangled them both. She kissed him when she rolled over on him. "I won," she pulled the necklace out of her mouth and tied it around her hand.

"How disgusting; is it everything you put in your mouth?"

"You don't object when you're the one," she kissed him again, hair flowing down to cover their faces.

"Are you saying I'm disgusting?"

He wanted to sit up, but she pushed him back with her palm on his chest. For a woman, she was fairly strong. "I thought you liked all of it dirty."

"Hence the trash talk?" He giggled.

"You would know, Trash," she said.

He frowned and hissed. She bent over and forcibly kissed him. She could feel him underneath her. She pulled the sheets aside to let him in. He wanted to say something, but she started to rock back and forth, and soon, in the throes of sexual pleasure, he changed his mind. This had been one of their weekend rites since they had been married.

When they were both lying down exhausted on the floor, she crossed her arms and legs around him. He usually sneaked away when she was sleeping, and she didn't intend for him to go anywhere today.

"You know you have to pretend to be sad, right?" He asked.

She nodded, and her expression turned to one of sadness.

"I didn't say now," he turned away.

"I know, it's just that I'm worried about our son."

"He isn't dead; they'll both be fine soon," he said it with confidence.

"I'm not talking about the twins."

He shifted his gaze to the ceiling. "Elzaiya would be alright," he said, his confidence trailing away.

***

The car swerved into the bush, hitting a tree. The headlights smashed, and all of them woke up with mindful alertness. For a moment, there was silence, and then the conductor shouted, "Who off light?" Even in this critical situation, Machiavelli laughed. He had to keep quiet, though, when he started to feel the other passengers' angry faces glowering at him. They were the only vehicles on the road; well, not technically on the road, but they were the last ones driving down Okene Road, which was notorious for robberies.

There was a pregnant woman in the car, and with the way the driver was behaving, they would not be leaving anytime soon. Also, the accident didn't feel like one, more like an orchestrated incident. This might be a setup; he became afraid and voiced his fears like the average Nigerian.

"Abeg, I wan go piss."

This request on a bus meant that someone else would remember they had to pee, and before long, most or all of the passengers would be on foot around the area where the bus was accidentally parked.

"Nothing do the car. We go soon fix am enter road." The driver said grudgingly.

"Shey na only piss he wan go piss." The man in front said.

"I no know oh." Some women at the back added.

"Brother, come down, me sef wan enter bush," a boy said.

Before long, they were all on the ground while the bus driver tinkered with the engine of the car. Machiavelli observed him closely for a while before concluding that it was a set-up.

There was a girl with whom he had been chatting in the car. She saw him edge into the bush, and she followed, finding him crouched behind a thicket. He seemed startled when she laughingly crouched beside him. "So what are we doing here?"

"Observing," he whispered.

"Why are you whispering?"

"Shhhh…"

"Don't shush me," she said.

"Lower your voice, damn it!"

"Why don't you make me?"

She wasn't taking the situation seriously, and he understood why. She perceived him to be a playboy, and she was right. His demeanour did not liken him to someone who took life seriously. Why not take the opportunity? He wondered.

Without warning, he kissed her. She seemed to have been waiting for it. She hungrily took the kiss and giggled in his mouth. When he pulled back, she attacked his lips and kissed him again. He got the hint.

Machiavelli did not believe in a rigid line of good and evil; he believed that there was a line, but it was squiggly, and each circumstance…

damn it. He didn't need to explain himself; life was short, and every moment counted whichever way the living wanted to count it.

He pulled her gown up and indulged himself. They were just finishing when they heard the first gunshot and people shouting. They trembled with satisfaction and fear and lay crouching in the bush as the shooting and shouting continued.

When the sounds died out, they heard a car drive away with the headlights flashing a little too close to where they hid. For hours, they hid there, not saying a word. It was very early in the morning, after they had dozed off, that she woke up to see that he was gone. She didn't know what to do; she had really liked him and enjoyed his company. Now she didn't know if she should miss him first or check the site of the accident. As it was the only option that involved actual movement, she left to check.

There, lying on the grass, were the mutilated bodies of all the passengers. Their belongings were intact, but body parts were gone—some heads, some hearts, some kidneys, and so on. But this was a massacre, and she knew it.

She would have fainted, but she didn't know what to tell the police when they came, because they would not believe that she'd gone to ease herself or that she didn't know anything about it. After all, she had been with some guy in the bush, and so, with very unsteady legs, she ran.

Elzaiya was the one who named him Machiavelli. There were large tunnels that ran under the Quinns' residence; he had them all mapped out in his mind. Not being able to go out by day, he had started to scout the compound and had discovered this secret passageway, one of which opened at the train station.

He was just four years old, and had his parents known, they would have freaked out and most probably imprisoned him until he was an adult.

He was walking the streets at 2 a.m. that Friday evening when he saw the boy sitting under the streetlight, trying to get some heat from the warmth of the light. He had felt that emotion they termed "pity". After observing it for a while and deciding that it was harmless, he moved closer to inspect it. The boy had awoken, and both had been startled.

"Get away from me!" The boy had yelled.

Elzaiya had observed him like a doctor performing an autopsy.

"Are you deaf?"

He kept on staring at him. He sensed that the child was afraid, but he was curious. He sat down. "Why aren't you in your house?"

"Why aren't you in yours?"

"I sneaked out. What about you? Do you prefer sleeping outside?"

"I don't have a house," the boy said.

"But your daddy must have one."

"I don't have a daddy."

"Oh! Then surely your mum should have–"

"Shut up and leave me alone."

He was concerned as to how a boy his age could not have a house to live in. He did not know what poverty meant or what it felt like to lack something.

"I have a big house. Would you like to sleep at my house?"

The boy had looked at him for a long time, undecided, and then Elzaiya had told him that he had to go. The kid had waved goodbye, and he had left.

The next day, he went out to meet his new friend with some food and a blanket. "I know where your house is." The boy had said.

He smiled. "You followed me."

The boy said yes.

He shared the meal between them. After that and some drinks, they were laughing at the jokes the boy made. Elzaiya found that he preferred the boy to his brothers. They did not understand him most of the time.

"Why are your eyes greenish-blue?" The boy had asked one day as they ate under the streetlight.

"I was born that way," he answered. Then he asked the boy who his parents were.

"I never met any of them, never heard anything about them. I just stay here because, as far as I recall, I've always been around here."

"That's a terrible fate for a child."

"You're not older than I am." The boy had laughed.

"Not physically. But most times I feel I am way beyond my age."

"Let it pass; you'll be alright."

"What's your name?" Elzaiya had asked. They had been night friends for two years, and they hadn't asked each other's names.

"I have no name."

"Today is my birthday. Would you like it to be yours too?"

"Of course." The boy was delighted.

"So make a birthday wish."

"I wish I had a family," the boy had said and had suddenly become sad.

Elzaiya understood. "From now on, your name will be Machiavelli. And since I'm not old enough to be your father, I will be your godfather."

"Who is Machiavelli?"

He'd laughed. "Only one of the most politically dangerous men in history."

"And what is your name?"

"My name is Elzaiya."

They had talked and laughed well into the night, and he had slept on the streets that night. When he sneaked back through the tunnels with Machiavelli behind him, they were both apprehended by his ever-diligent father, who questioned them separately and intensely. And who, after much thought, had decided it was best to keep Machiavelli in the confines of the Quinn castle.

Quinn did not seal the tunnels, nor did he inform his wife of their son's exploits. He only told her that he thought it best if their son had someone his age to keep him company, so he had acquired a boy his age. She had agreed.

Machiavelli then became a part of the family and was Elzaiya's right hand. He had his intelligence, even though he couldn't measure up to it in all aspects, but by constantly being with Elzaiya, he stood well above the twins. Elzaiya's intuition was what he lacked, and so he never failed to listen when Elzaiya gave him a course of action, no matter how stupid.

The car dropped him under their special streetlight, and he stood there for a while, enjoying the night air. Elzaiya might be a genius, but they were crossing dangerous lines. He was still in his thoughts when the tunnel gates clanked.

4

HARLEQUIN IS DEAD?

The gloom he met was not what he had hoped to experience on his return. Because of the mysterious circumstances of his brother's death, the media had been stalled. Two laws allowed the president to resign from his duties as head of state. It was either that he was fatally sick or mentally unstable, or he wanted to, by cunning, kickstart the games. Whichever one it was, whatever happened to the president was the business of the public. They lived in transparent times, but this was a different case.

Merceides was welcomed by a grave atmosphere. His parents were at the dining table, as was Dr Kendrick, with uneaten food in front of them. His mother seemed to have been crying. Denise trailed behind him, awed by the simple sophistication of their mansions.

"Thank God you're alive," his mother rushed to embrace him.

"What happened?" He asked with concern.

"Who is your friend?" Quinn asked as they shook hands like teenagers.

"It's a long story; I'll fill you in after I know what happened."

Elzaiya and Machiavelli watched the happenings from behind the glass of the upper rails that overlooked the dining hall.

"How do you think he will react?" Machiavelli asked.

"A thousand Dollars says his jaw will drop, he will grab the edge of the table, and, trying not to cry, he will storm out."

"In that sequence?"

"Uhum! What do you think he would do?"

"I think he will try to hold it in, but he will cry and tearfully walk out."

"One thousand Dollars?" They both agreed. Elzaiya smiled, and they shook hands.

"Sit down." Quinn was saying.

"Just tell me. What happened? Is something wrong with Harlequin? Cos…" He checked himself and kept silent. There was a visitor, and the existence of their third brother was a secret. "How is Harlequin?"

"Harlequin…" His mother started and burst into tears.

Denise seemed more surprised than Merceides was. He turned to look at her first, and then he held on to the edge of the table so as not to faint. It had been an exhausting three days already.

"Come on! Really?" Machiavelli was not enjoying his reaction.

"Shhh… One more move," Elzaiya raised a finger.

"But I… he was so…" Merceides stammered and swallowed his words, trying to maintain his composure in front of his new friend.

"It will be alright, son." His father said.

"You always say that."

Merceides turned and stormed out of the hall. Denise, with a solemn look on her face, mouthed 'sorry' and ran after him.

"Come on, it's not like you need my money," Machiavelli said to Elzaiya, who had opened his palm.

"Well, then I have a favour to ask."

"I think I have enough money to spare," Machiavelli started to punch into his phone.

"Come on, it's a very small favour," Elzaiya said, pushing the phone aside. "It shouldn't hurt much."

"That's exactly what a pedophile will say. "What is it now?"

Elzaiya whispered something in his ear.

"You know, I don't hear the devil trying to tempt me, and sometimes it scares me to know that it's probably because I'm already living with him."

"Time is running out, Avelli; you'd better hurry before I find it out from somewhere else."

"Yes, Satan," he bowed mockingly.

"You know I love you, son."

"Yes, Abraham, and I go on to become the lamb for sacrifice," Machiavelli jogged down the stairs.

Elzaiya smiled. He'd missed him when he was away. He just hoped the boy didn't put himself in trouble. He was about to turn away when a guard came in. He bowed to the family, and Quinn smiled at him.

Quinn was kind and modest, humble to a unique degree. He did not forget where he had come from, and even though his sons had never experienced poverty, he had taught them the value of humility. He watched his father attend the guard. The man smiled and trotted off toward the east gate.

"What's the matter now?" Aaira asked her husband.

"Some Igbo girl is at the gate looking for Machiavelli."

"Is he around?" Aaira asked excitedly.

"Yes. Why are you so excited?"

"I will excuse myself now." Dr Kendrick bowed.

His parents thanked him and continued their discussion.

"I love the muse being around; he makes Elzaiya happy. Be honest, when do you ever get to see him smile?"

Elzaiya smiled.

"Hmmm." Quinn nodded and picked up an apple. "I'm starving."

"Come here then," Aaira giggled.

"Oh, please!" Elzaiya sighed and averted his eyes as their romance started. There was a knock at the door, and the guard came back in, escorting a girl. She was dishevelled and dirty; she looked like she had been running from something. Elzaiya bent to get a better view of her. In the same instant, Machiavelli joined him.

"Who are you?" Quinn was asking.

"Who is she?" Elzaiya asked.

Machiavelli said it must be some random girl. The girl said that her name was Cairo and fell to the ground in a faint. "Oh!" Machiavelli exclaimed.

"You couldn't zip it and leave it that way, could you? You had to share with whoever wants to drink from your goddamned fountain of youth."

"Don't freak out; I didn't know we would meet again."

"You didn't… Are you even listening to yourself?"

"I'm not as moral as you are; I try my best. We all have our flaws."

"Avelli, I know you do try, but you can't just sleep around with any girl you see. What if you catch something? Did you even for a second stop to think about the consequences before sticking your… Arrgghhh!"

"She wanted me to."

"Is that the best defence for this kind of situation? You would blame your actions on the poor little horny thing?"

"Which of them?"

Elzaiya paused to laugh before proceeding. "You're not even taking me seriously, are you?"

"I am; it's just that you've got very high standards, and I can't measure up to all of them."

"I'm not saying…" He reconsidered. "It's fine."

"I'm sorry," Machiavelli said.

"There is no affordance for bemusement, Avelli, not at this hour."

"I will be focused."

"I trust you; do not disappoint me," Elzaiya said. Machiavelli did not reply. He knew well enough that he was the only person to whom that statement was a bit of advice. To everyone else, it was a threat.

One day, when they were 12, they had been walking around at night; it was just past midnight, and the whole street was dim. They had come upon a gang of four who had stopped them and tried to bully some money out of them. Elzaiya could bear verbal insults, but he couldn't endure being manhandled. These guys had threatened to beat them up, and Machiavelli had stood up to fight them. They beat him up and kicked him over to the kerb.

Elzaiya, who had not spoken or shown any emotion, now spoke calmly, unbothered by what was happening. "Guys, it is sparing that we meet like this on such an evening. To preserve the serenity of this evening and our delicate fragilities, would it not be best if we settled in peace and went our way?"

They had laughed at him, and the leader of the gang, who looked about 18, had approached him and placed his hand on Elzaiya's shoulder. It happened too fast for Machiavelli to structure his explanation correctly. With an eagle's move, Elzaiya swung his hand out from his coat's pocket and smashed the face of his watch into the eye socket of the leader. The glass shattered.

The boy seemed to have been blinded and shrieked in horror as he held his hands to his bleeding face. Elzaiya raised his leg and kicked the boy in the torso. He fell to the ground while the others watched, horrified.

"I tried to talk this away, but you thought you were the owners of the street – sharks out for blood. Well, come on then; try and devour me," he threatened with chilling impudence.

The other boys seemed unsure of what to do, now that their leader was on the ground. Machiavelli, who had stood up, was awestruck. He knew Elzaiya to be gentle and fragile, but this violence was something dark. The Quinns, as he knew, were not violent people. He kept silent, fearing that the rage could turn on him.

There was a bin beside the road, with its aluminium cover lying on the grass. Elzaiya went to it and, picking up the cover, started to clean it with his handkerchief. The gang leader who had stood up now rushed toward him.

With delicious ferocity, Elzaiya turned and swung the edge of the cover into the guy's face. All of them heard the bone breaking and the gasp as the guy clutched his face before crashing down to the pavement. But that wasn't enough. Elzaiya bent and started to scratch at the fallen guy's neck, and, horrified, the others watched as he scratched the boy's skin open, and then, with blood dripping from his nails, he turned to face them.

"Take your friend away," he said fearlessly. "His parents would ask what happened. Tell them that he climbed up a tree and was attacked by a wild cat. He hit his head on the edge of a bin and is only suffering a mild concussion. I hope, for your sakes, that you learn to allow other people to enjoy their evening in peace," he moved away from the body and let them carry their leader away.

He found a tap to wash his hands, and they continued their stroll as if nothing had happened. For a while, none of them spoke, and then Machiavelli asked. "What if you had killed him?"

"I had the intention," he said nonchalantly.

"He is not an animal, he is human."

"So are you, and he could have done the same."

"No, he would not. I wouldn't have let him."

"Hmmm!"

"Is that all you would say? Hmmm!"

Enraged, Elzaiya had turned toward him. "We sally into situations thinking that we have them well under control." The truth, however, is that we can only anticipate under presentiments and scheme into the future with the hope that it favours us well enough to align itself with our ideates, but what if it doesn't? What if we choreograph for all the possible futures there are, and in the end, the future itself restructures itself in ways our slight minds can't even intuit? After all, we are but grains in a labyrinthine hourglass, shifted by the design of agencies pre-eminent to us. And when a grain of sand gathers to a stone to clog the passage of events, the maker cracks the glass, and out we spill: sand, stone, pebble and all. And what will you do then? Being merely dust? Inasmuch as you have no real power. What would you rely on then, if not yourself? A friend, God? An angel or, in the very worst case, your hatred, your fears, enemies, demons or the devil? Something will always rise to abet you if you let it. But let it come from within, and let it be within your grasp to cease; don't you ever for a moment buy into the overhyped chimaera that you, yourself, with your conscious mind, are in control of all your gestures and addresses and how all affairs play out. You can never be certain. You can only seize control and sway where you see you can command it; and if loaned, use it for your advantage to the extent that it doesn't come back to prevail over you."

"She is awake." Dr Kendrick came to meet them outside the room. "And she is asking for a certain Machiavelli," he added with jest.

"Thank you, doctor."

"Will you come with me?" Machiavelli asked Elzaiya.

"Sure." They slipped into the room and closed the door behind them.

She lay on the bed, a bit pale but cleaned up and well-scented. The Quinns sure knew how to change your look. She was beautiful, Machiavelli thought. He had not really looked at her, as he figured he would never see her again. "I didn't know where to go," she said as he sat down on the bed beside her.

"It's alright, we will take care of you."

He took her hand, and she started crying. Machiavelli held her to his body. Elzaiya opened his hands, signifying that he should ask her why she was crying.

"You're safe now, Cairo," he said.

"They killed my uncle and my stepsister," she sobbed. "It wasn't some random killing; they were looking for me," Machiavelli pulled away to clean her eyes and look at her face.

"Who are you?" Elzaiya asked.

"I'm Cairo, an illegitimate child of the Sultan, and I think we are being hunted."

***

Sarki was worried. "What do you mean you can't find my daughter? It's been four days already. No one has received a call asking for a ransom, and nothing has shown up to tell me she's alive or dead. Dan ubansu! Are my people just incompetent or what!" He banged his fist on the table, and Emerson's glass jumped. He had his AirPods in his ear.

"Have you even been listening to me?"

Emerson reduced the volume of the music. "She's just a girl... Maybe you were too hard-handed, and she's decided to weasel out of your grasp for a while; don't overwork yourself."

"You don't care for children; how would you even know enough not to be overworked?"

"Hasn't that been wise of me? Between you and me, look who's having a good time."

"You godforsaken..."

He smiled and increased the volume of the music, drowning his brother out.

He had sent some of his thugs to take another one out. One by one, he would take out the wretched lineage until there was nothing left in the way.

He removed the earpiece and frowned as if in serious thought. "Have you considered the possibility that your daughter might have been abducted by the Quinns?"

Sarki, who had been raging, now turned to his brother. "I thought about it, but not deeply. They are not evil people; they would not kill my daughter."

"A child for a child; it sounds fair to me."

"But I didn't kill their son."

"No, you see, you're getting your tenses all mixed up again." Emerson stood up for the sake of emphasis. "You failed to kill one son and are denying the devoir that comes with killing the other son. So my guess is, they are involved."

Sarki disagreed and then paused as if frozen in a eureka moment.

"What is it?" Emerson asked.

"What if we have another enemy in between? I have more than one enemy; the Quinns are just up on my list."

"That is a go-around, but if that is the case, you don't need me here. The Quinns are my concern, and if you don't intend on getting my revenge and the power you seek, then I'm afraid I am not interested. Have I not already made it clear from times past that your politics is not my thing?"

"Yes, brother, I know." Sarki came to stand with his brother. He was sturdier than Emerson and looked like the typical Hausa man. He was not close to his brother in physical beauty, but that was balanced out by the amount of power he had. With wealth, he was not required to be handsome to be attractive.

"I have no son, and you have no children," he poured some wine and gave his brother a glass.

"I thought the sultan and all Muslims didn't take alcohol?"

"Who told you it was alcoholic?" Sarki smiled. Emerson took a sip. "Oh my!"

Sarki laughed. "As long as it doesn't get out; by the way, it is non-alcoholic as the label says." Emerson shrugged.

"As your only daughter has been kidnapped and you have no son, who will be your heir?"

Sarki was sober. "All the men in our bloodline are dead, save for us. I was hoping that my daughter would get married to a devout man and their son would become the heir."

"A man as devout as you?"

"I know; it sounds a little hypocritical, but can you judge me? I was not meant for this position."

"You can't lie to me, brother; you coveted the position ever since you were a child. You would sit on our father's throne and play king when he was away. You slept with his maids and did as you wished because you assumed it was rightfully yours. I was not going to fight you for the throne and power you hankered after."

"You showed no interest in it, brother. Our father wanted you, the son of his favourite wife, to be his heir, but you wanted to go dancing."

"Am I dancing now?" Emerson glared at his brother.

His gaze was so terrifying. Sarki found himself apologising. "I didn't mean to annoy you," he continued, "I can't have children. It's something we inherited in our bloodline. The fault is mine, just like it is yours. My daughter was a miracle."

"I don't want children. I have no need of them." Emerson said calmly.

"So this is how our bloodline ends?"

"Your wives will conceive," Emerson said with reassured ease.

"Insha Allah," Sarki said.

"Not by his grace, brother, but by our means. We will make them bear, and you will have an heir."

"We?" Sarki wanted to be sure.

"I do not need children," Emerson said. "I will not question if it's mine, just as I've not asked after all these years about the origin of your daughter." Sarki gasped.

"Have you forgotten the past so soon?" Emerson faced him with a weird smile.

***

Elzaiya closed the door behind him so they could talk. Machiavelli would fill him in. It was 11:23 p.m., the house was quiet, and all the lights were turned off or dim. The guards who were awake kept watch in shifts of three. He smiled. If they knew the level of security in the building, they would gladly fall asleep without worry.

He was staring down from the window when the kitchen door opened. It was the girl that his brother had brought home. She should be about a year older.

She wore something like a sari, an Indian-type nightgown that was parted in the middle to show the full extent of her everything. She had black pants on. She held a glass of water, an apple, and a banana. She could have been mistaken for a 20-year-old, but he would not be fooled.

Her body looked like that of an Amazonian princess—not Wonder Woman—but it cut close. She had a very appealing shape, but she wasn't the first beautiful person he'd seen, and somehow, she was just a little bit more beautiful than Cairo. Her complexion was caramel, and he started to wonder why he was comparing her to confectionery. It's been a long time since he'd taken chocolates. He looked at her lips and averted his eyes. This was calling trouble upon himself.

They both looked shocked to meet each other there.

"Aren't you supposed to be asleep?" She asked with authority as if she were a member of the family. He wanted to laugh. Did she mistake him for a guard, the potter, or a common house servant?

"I would soon be on my way, ma'am," he turned to leave.

"Stay right there," she came to where he stood. "Are your parents African?" She asked.

"Yes," he was used to being asked that because of the colour of his eyes and the freckle-like spots scattered on his skin, which were visible from his neck down.

"How old are you?"

"I'm old enough," he said.

She dropped the apple. It rolled down and settled at the edge of the wall. "Go and pick it up, boy."

He normally would not have, but he wanted to know what kind of game she was playing. The apple was resting in the darkest corner of the corridor, and it would take some strong looking to find it, as the lights were off and the moonlight didn't reach that corner. He walked slowly into the darkness and started to grope for it. He found it in the corner. When he turned, she was standing behind him. "You're no servant," she said. "Who are you?"

He swallowed. There was something about this situation that felt like a déjà vu. He kept silent and stared.

She dropped the glass on the ground and started to peel the banana. "You don't smell like a servant, and you certainly don't talk like one," she put the length of the banana in her mouth and pulled it out slowly.

He felt his heart skip.

She giggled and allowed her spit to drizzle down on the banana. "Do you want a bite?"

"No, thank you. I am quite full," he found it hard to talk. His hands were trembling, so he clenched his fists. She took his hand and kissed the back of his palm, then bit lightly on the side.

"Poor thing, I know how full you are," she placed his hand on her breast and moved in to kiss him before he could resist. Her kiss was strangely satisfying. Her lips had no restriction on the amount of hunger she wanted him to satisfy. She tasted like bananas and pushed him deeper into the shadows, literally as well.

He gripped the apple tightly until his palm started to ache. The gown slipped off her back and hung from her elbows. She left his lips for his neck.

"Give in," she breathed into his ear.

When she discovered he was still holding the apple, she pried his fingers off of it and slipped his hand beneath the gown. Her skin on his hands sent him to strange, animalistic places. He squeezed her gently and started to kiss her neck.

"Yes, just do as you please," he let her drop her hands, so the gown fell to the floor. And then he turned her to face the wall.

Normally, he would have questioned the whole situation, but there was a foggy feeling in his head, almost intoxicating, as if he had been here, doing this, at this time, in a past life. If she felt the same way, then certainly they were not in control of what they were doing.

"Make love to me," she murmured. He hoped it did not echo.

"Are you sure?"

"Please," she said this while leaning into his body.

She could feel that he needed her as much as she needed him. She still didn't understand why. When the person who was interested in her was fast asleep in his room, and she liked Merceides, but this person...

She unbelted him and slipped her hand in. Without warning, he turned her around and held her close. His hand was on her breasts, and the other trailed down her legs.

"Please."

"Not today," he replied. She struggled to get away, but he held her tight.

"Breathe," he said coolly. She felt the sweat from his hands trail down her cleavage. She felt strangely comforted by the way he held her.

"Breathe," he said again.

"When will I see you?" she asked. He bent to pick her gown up to put it back on her body.

"Tomorrow morning."

"You can't leave me like this tonight," she complained and held his hand. He picked up the banana from the window where she had kept it and handed it to her. She hissed, and he grinned.

When she picked up the glass, she wanted to ask his name, but then the lights came on at the other end of the corridor, and Merceides' door opened.

"What are you doing up so late?" He rubbed his eyes.

She turned, but there was no one else there. "I was wondering if my dad ever thought about me, if he cared for me as your family does you," she said and drank from the glass.

He came close and stood beside her. "You're a wonderful person. I'm sure he does."

Elzaiya watched through the crack of the door at the far left of the corridor. He closed it silently and buckled his belt. Machiavelli found him scrolling through his phone, muttering, "I think we may have underestimated our foe."

5

EMERSON HAS FAMILY

She couldn't sleep, and neither could he. It was the banana; it wouldn't get out of his head. He kept tossing around, but there was no point in trying to sleep. Seriously, why did she have to do that to the banana? Poor banana. Banana, banana, bana... shut up! Please, just shut up about the banana.

He sat up in bed, glaring into the darkness. He should have just let it happen, shouldn't he? What did he have to lose? Everything, dummy! Where is the separation if you give in to base desires? The superior man and what they chose to do. Unconventional stupidity... the road less travelled. His brother had an upward spike in his feelings for her. What to do? Her presence felt so strong, just like her body was firm. Those soft...

"Get out of my head!"

He lay back down and closed his eyes, but who was he kidding? All he wanted to do right now was just feel that hot breath and...

"What is wrong with me?" He sat up again in a bid to distract himself, but the length in his trousers was not helping. You need to have this. It was telling him. No! I don't. I want it, but I won't do it. It's an unimportant urge.

It was hard to battle with desire. His urges conflicted with his moral values. And on the other hand, constant strife with oneself, even for the sake of idealism, was its own problem. All these things were, in the end, addictions. Now he was just quoting Carl Jung. What did he think? He was thinking about her, and they were not all the right thoughts. Why deny himself this small thing? Wasn't it just a fleeting lust that, once satisfied, will go unpunished? But nothing happens without due consequence. He put his face in his hands and got out of bed to pace in the room. He realised the futility of the action and went to lie back down with his feet touching the floor, wondering what she was thinking about.

Denise tossed and turned for an hour until she couldn't rein in the thoughts anymore. How stupid could she have possibly been? Making a fool of herself to him, whoever he was. What sort of fascination had pulled her toward him? It had been so instinctive that she couldn't help herself. It all felt strange. It was not just his eyes or his manners; it was everything. He was tormenting her from where he was. She had thrown herself at him, thinking she would be the one in charge of the situation, and now here she was, wanting...

Merceides was in the outer room, and her door was bolted shut. She wished for someone to come and quench her thirst. But if it wasn't him, she knew no one could. Each hunger had its food, each twinge its remedy. She slid her gown off and let her hands roam her body as she replayed everything.

She pulled her pants off, so she was totally naked on the bed. With one hand scouting her body, she let her fingers indulge themselves. Closing her eyes to visualise what she wanted, she started to disrupt the peace of the sheets. And forgetting that she was not alone in her home anymore, enjoying the pleasure she gave herself, she moaned aloud, while Merceides lay in his bed, listening, wondering if she was thinking about him.

Sambisa Forest,

3 Months Ago

Bala Sarki walked like a god to his seat among the crowd as they chanted, "Rai'n ka ya da'de' Sarki." Words fit for any king. He smiled and looked down at the crowd. These were his real followers, the covert reason he amassed so much power. They were the tools he would use to clean out the Kafiri scum from society.

"Abokai na…"

The crowd hushed to listen with massive curiosity to what he had to say. Being the sultan, he was to serve as a bridge of peace between the religious factions in the country, but he had a separate agenda. Religion was for the poor; those who were starving were the ones who depended on God for daily bread. His had been sliced and buttered long before he was born. What he was doing was ensuring that the dough and oven never left his house.

In truth, he detested them. All these Almajiris convened, looking to receive alms at the end of the talk. Ignorant children, nothing more than tides looking for someone windy enough to blow them in any direction they choose. They would never know what real power feels like. He almost pitied them, but their lives needed a purpose, and if he gave them none, would his enemies not give that to them for far less than he would?

It was wise to control these stupid elements because, when the time came, real power always fell to the people. And he knew enough to know how many empires had fallen when the people revolted. "Jama'a! Lokaci'n mu ya zo."

Their artillery lay in caskets piled up behind a fortress at the far end of the jungle: explosives, guns, daggers — whatever people needed to kill each other these days. All of them were military-grade weapons. When the time came, they would own this country.

Coming from a long line of religious men, he had watched his father negotiate and keep the peace between the ethnic groups and religious factions in the country. But why should they tolerate what could be eradicated? He had no care about what anyone worshipped, but standing in front of these people today, he had to be a firm believer in the bias that they, the Northerners, were the real owners of the country. If he could use religion as a tool to wipe out the competition, why shouldn't he? It's not like he would be the first evil man in history. All hail Hitler! These people needed a jihad, a cause to make them feel like true believers, and he would give them one.

"We need to take back our country." The interpreter was speaking in another dialect. Not all these men spoke Hausa. How amusing. He did not even know the difference between "bahilache" and "bahaushe".

Unlike the other rallies where he just came to inspire general unrest, he had a real target this time. Even though they were not Northerners, the Quinns were loved by the public. Arden was from the southern oil state but had grown up with the Northerners, who, over time, had come to accept him as their own. Aaira was a Muslim, and even though she went to church and did whatever the hell women did, she never left the Islamic faith, which was a very daring political move.

After their wedding, Aaira had edged her way into politics, finding a seat in Congress, and with time had gained more support after installing some more Muslim women who each bettered their community, respectively. She had resigned to her estate after her children started their university education, and just when everyone thought the Quinns were anti-political, the twins had joined Congress and, six years later, had both run for the presidential seat. Harlequin had won when his twin stepped down, and the people had fallen in love with the sons of Aladdin.

From his first year in office, it was clear that he was a wise choice. Like the coronavirus, he had started small, slum by slum, until the city of Lagos equalled the Western civilisation, and then he had seeped into the Western states and, through diplomacy, had coerced their governors to ensure development at all costs; visible development, he had said.

In no time, the western states were well accounted for, and the east, with their natural zeal to compete, had decided to do better. With his second year in office, he had focused all his strength on building a Northern region that was unlike what the history of the country had ever known, and he was halfway there, but Sarki could not let him. He could not let a Kafiri take the glory that was due him, because if Harlequin accomplished this, the people would slowly realise that civilisation and modernity were not as evil as their teachers taught. Alongside that, all that would be left would be for subsequent presidents to consolidate on what he had started, and God forbid that he comes second after Harlequin in history. A bloody Kafiri; a half-blooded Iyamiri.

The other meetings had been on how to thwart the developmental plans for the North. He smiled and looked down at the people. If only they knew the things they lost by their bombings and violent acts, they would weep and curse him or stone him to death.

"We have to take out the president without inciting a war." The interpreter was saying. "I will thereby choose a select few from the best strategists among you, who will aid me in making this goal a reality. The North belongs to us, and we cannot be ruled by an unbeliever. Our time has come!"

"Lokaci'n mu ya zo." They all chorused back. Sarki waved and stepped down. He was escorted to an inner room by the organisers of the rally. It was there that they decided it was best not just for the president to die but for his brother as well. It was Emerson's idea that he had insinuated. The people were in love with them, and being smart, if one were no more, it would only take a tiny stroke of good luck to stop the other from running for the post. But in the case that they were both eliminated, there would be no one to stand in their way, and then their people would flood the council, and after running for the seat, one of their indigenous sons would be in power to do the bidding of the Sultan as he saw fit for the good of the nation.

In the darkness, a young man, whose face was shrouded like the rest of the zealots, was sent to scout the surrounding area and to keep watch. Finding a safe spot, he brought out a tiny beeping device from within the folds of his cloth and started clicking a message in Morse code.

***

Elzaiya had called the meeting after Merceides left on the adventure he had warned him not to embark on. Harlequin had flown in from Lagos the previous night and thrown a mini party. They were wondering if he would show up early when he came in, all washed up and ready to have a good day. Elzaiya smiled. He had no idea how his day was going to turn out.

After nodding and sharing pleasantries. They all turned their attention to what he had to say. He put his hands on the table and looked at his brother. Honestly, he preferred Harlequin to Merceides. He was a lot more rational and nicer to him. They had even had some good brother moments together.

"We have received some very unsettling information," Elzaiya turned to Machiavelli, who shared, in narration, the contents of his research.

There was silence at the table. "I assume you've already come up with a plan then, brother?" Unlike his twin, he trusted Elzaiya.

"We have a plan," Elzaiya said, "But it might sour you up a bit."

"Try me," Harlequin said.

"How would you like to die?" Elzaiya asked.

Harlequin looked at the greenish-blue eyes that seemed to see into his soul and knew that he was not kidding.

***

Many years ago, when they were just teenagers, Sarki had brought his brother to a building he used as a secret hideout. Here he came to smoke and do any unlawful deed, he didn't want his father to suspect.

The building was an empty military bunker with a lot of rooms that looked like they were built for half of the Nigerian army. It was so large that he dared not walk past the first compartment. They were the only ones who knew about the location, but that was for a while. After sneaking to the place for some years, they stopped being careful, and one day, Quinn, picking up fruits, saw his friends go in through a trapdoor. He hid for a while and watched what they were up to. After some hours, he saw them come out with bottles of booze and cigars, and he knew that this was their getaway. After they left, he went in and assessed the building.

He knew what it was. His father had told him about this bunker, built in case of an unforeseen event. There were three bunkers like this in the regions of the country, but only a few knew where they were or that they existed.

He was awed by the design of the place. It had one entrance, but that wasn't what his father, the renowned engineer, Jacob Quinn, told him. His father had the blueprint, and he had used it to practise complicated designs more than once.

He found twelve trapdoors, with one of them leading into the main town. It was late at night when he finally found one in an uninhabited bush. He never shared the secret with anyone else but Elzaiya.

Elzaiya started designing the compartment Sarki and his brother used the same way he designed the one in the submarine: by making duplicates of everything and making sure nothing could be traced back to him.

"Why do we need the site of a kidnapping when we're not going to use it?" Machiavelli had asked.

Elzaiya had explained that they needed a place that would not be searched so that when Nadia got out and they asked where she was found, she would pinpoint the location, as would her rescuers. That way, no one would guess that she was held underwater—not even her. She'd vanish into thin air and reappear right under their noses.

Now that Harlequin was dead, the next part of the plan involved his funeral. They were to stall his burial for as long as they could, till the rest of the plan fell into place. "What's the other part of the plan?" Aaira had asked.

"We kidnap the Sultan's daughter."

"How does she fit into the whole thing?" Harlequin had asked.

"Your father has lost a son; his friend has lost a daughter," Elzaiya said.

"Yes, and so?" Harlequin did not get how the dots connected.

"Bala Sarki has no son. Whoever marries his daughter will be the interim sultan until their son is born. His daughter is the key to his religious power. Without her, he cannot feel comfortable about the title he loves dearly. So, when she isn't in the picture, he will become desperate. He'll try to keep the news quiet, but we'll spread it just as he'll spread rumours about the president's demise. He will be paranoid, thinking that his power has started to crumble; his fight will lose momentum. This will buy us time to injure him better. When he is desperate, his enemies will start coming for him, but most importantly, so will his allies. And we need to know who supports him so we can know what we are up against. When we want to bring him down, we will go for his friends after his enemies are all on our side. We will then strengthen our political footing, and since we know how he intends to disrupt Harlequin's plans for the North, we would play right into his hands and then change our strategy. Also, we would ask him for the most ridiculous thing."

"Which is?"

"He would want to come to Harlequin's funeral to make sure he's dead. He would want to gloat, so we would show him that we are helpless and then beg him to use his power to protect the only remaining son."

Harlequin nodded. He knew that Elzaiya and his father were hiding something from him, but this was good enough information. He believed that whatever they hid was for his good.

It was morning, and Elzaiya had slept far into the day. His laptop was dead, so he plugged it in and put it on before getting out of bed. Nadia was still asleep. She had slept quite late, too. She seemed to be enjoying herself more than he was.

Today was going to be a good day. Deep down, he felt it would be a very eventful day. As he jogged down the stairs, he wondered what Machiavelli was doing.

Cairo had told them that the Sultan had a son and three daughters outside of marriage. The son had died in a swimming pool when he was 12, and a girl in a car crash. These deaths would have been random except that weeks before their deaths, a man had come to confirm who their father was. He came with a doctor who, after ascertaining their DNA, left. The boy had wanted to travel back to boarding school and had drowned the next day, while the girl, who was on a journey, had had an accident, and no one survived.

Her mother was in the military and had learnt of the children's deaths through a colleague who had traced their origins. She had told her to lie about who her father was whenever she was asked. She had been approached by the same men in school, too, but she had lied. She said her father was a trader who had died sometime after she was born. She had come back from school to find their house broken into.

Her mother had said it wasn't safe and had sent her to stay with her uncle. Things had been fine until her uncle decided to travel, and so they had been on their way, accompanied by her stepsister, until the accident and the killing.

Elzaiya jumped down the last stair to meet the family at the table. Dr Kendrick, Mum, Dad, Merceides, Cairo, and Denise. Her eyes met his, as did everyone else's. He had mastered his emotions too well to let them betray him now. He was walking over to the table when Machiavelli slipped down the stair rail. He stood beside him and flashed a smile as they walked to the table together.

"Boys, you look positively radiant. Have you been up to any mischief lately?" Quinn asked.

"Don't ask questions you don't want answered." His wife said.

Elzaiya pulled a chair opposite Denise, whose lips seemed to have become fuller. She looked like a rose petal in the light of the sun. He did not look at her, but smiled at his brother, who nodded.

Machiavelli, who had sat opposite Cairo, smiled at her. She seemed to have a hard time adjusting without him around. She seemed relieved. He could tell by her smile that it was genuine.

"I have a feeling today will be spectacular, sir," Elzaiya said, looking squarely at Denise.

He and Machiavelli knew enough to be formal when they had visitors.

6

WHO'S IN CONTROL?

With the president out of office, it was the duty of the secretary to handle his affairs and make certain that his agenda was carried out. But she wasn't just his secretary. Navina had a blinding crush on Harlequin, and why not? He was as good as he was handsome. She knew the twins well. She had got to know them during Harlequin's victory party. While his brother was one to rouse, Harlequin was more of a strategist. Unlike other leaders who had dirty secrets and sordid pasts, he was clean, humble, loving, and kind. As if he were born to be president at this time in the country's history.

Sometimes, when they stayed working late into the night, he would buy food and serve her some. He didn't speak much, and he didn't have to; his actions carried a lot of weight. Some nights ago, he had been worried. It had been visible by the way he paced and felt his forehead as if checking for a fever. She had come in to say goodbye, and he had waved her away. She was bothered and asked if everything was okay. He'd just smiled and said it would be fine. With all his transparency, he was a closed book.

At that moment, she had stupidly spilt how she felt, telling him that it was okay to talk to someone because people were willing to listen. He had stared at her blankly until she started to feel stupid, and then, when she turned to go, he had pulled her back and kissed her. Then he apologised, saying he didn't know if it breached the ethics of her religion. She had kissed him back, and flinging his suit aside in the locked office, they had made love, after which he drove her home.

In the morning, she had made him some food, and he asked how she would like to be with him as his… he couldn't seem to finish. She told him that she would have to break a few hearts, but she would love to be his, as he liked it. He had laughed and had given her a golden bracelet, whispering some words in her ears.

At work, he had gone to his office, and she had organised everything as always. This time, he had told her to go over it once more. When she had come in to tell him that it was all ready, he had smiled and nodded.

It was exactly noon when the shot sounded. The Secret Service was already on their way, and he was covered up and rushed away before she could blink. She hadn't heard anything since; she didn't know if her harlequin was alive or dead.

The press was on its way. They were not supposed to have heard about this. Harlequin was not dead yet, she told herself. But the sounds of reporters and cameramen dragging their gear and shoes as they walked to the president's office made her doubt otherwise. There was a knock at the door.

"Come in," she said coolly.

She had moved into the office. She would entertain them in hers. It was a democracy, and they trooped in as she stepped out to meet them, closing the door to the president's office.

They stood with different facial expressions, like a box of emojis—emojis who knew their rights. How the times had changed.

"You have been Harlequin's secretary of state…" One of them spoke.

She answered as honestly as she could without divulging any sensitive information.

"Is it true that the president is dead?" One of them asked amidst the throw of questions. She tried her best to ignore it. But another journalist took it up until they were all asking the same thing.

"Is President Harlequin dead?"

She said it was a question meant for the Secret Service.

"A convoy was reported to have carried a dead body into the Quinns' residence…" Another reporter rattled on. "Since his brother is still alive, as are the other members of the family, shall we not ask to confirm, since it is our right to know if the president is dead?"

"The president was fatally injured in office," she said. "But as to his real state, alive or dead, only the Quinns or the Secret Service can honestly answer. If you intend to know the truth, just like I do, then you should ask them."

She excused herself and left them to their deliberations. When she closed her door to the noise, she broke down, realising that Harlequin might be dead.

Sarki turned the TV off and smiled. Things were looking up.

***

"He isn't wasting time." Quinn entered behind the boys, closing the door to the study.

"As expected," Elzaiya looked at Merceides. He wondered what he could be thinking about.

"What?" Merceides asked when he caught him staring.

"I was wondering if you would like to say something," Elzaiya said.

"They say Harlequin is dead; I believe it's a lie. But even if it were true, I know no details of his death. I returned from a long trip to hear that my brother is dead, and we're moving on like nothing happened?"

Quinn wanted to speak, but Elzaiya had something to say.

"A trip that I warned you not to embark on. Tell us, Merceides the murderer, what did you find out on your trip?"

"What are you getting at?" Merceides stood up.

"Maybe if you tell us everything, we could try to be a lot more specific, too. You travel, and then we hear that a seer has been killed and a fugitive is on the run. The same seer you went to see. And then, you return home; it's too early for someone who wanted a four-month vacation. But you don't come back alone; you drop by with a strange lady — the daughter of our enemy's brother, I hear. The least you could do is respect the fact that we are trying our best to feign cooperation regardless of the circumstances."

Merceides stared at his brother with hostile suspicion. The young man had no fear in his eyes as he stared back at him. There was something in those eyes that was vacant, leering, daring him even to do something. He did not need the seer to tell him that his brother was dangerous.

"Ah! … the seer," he turned from his brother.

"What happened with the seer?" Quinn asked, bringing down the tension.

Machiavelli was tapping impatiently; he wanted to be with Cairo. The girl seemed to have bound him with a spell.

"Her words were disjointed; I couldn't place them."

"When are those seers ever forthright? All they do is flimflam and feed off people's superstitions," Elzaiya scoffed.

"You would think so. But she said some things that made sense."

"So, what did she say?" Machiavelli couldn't mask his impatience. Just like Elzaiya, he didn't get along well with Merceides.

"She asked what happened to my brother; she said there was something impure about him. And then she said we had no future without him. that his shadows are our saviours, and yet he is everyone's darkness. That he is the greatest of us all, but he will fall unfailingly by the hand of God."

"Honestly, I have no interest in the erroneous speeches of booze-sipping fanatics," Elzaiya said. "What happened after that?"

"I think I killed her," Merceides said.

"What?" Quinn pulled at his beard and looked at his other son from the corner of his eye.

"No, you didn't," Machiavelli gibed.

"And how are you sure?" Merceides asked.

"That's because you were drugged," he turned to Merceides. "Dr Kendrick performed a test on the water droplets left in your flask. Luckily, you did not pour it all out, seeing that you were in a hurry. It turns out you were drugged strongly enough to affect your perception of time. It's the manipulation of an old drug for specific effects. You know how doctors are; he's still in the lab trying to create his version of it. Says it's wonderful and all... The point is, you were the target. You were to be lynched. The killer wanted you to think you killed her, and then you were supposed to die from deserved justice."

"And what about the girl, Denise?" Elzaiya asked.

"She was the one who saved me," he told them how she had taken him to her house and decided that they should come back to the country. "By the way, she said her father was around."

"Emerson is in the country?" Quinn's insides soured.

"Yes," Merceides said.

"We have to be careful," Quinn spoke as if in a trance. "There are too many bad omens surrounding Emerson. We should prepare so as not to be caught unawares."

***

During breakfast, they exchanged eye contact. She had come to know that he was someone important to the family. He certainly seemed to have a lot of admiration from all members of the family, except Merceides. So she knew not to ask Merceides about him, so he wouldn't feel jealous.

The older Quinns had been the first to leave the table, followed by the doctor who had told Elzaiya to come see him later. The other guy, whom she did not know, had left with the other girl, and Merceides had told her that he wanted to go talk with his father.

She had told Merceides not to bother trying to keep her company. He had agreed after much persuasion, and she had decided to roam the gardens, hoping to run into this Elzaiya. His light brown skin and tangled, curly hair made him look Arabian.

He wasn't as muscular as the other members of the family, but there was something aside from his physique. A dominance that the others couldn't equal. He had an animal inside that he struggled to control. It was there in the fierceness of his looks, which betrayed a determination to achieve anything he set himself to. He was a boy king.

She found a small house shrouded by trees at the far end of the estate. There was a brook flowing in front of it. Steps were built to form a bridge across it. She climbed up and found the front door open; there was a servant inside.

The maid looked quizzically at her to make sure she wasn't lost.

"Sorry, ma'am, but I don't think you're in the right place," she said.

The maid was about 13 years old.

"And where am I supposed to be?" She asked, surveying the apartment. She liked it. The design was simply artful.

"This is Elzaiya's place." The maid said. "Only he and Machiavelli come here."

"Great," she replied. "Leave! And if you meet him on the way, tell him that he has a visitor." The maid bowed reluctantly and left.

There was a picture half-painted at the far end of the room; the brush was still fresh with paint. It was the picture of a bird swallowing a bird. But from another perspective, it was the face of a man with a moustache growing on his tongue.

She was dazzled by the artistry. On the table beside the painting was a black journal with reflective covers. She opened the book and read the first lines:

"Wherewith that many a man was led by the tides of fate and destiny; he is but a rocking boat cruising delightfully on a violent sea. But to other men, nay, neither. That man wills his way into all things. And if his will be strong, he advances thither."

"I see you've made yourself comfortable," Elzaiya said.

He had come in quietly and was standing behind her.

"May I present you with some caviar too?"

She appeared flushed.

"There's something about you, Denise. Care to tell me what it is?" He moved closer, digging his hands into his pockets.

"Maybe you should tell me. Do I make you grow a moustache on your tongue?"

He laughed.

"I'm not sure if you've noticed, but..."

He reached over, impulsively, and kissed her lips, then asked if she would like to see the rest of the house.

Merceides lay on his bed thinking through the prophecy for the fifth time that day. He wasn't a true believer, but he agreed that sometimes people were directed by greater forces to be able to see visions of the future. And why should that vision be clear? Seeing that every man could as well wake up and take a path not in line with the future foreseen. If a man was shown death in his future and did what he could to avert it, was that not the purpose of that prophecy, to save that man's life? Was it then mere gibberish?

He would meet his dad later to talk things through. He wondered where Denise was and shrugged. Why was he carrying a torch for her? Was it a reverse case of the girl in the tower? She had come to see the country; it didn't mean she was in love with him. He was being sentimental.

He fell asleep with those wandering thoughts.

***

After showing her the garden he had planted and the vines he plucked his grapes from, he showed her the water fountain on the other side, which collected the water from the brook into a small dam, then the engine he had created to serve as an electricity generator powered by the water's flow.

When they got back into the house, it was still noon, and the sun was high and hot. Most people dreaded coming out at this hour, which meant that half the household would be too occupied to come this way, except for Machiavelli.

"I want to see the bedroom," she said.

"This way," he led her down the corridor and opened the door on the far left. "This is my room."

"And the other?"

"It's for Avelli," he stood by the door.

"You're the only one who calls him that," she sat down on the bed and started to take her sandals off.

"Would you rather I tell you why I call him that?" He said, "Or should I help you with your sandals?"

"You lack such humility," she laughed mockingly, removing one sandal.

"I don't intend to do it humbly," he went to where she was and, kneeling, unbuckled the other sandal.

She placed her hand on his head and ran her fingers through his hair. It was light, almost watery. His beard was almost blue-black from the sun's rays, and it reminded her of someone.

He took the sandal off and raised his head to look at her.

She pulled his hair, so he came to her. "I'm not always like this. It's just that you do something to me that I can't explain. It feels like a…"

"Déjà vu," he completed it.

"And I lose control whenever I see you; every time I think about you. And it's stupid because I only met you yesterday, but it feels like we've always been together. As if we were always meant to meet. But you should understand that…"

"I know, me too," he said.

She stood up and turned her back toward him. He slid the zip of the gown down and let the dress fall off her body. He unhooked her bra, and then, with deliberate hands, pulled her pants down. He held her close to him, placing his hand across her breasts. He could feel her heart pounding loudly.

"What about Merceides?" He whispered.

"I don't know what will be," she said.

"Will you do anything I ask?" He asked in sweet, seductive tones that felt like piano sounds to her.

"I don't know, but I'll try."

He kissed her neck and covered her breasts with both his palms. She was already moaning before his hands found their way down to pull her thighs apart.

7

WHAT MY BROTHER FINDS

Emerson was never habituated to his nightmares; he woke up screaming. His mind had conceived the same thing again. He had been buried alive, naked, under a sea of flies. There were goosebumps on his body as he shivered.

It was 2 a.m.; damn the time!

He crumpled out of bed, trying his best not to wake the woman beside him or the others that filled the bed like a human swamp. He crossed their naked bodies and put his white shirt on. White was the colour of purity; wearing it gave you a saintly aura regardless of your proclivities. He left the room to stand on the balcony. Unfortunately, his brother was already there.

For the love of…

Sarki turned to look at him. They had both been in the room together, sleeping with his wives and concubines in mindless debauchery. All in a bid to produce an heir. He remembered now when it had happened the first time.

After the death of the first set of children, Emerson, whom he had approached, had made a suggestion. They had slept with each wife until Nadia, along with 12 other children, was born. Sarki didn't remember the events of that night; he had been drugged.

The truth was, he had not been able to perform. The children had died regardless, except for Nadia. "Couldn't sleep?" Sarki passed the cigar; he waved it away. Smoking for him had just been a teenage rebellion.

"So it seems," he said. "Why are you up?"

"I was just thinking about the future: heirs, legacies and all."

"Things will be fine, trust me." Emerson had had it all planned out. He had someone in the palace who constantly switched the Sultan's vitamins to infertility pills. In the case that the Sultan managed to get his wives pregnant, the children were to die of natural causes. When the Sultan was desperate, he'd call his brother for help. And that would be the signal for the execution of his plan. But heaven had spat on him, and he too couldn't have children. Yes, he had a daughter, but so did his brother. He preferred a son, a model in his image. It was a good thing Nadia had been kidnapped.

"The press came to the house today." Sarki interrupted his thoughts.

"What did they want?" Emerson pretended to be flabbergasted.

"They wanted to find out if it is true that my daughter has been kidnapped."

"I thought you paid them heavily to keep it a secret?"

"I did. Someone must have let it slip."

"Wow! How chary of you, brother. I assume you're telling me this, seeing as you expect me to come lick up your vomit?"

"Not per se, but yes, if you can." The clause was a challenge, and Sarki knew that pride in himself would make his brother accept a challenge. For such a divine being, as he claimed to be, he was vain.

"You should pledge a reward for anyone who finds your daughter. As there have been no demands for a ransom at this stage, I believe it's a wise call."

"I'll think it through," Sarki said. Sometimes he wondered about his brother, if he was truly on his side. What did they say about smart? If the object had a mind of its own, it was not to be trusted. He believed it was better to coexist under debatable trust, from humans down to smartphones. A man needed an obvious flaw, and his brother seemed to have none. But there was no cause to worry. Emerson had never married, and whatever children he had fathered had died. Well, as naturally as children do. He was on the same level as his brother. They both had no heirs, and that was good enough for him.

He smiled at his brother, who smiled back. "Sure you don't want a cigar?" He asked again.

***

He woke up with his heart racing; it was 2 a.m., and another nightmare. A hand was curled around him. *Shit!* He looked at Denise, who slept peacefully beside him. She looked happy in an off-kilter kind of way. He couldn't place what he was feeling; it was outré.

The sheets covered her up to her neck; otherwise, they were both naked.

He had been dreaming about death again. Never anything else. Dying in his dreams had become a familiar spiral for him. On some days, he'd wake up feeling half-dead and sometimes slightly wounded. He knew who killed him, but he was never angry; he felt he deserved it.

"Why are you awake?" Denise stirred.

"It's nothing."

"You seem worried."

She sat up, and the sheets fell to reveal her upper body. He stared at her with deep soul-searching eyes that glowed like fireflies falling off a broken rainbow.

"I'm fine. I was worried that Merceides might be looking for you," she held him. He could feel her heartbeat.

"Why is your heart racing?" He asked.

"I don't know," she looked at him.

Was she scared of something? He wondered. His brother would make a scene if he found them out. And then there was the question of what future they had together. The future… he focused his gaze on her.

"What's wrong? You're scaring me," he put his hands under the sheets. Her lips parted. He kissed her and continued moving his hands. Her legs were shaking and fluttering under the rumpled sheets. Suddenly, he stopped and broke the kiss. She was nearly out of breath. "Tell me your secrets," he said.

***

"Father, do you think the prophecy might be true? After all, something has happened to my brother, and there is something impure about the other one."

"You're overthinking it," Quinn laughed.

They were in the study that smelt like a thousand books crammed into a bottle perfumed with that special odour only old books had. The scent of early morning blossoming roses came in through the open window.

The twins were their father's replicas. Just an inch taller than he was, with big frames that made them look like bodybuilders. They shared his brown complexion, black eyes and hair, whereas their father shaved his head and kept his beard full, the twins kept all their hair. Merceides kept his low, while Harlequin kept a full afro.

Merceides uncrossed his legs. "Really? You wouldn't even consider the fact that it might be true?"

"What would you want me to say? That I believe the seer's words? You know that I'm a sceptic, and it'll take some convincing, but to be honest, I thought about it too. It involves my sons, doesn't it?"

"That is satisfying enough," Merceides said as the door opened.

Machiavelli and Elzaiya were almost alike, except that Machiavelli was a bit taller. Neither was as tall as the twins; they were at most just a little above 5 feet 9.

While Machiavelli had a rectangular face, Elzaiya had a full oval face like his mother. Merceides only now noticed that Machiavelli had dimples. He wanted to ask if they had seen Denise, but this wasn't the right time.

They exchanged greetings, and Quinn went straight to the issue at hand. "The press is waiting outside our gates. They want to confirm if the president is dead."

Merceides sat upright. "I would like to know that too, cos there is something sketchy about you lot."

"You wouldn't recognise sketchy if they sketched it out for you," Elzaiya mumbled. Machiavelli chuckled.

"What was that?" Merceides asked, standing up to tower over them.

"We don't tell you things for your own good because you don't like to stay in line. Maybe there's something wrong with one of us, and it could be you, just like that featherling said before she was snapped off her mortal coil. So please, do us a favour; be sketchy along with the rest of us, and if you do it well enough, we could consider churching you into this holy grail of hypocrisy you so want to be a part of."

There was a tense silence in the room. Elzaiya had his hands in his pockets while his white shirt relaxed on his body. Machiavelli dared not interfere. He looked at Quinn, signalling that he needed to do something.

Quinn averted his gaze. Let the boys become men on their own terms.

"Maybe it's you that'll be snapped next time." Merceides finally said.

"Come on, big brother, you don't want to soil your hands with my blood."

"I will talk to the press," Quinn announced. "Merceides, you will take care of the burial preparations," he handed him a to-do list. "Machiavelli, you will take care of the house, and Elzaiya, I want to talk to you."

"What do I get to do?" He asked.

"Nothing. You will stay beside me like the IT personnel you claim to be, so you don't get into anyone's bad graces."

Merceides looked the list over and turned to go.

"I'm sorry," Elzaiya said. "I'm just upset that you don't at least consider it when I tell you what I think is best for you."

Merceides turned to look at him. His brother was as diplomatic as both parents combined. "You are the best of us," he said, and walked away, leaving Machiavelli behind.

"You should learn to fight only worthy battles," Quinn said to his son. "Sit down," he cut him off as he opened his mouth to speak. "I am not interested in what you want to say. When the press comes in, you will stay out of sight. I don't want you on TV. Just observe, blend in, and listen."

"What will you tell them?"

"That the president is dead. A murder staged as a suicide."

"That's fair enough."

He was turning to leave when his father called him back and recited the prophecy in full detail.

"Yes, Father, your memory is as sharp as ever," he laughed and continued to the door.

"Your mother is worried about you," Quinn said. "Do you still have nightmares?"

"No," he turned. "Not for a while now."

"I think you, most of all, should heed the prophecy," Quinn said.

"You're getting old, Father; it's normal to start being spiritual."

His father threw a pen at him. He ducked. "You see, you can't even aim right," he picked up the pen and slid it into his pocket.

"I'll think it through, Father," he closed the door.

Quinn sighed and sat down. Today was another strategic manoeuvre. It was not easy being the president's father.

***

It was drizzling, and the minister took his time as if the dead cared what he said. The rain seemed to pretend along with them. Those who mourned, those who were sad, and those who had come to make sure the dead remained that way.

"For god's sake, be done already," Elzaiya complained, lowering the umbrella.

"We're at your brother's funeral; behave," Machiavelli whispered.

"Would you like to take his place?"

"If you're not the last face I see bending over me, maybe I'll consider it."

"And here I thought I was your friend to the death," Elzaiya shifted a step so the rain could touch down on Machiavelli.

"How deplorable of you," Machiavelli cursed.

"It's not like funeral laws dictate you look good through and through. A little rain matting your hair will make you look the perfect fit for a wretched cousin," Elzaiya smiled. "By the way, why aren't you with Cairo over there?"

"Deaths seem to be a sore subject for her. I cracked a joke, but she didn't find it funny."

"Which one?"

"A priest, an angel, and the devil walk into a bar."

"Hell no," Elzaiya exclaimed, laughing.

"You see, she didn't allow me to finish."

"Ashes to ashes, and dust to dust…" The preacher said.

"If the person wasn't cremated, there's no point using ashes to ashes. All this mindless legalism…" Elzaiya complained.

"You'll make a fine contemporary priest, my friend," Machiavelli mocked.

Quinn turned. They looked down at their feet, pretending to be solemn.

"I wish I could do the puppy eyes; girls love that stuff," Machiavelli said.

"You have no clue what girls love."

"How would you know when all you feel is apathy, pride, and egocentric cynicism?"

"I'm proud of how well you know me. Hey, maybe you should write a book about it, Fucker!"

"Why, maybe I would. I'll be sure to remember to read some pages at your funeral. I do have the feeling I will be around long enough to hashtag your evil ass to the place it deserves to be."

Elzaiya made the sign of the cross, and Machiavelli stared at him till he turned to look at him. "What?"

"I was waiting for hail and brimstone. I thought the world had come to an end," Elzaiya moved away with the umbrella and left him standing in the rain.

"Of course," Machiavelli moved again to stand with him. He should have brought his umbrella.

After the burial, Cairo left the crowd to meet Machiavelli, who was waiting in the car to take her home. She passed by a man in a navy-blue suit who stood at the edge of the burial grounds. He seemed to have arrived then. They were both too preoccupied with themselves to notice each other.

Denise had not come to the funeral. She had stayed in Merceides' room. He had found her standing in front of his door at about 5 a.m. When he opened the door for her to come in, she pushed him back in and locked the door behind her. Everything else had happened on its own. He asked where she had been, and she said she had found a small house in the compound. "Elzaiya's casa," he had said.

She had laughed and asked when he would be back. As soon as the funeral service was over, he said. She told him that she would be sleeping in Elzaiya's apartment if that was fine with him. He thought it over and, after concluding that his brother was harmless, agreed.

Elzaiya stood under the drizzling rain, waiting for his parents to do their thing. He thought about his night with Denise. Would he be judged as good or bad? He had not made love to her. He couldn't; he had not done that with anyone before.

He sometimes questioned the paradoxical nature of his morality. He understood when others did it, but he had his standards — or were they expectations?

Her body made him feel like a different kind of creature. She was smart and happy. How do people stay happy? Was it by acceptance? The truest thing in the world was how hard it was for intelligent people to find happiness. He looked at his parents. They looked happy, and they were the two most intelligent people he knew. Their sympathisers had thinned, and the only person left was the predator.

The Sultan approached his parents. He could almost taste blood in his mouth. He gritted his teeth and watched them shake hands.

"We heard that your daughter was kidnapped," Quinn said.

"Insha Allah, she would be found and justice would be served."

"We would, in our way, pool our resources to help you secure your daughter," Aaira said.

"I would be most grateful. And if there's anything you would like me to do in my capacity, please let me know; believe me, I know how hard it is to lose a child."

"Actually, there is one very small thing," Aaira said, and Quinn frowned. It was obvious he didn't want to share that in public. "My husband may be too proud to ask; you know men and their ego."

"Anything. A man will help another man to rise; that is how the world is designed. One palm rinses the other."

"Just as a hen needs both legs to scratch the ground," Aaira said. "The thing is, I have lost one son, and I am not willing to lose another one."

Sarki swallowed. He hoped his plans had not been found out. He frowned and held her hands in his as she went on.

"We have a son who is too stubborn to listen to us. Regardless of what we say, he still thinks it best to run for office. I am scared because I believe that my Harlequin was not the type to commit suicide. Everything was fine, and then he was dead. They say he killed himself, but I know he didn't. We are peaceful people who do not wish to exhaust ourselves playing revenge. I want you to use your influence to protect our son, my only child," she trailed off into tears, and Sarki was forced to elicit more sympathy. The press inched closer.

"I promise, I will try my best to protect your son; after all, he is like a son to me."

"Thank you," Aaira said tearfully. "We would be eternally grateful," Quinn added.

Elzaiya finished his observation and turned to walk toward the car when he bumped into a man. His cologne smelt terribly expensive, and his cufflinks were custom-made, as were his shoes. His white shirt was of the softest and most delicate but expensive fabric, and his navy-blue suit was the perfect fit for his immaculate frame.

"I'm terribly sorry, sir," he apologised.

The man was not offended. "Nice suit," he said, complimenting Elzaiya's navy-blue suit that was almost as expensive as his and was tailored to be perfect on the owner. He had a slight accent that could be mistaken for British.

"Thank you, sir. Though I believe that mine is nowhere near the excellence of yours."

"You flatter me." The man said. "But why navy-blue? Isn't black the colour for a funeral?"

"The dead don't care what we wear to their funeral. It couldn't make them any more dead," he apologised, as it was offensive to some people, and then went on as the man waved him on. "Besides, navy and rage blue are sensibly mature colours, fit for royalty, I might add. Black is too common, and white is courtesy. Bright colours only reveal the degree of vulnerability or stupidity in a person. For me, the other colours just don't fit. But of course, I am prone to being biased."

"I like you." The man smiled and tapped his shoulder. "I hope we meet again soon."

***

"Why didn't you come to sympathise with the family?" Sarki asked later when Emerson settled beside him in the car.

"The mud would ruin my shoes."

Sarki shook his head and looked at Emerson's shoes. "They asked me to do what I could to protect their other son. Can you imagine?"

"They did?" Emerson's interest was visibly piqued.

Sarki narrated what had happened, and Emerson, after laughing awhile, explained the humour.

"If anything happens to their son, you will be held partly accountable. You have given them your word, and I assume the press was listening. It will be in today's news whether you like it or not, and all eyes will be on both of you. If any harm befalls that boy, it will be noted that you made a promise you couldn't keep. Something as little as that can disqualify you from the games."

"Curses! So, what do we do now?"

"We wait; we just have to wait for something to turn up," Emerson said with usual optimism. "Something always does."

They were both silent in the car for a while before Emerson asked. "I met a chap in his early twenties; he struck me as someone of great importance. He wore a blue suit and had remarkable qualities. Do you know who he was?"

"You mean to ask if I know the younger version of yourself that you just described? No."

"Hmmm..." Emerson stroked his beard and dismissed the thought. There was no younger version of him around, but if there was. That boy was close.

***

Elzaiya was surprised at the kind of man Emerson was. He struck him as a good person. He looked refined and had stately manners. He spoke with a certain suaveness that only years of confidence in intelligence and getting your way could allow. Maybe that was where Denise got all her good qualities from. He hoped for her sake that he was good. He would hate to find dirt on her father.

When they arrived, Elzaiya alighted on the path that led toward his house. He had things on his mind. When he got to the house, he met Machiavelli and Cairo making out on the sofa. Her bra was on the floor, and his hands were all over her...

"Get a room," he hissed as he passed.

"Come join us," Cairo said. She stood up to face him. Her breasts were almost visible with the way the spaghetti strap of her gown hung on her arm, slightly about to fall. She walked over and put her hands on his shoulder.

"Machiavelli doesn't have any plans for me; he shouldn't be jealous. Why should he keep me to himself?"

Elzaiya did not move. He just smiled and looked at Machiavelli over her shoulder. "And how did you come about this astute claim?" He asked.

"He has slept with me once, and he wants to do it again. I figure when he's bored, he will want someone new. Why should I bother trying to convince him that I'm worth keeping if I know my worth? Isn't he supposed to prove himself to me?"

"I think I like you," Elzaiya said. "Sometimes Avelli can be as dumb as a doorknob, but I think he's been around long enough to know good things when he sees them. Aren't we all stupid enough to throw things away only to repurchase them at a much higher price in the future and call them vintage? I think he will come around in time."

He raised his arms to take hers away, but then he suddenly held them up and looked into her eyes. He moved closer and whispered something into her ear. She giggled and ran to where Machiavelli was, where she kissed him. Machiavelli waved him away as things started to get intense. He smiled and went toward his room. He paused at the door and went to the freezer at the end of the corridor to get a bottle of water. When he got it, he paused again at the door. The passageway smelt different. He opened the door and stood outside for a while before stepping in and closing the door.

The shower was running, and there were clothes on the floor. Denise.

He looked at everything in the room; his laptop was the way he had left it. He dropped the bottle on the table and sat down on the bed. She finished in the shower and came out, wrapped in a towel.

"Go and bathe; you look grave," she joked. He smiled and removed his suit. He hung it and took off his shirt and then his shoes. "I'll be waiting for you," she said.

"We'll see," she stared at him, waiting for him to finish undressing. "Turn around," he said.

"But you've seen me naked."

"Turn around," she turned, and he took his clothes off, wrapping a towel around his waist. He walked into the bathroom and turned the shower on. She was applying her cream when she heard his laptop beep. The screen came on. There was a video signalling to play among the lock screen notifications. She tapped on it, and a video clip came on. It was a recording of some sort. A guy was talking to a girl. She thought it was some sort of bizarre pornography until she saw the girl's face. It looked very familiar.

"Oh my God!" she gasped with shock as she recognised her.

She stared at it for a while and then minimised it back to the way it had been. The laptop screen went off again, and she went on with her preening.

When he came out of the bathroom, he stood staring at her. When she turned to look at him, she forgot all that she had seen in the overwhelming desire that engulfed her.

She knew there was something about him, and if he was dangerous, she didn't want to know; she just wanted to … He took the towel off and reached for the cream beside her. She tapped his hand away and, putting her finger in it, scooped out a bit and started to rub his back. When she went lower, he didn't object. Nor did he say anything when she pushed him to the bed and took her towel off. He just stared at her, cold and silent. She kissed his chest and his stomach, and then, looking into his eyes, she took him in her mouth.

8

SAVING NADIA

An Uneventful 46 days Later

Levine collapsed on the way to his room. Elzaiya was watching, but it wasn't yet time. He glanced out the window at his brother strolling down the garden with Denise. The walk was meticulous; the art of courting was coffee that he wasn't thinking of pouring into his cup.

She was laughing over something he'd said. He smiled. In this cruel world, how easily love came to some people.

She still sneaked over to be with him. When would their escapade stop? He was only allowing her to develop feelings that would only cause hurt in the end. A part of him wondered why he should care. The other part, which he still wouldn't call the better part, told him to deal with it.

He knew he should tell her to stop, but he couldn't. He wouldn't deny the fact that he was attracted to her. This thing shouldn't move beyond that. He closed the curtain and continued his vigil.

When Levine regained consciousness, he arose with the realisation that he was close to the end. He waited until evening before sending the signal. Elzaiya would tell him what to do.

***

Sarki had increased the reward for whoever found his daughter. The people were frantic, and everything was being searched. Suspicious movements were reported, and some of his enemies were even arrested and tortured, but to no end.

Emerson, on the other hand, seemed happy. "You seem to have given up hope," he patted his brother's back. "She would be found."

"I don't think so, Omar," Sarki said. He was the only one who called him that, like their father had. Emerson despised the name.

"You always said that a man with power could achieve anything, and here you are, bent over because you can't find your daughter."

"She is my only hope of having an heir; she is our only hope of carrying on this legacy."

"She was, brother!" Emerson shouted. This pitiful dependence on the girl exhausted him. It was like talking to a child. "You might soon have a son."

"That would die as soon as he is born," Sarki yelled back. "She is the only one who survived."

"I understand." Emerson sat beside him and passed him a glass of wine. Sarki turned it down. "I wonder how the Quinns felt when you murdered their son," Emerson spoke soberly.

"I didn't." Sarki shot him a dirty look.

"You keep saying that, but why should I trust you — you who would do anything to get what you want?"

"You think this is the right time for this?"

"I'm sorry," he apologised. "I tend to overreach sometimes."

Emerson stood to refill his glass. There was a knock at the door, and the guard motioned to Sarki that the messenger was from within the palace. He waved for them to be allowed in. The maid stood at the door and knelt. With sad eyes, she looked at the Sultan, and his heart melted. Hope and expectation slipped away.

"Mai ya faru?" He asked.

"Ta zubar da ciki." The maid replied humbly.

He stared blankly, motionless, for a while, and then waved her away.

She genuflected and then bowed at Emerson, who smiled at her. She walked away like the wind, leaving Sarki emotionally incapacitated. Emerson sat back beside his brother and continued his drinking, another glass beside him.

After a while, Sarki stood up and was pacing the room when he got a call. He moved to the far end of the room. After listening to what the speaker had to say, he smashed his phone in a fit of rage. Emerson smiled within himself. It felt good to be home.

Sarki sat down, sinking into the sofa just like his depression had on him. Emerson didn't feel pity; he didn't understand the concept. He was always of the opinion that the inability to feel was a sign of true transcendence to divinity. It gave you a clear mind; it elevated you to the status of a god.

"Drink?" He suggested.

His brother took his glass, so he filled another, and they drank in silence.

"The police have still found nothing," Sarki said.

His brother patted his shoulder as a sign of comfort. He might not feel it, but he had taken his time to learn the essentials. Sarki sipped his wine, wondering at the game his brother was playing. If he had a daughter and feigned ignorance of her existence, then he must either have a plan or be plainly mad. It better be the latter.

***

"It has to be done tomorrow," Elzaiya emphasised.

"Tomorrow is a market day; what if we get caught?"

"I assure you, we will not get caught."

"You're not God," Machiavelli went on to list all the reasons why it was a bad idea. Elzaiya wasn't going to change his mind, on the basis that if Levine died before the time, it could change their plans. "So why do it on the busiest day in town?"

"It's because everyone would be busy, and busy people look suspicious. You wouldn't search the whole damn town for goods that the town would deliver, would you? You wouldn't hinder the movement of the whole town in search of your daughter, who is most probably held up in some unknown building. And only a fool or a madman will take that risk of moving her in public."

"So, what is this genius plan?" Machiavelli asked, finally giving in. Elzaiya proceeded to share the details.

They both will embark on the quest to find the Sultan's daughter. Machiavelli was worried about her seeing their faces, but Elzaiya said that was the whole point of saving her. It was crucial to the Sultan's being indebted to them.

"But, Avelli, you'll be there for a different reason."

Machiavelli gave him a puzzled gaze. "You have to make sure Jason Levine dies tomorrow."

He stared at Elzaiya like he had cracked a joke, then gasped in horror when he saw he was dead serious. "Dies like Harlequin's kind of death?" He was not a murderer, and he would not kill, not even under Elzaiya's orders.

"No! He dies for real."

"God have mercy on your soul, but I'm not killing a man," Machiavelli spoke with a declining note of moral finality.

Elzaiya smiled; at least now he had a rigid moral stand. "I'm not asking you to kill him. All I'm asking is that you make sure he dies."

Machiavelli gestured that he did not understand. Elzaiya went on to explain.

"Jason Levine has cancer; he volunteered for the job. He wanted to commit suicide before we met. I asked him to live his life out, and I would make it worth his while. He has a son, whom I take care of. Just anonymous gifts, donations, and a scholarship. The sickness is now fatal. In about a day or two, he will be gone, but some pills will give him a quick and painless death. He has others that he would use on Nadia to also give her a slow, painful death.

But before that, he will put her to sleep while we move them both to the site on land. Fifteen minutes before the sleeping drug wears off, he will paralyse her. When she's awake, he will inject her with poison and set the place on fire. She will watch him inject himself too; she will see him die, and then the smoke will rise."

Machiavelli smiled when he got the plan. "The smoke will draw attention, and we will find our way in to save the girl. But what happens from then on?"

"Nothing. Our part has been played."

Machiavelli nodded. He left after they had finalised the plans. It was 7:15 p.m., and the night was still young. Machiavelli was going to meet Cairo.

Who knew that it would take just a girl to make his Avelli a responsible man? Denise would be with Merceides, and as usual, he would be the only pea in his pod. He flipped his laptop open and watched the girl on the screen. She had on a blue T-shirt and tights. Her hair was loose on her shoulders. She turned the TV on and crossed her legs on the bed, eating popcorn, while her diary sat on the arm of the chair. She ate like a stoic. She did her yoga in the room, among other exercises. She was going to die, and yet she wanted to be fit.

Once, when she had been sad, then enraged, she had not eaten and had started to have conversations with herself. Now she was calm as a lamb, almost as if she knew she would die tomorrow. He closed the laptop and started to go through his shirts. He made sure the door was locked before he opened the secret compartment in his closet. He picked out a bulletproof vest and tried it on, in case things didn't work out tomorrow, as planned.

Levine slid the food in and asked her to give him the garbage bag. She passed it to him and was shocked at how pale he looked.

"You don't want to save yourself?"

He said nothing.

"So how am I going to die?" She asked.

He coughed, wheezed and spat out blood. "Anyway I see fit," he said. "Start saying your prayers."

"You're a good man," she said. "I'm not saying it so that you'll reconsider; I'm just saying, you're a good man to whom life has not been fair."

"I was," he said and shut the door.

He wanted to live his final moments in peace. He knew that his son would have a bright future because of his sacrifice, and that was more than enough. He was grateful for their meeting.

He was buying the pills when he ran into him at the pharmacy. Elzaiya had looked at him and told him that there were more honourable ways to die. He had denied his intentions and said he was not answerable to anyone. He had left the pharmacy angrily, but Elzaiya had passed by with his car and had told him to get in. He had driven him home and was surprised he had no family. He had told him his story, and Elzaiya had told him to change his mind, but he said it was made up, so he had told him to wait. Two weeks later, he was in the living room watching a movie when his phone rang.

"Meet me in St Patrick's church near the old barn. I need a favour."

He had met him there alone, and Elzaiya had made him the offer.

He had said it was giving too much, but he had insisted that he wouldn't see the child not finish college and become responsible. And so he gladly accepted the role. He was going to die tomorrow, and he didn't regret that. He felt satisfied, knowing that, in the end, his life had been worthwhile and he would receive justice.

The gun in the cupboard was loaded; he was also a great shot.

***

The market was just opening when Machiavelli set up the tent. There were shops and kiosks, but the tent owners were the headache of the market. They set up a tent at any location they wanted.

Today, he was going to be selling Persian rugs, along with Egyptian cotton sheets and the best carpets in town. All of which they had rented for a very small price, with a bonus for the owner who told them that they could call to ask the price if anyone was interested in buying. He had been eager to help without question. Hakim was going to be the salesman.

The tent was placed on one of the exits that led to the bunker. It would take 20 minutes to walk from that exit to the copy of Nadia's room, and then it would take a turn around town to arrive at the point at which they were going to be exiting — the one that Sarki and Emerson used as boys.

Levine was to drug her food between 9 and 12. They would bring her out of the water in a body bag and fold her into a bag among others filled with second-hand clothing, which would then be moved in a wheelbarrow to the tent along with rugs and carpets, where they would be offloaded. Levine would go in through another exit, so no one would tie him to anything.

It was 11:47 a.m. when she finally fell into a drug-induced sleep. Levine sent the beep, and they dove in with their masks to get her, along with Levine, who couldn't swim. They loaded her into a large bag woven for that purpose and then drove the lorry to the market and offloaded them into the wheelbarrow at the gate, where they were stared at until they bribed their way in.

The lorry then drove Levine to the other exit, where he alighted.

Hakim parked the lorry alongside the others in the lot and walked to the tent, where Elzaiya and Machiavelli took the bag down the steps into the building after opening the hatch. They laid her on the bed in her room and scattered her clothes as they had been in the sub.

They waited until Levine breathed his way down. He had the drugs and another bag with him. And there was a room with a few of his belongings. They went over the timing of the injections again, and when they were sure everything was fine, they exchanged their last goodbyes and parted.

***

The first light she saw hurt her eyes. She blinked and tried to move her neck; it wasn't working. He came in with a fuel can and started to pour the fuel on the ground, around her bed, and out past the door. She could hear his footsteps receding.

She tried to scream, but nothing came out. When he came back, she saw that he had a gun. This wasn't a defensive pistol; it was a beautiful heavy-calibre gun that looked deadly – an original weapon of war.

He bent over her with a syringe and found a vein. He slid the needle in, and tears poured down her face. She was screaming in her head, but the sound was muted.

"This poison would kill you slowly; you would feel the pain that I've felt. The pain your father caused," he said.

She wanted to say something, but she couldn't. And then the pain kicked in. It felt like her head was repeatedly being smashed on a wall, and her body was already on fire. She was having spasms of contractions in her neck, and then they spread through her body until it felt like someone was wringing her like a cloth. Her eyes widened, and she started to convulse.

He stood up and, going to the far end of the hall, lit a match and set his room on fire. Given that he had not poured the fuel in a line that allowed the fire to enter her room, it would take about 20 minutes for the fire to reach her.

He took the pills and held the gun. Elzaiya had made sure the pills did not impair his vision. 15 minutes from now, he would be dead.

When they saw the smoke, they started to run while others watched. They had been sitting under a tree, and the Fulani boys with their cattle were not going to leave their animals to attend to some smoke, nor would the market women leave their goods.

They started to shout for help, and others ran along with them. Machiavelli was the one who tripped and found the trapdoor. He called to Elzaiya, and they went in, leaving the door open with the others too unafraid to come in.

Inside the building, they used special handkerchiefs to cover their noses. They were about to cross into her area when Elzaiya held Machiavelli and took a step forward. The gunshot brought him to the ground. Machiavelli also heard someone else crash to the floor. He was confused. He had not been comfortable with the plan, and now it had gone wrong.

He rushed to where Elzaiya was. He didn't know what to do. He was about to go get an ambulance when Elzaiya stood up and called him back. The bullet had smashed into the screen of his Samsung; the phone had been in his front pocket, which was zipped closed.

Machiavelli muttered curses and ran on ahead. The fire was increasing. Elzaiya ran alongside him, and they met the girl choking on the bed. Elzaiya went in. "Call an ambulance," he yelled when he saw her condition.

"There's no signal," Machiavelli said.

They carried the girl's trashing body out, past Levine's dead body. The fire had increased, and the smoke had attracted a lot of attention.

When they got out, people had filled the exit. They started to yell for an ambulance, and soon an ambulance arrived along with the firemen. She was immediately rushed to the emergency unit.

Machiavelli was waiting by the door when Sarki and Emerson came in. He rushed to meet the young man who had saved his daughter's life.

"How will I ever repay you? He started.

Machiavelli cut him short curtly. "It wasn't I who did the saving, sir; it was my friend."

Sarki went to meet Elzaiya, who was placing an ice pack on his chest. "I see the fire did a job on you. Thank God you're not hurt. I hear you are to thank for my daughter's life."

Elzaiya dropped the ice pack so Sarki could see the hole left by the bullet on his shirt. "It was all God or fate," he said. "I was lucky to get out alive, too."

"How come it didn't get through?" Sarki gaped, surprised.

"Sometimes it's the small things that save us," he produced his phone.

"Ah! The man of the hour. We should stop bumping into each other in dire situations." Emerson said from the door as he came in to join them. "This is the young man I was asking you about after the funeral," he told his brother.

"Oh!" Sarki really looked at Elzaiya for the first time and noticed that there was a semblance of his brother in the boy.

"Here's my card; call me up when he's given you the reward money, or, you know, to remind him if he doesn't." Emerson gave him a card.

"Thank you, sir," Elzaiya smiled and then said modestly, "I just want to make sure she's safe, and I would really love to get a new phone soon; that's all I need."

"You're very humble." Sarki said, "I like that in young men of your age. I'll get back to you and your friend."

"Excuse me, gentlemen." A nurse interrupted them. "The girl wants to speak to the person who saved her life." Sarki and Emerson turned to Elzaiya, who looked at Machiavelli and nodded.

"Alone, please." The nurse said.

Elzaiya went in to meet the girl. She was not even on a drip; she did not need to be; all she needed was an injection to clear the poison from her system. She would be good in hours.

She looked at him as he walked in to meet her. His brown trousers were black with patches of soot and were scratched in some places. She looked at his top and saw the hole made by the bullet.

"I saw what happened; I am very grateful," she said.

"It's fine. I would have done that for anyone."

"You'd take a bullet for anyone?" She asked.

"Oh!" He looked at his chest and straightforwardly avoided the answer. "I'm glad you're fine. But I'd love to get back home now."

"Of course, thanks again."

He smiled and turned to go. There was something about him. Beneath that gentle exterior was a burning need to do something deadly. Maybe she was being stupid, or being almost dead had made her start to see things more clearly. "Don't go catching any more bullets," she called after him, turning to her side.

He left the room and shut the door.

They were already at the door of the hospital when they met the Sultan and his brother. "We'll see you soon?" Emerson asked.

"Yes, sir. We just need to get this one patched up. He's always out for an adventure. I hope this teaches him to be careful next time," Machiavelli said.

They laughed about it, and the Sultan insisted that they come by his place the next day. They had to ask for something; they shouldn't be modest about it.

Elzaiya smiled. "I'll come get the phone tomorrow then."

9

BEING EVIL, TO DO GOOD

Corruption is a fire that burns everything in its path. A fire that doesn't burn itself out when there is nothing left to burn. Corruption was a contagious disease in the old republic. So commonplace that those who despised it were said to be insane. It was a wooden age, one that produced the worst kinds of men. Cynics, as the saying goes, knew the price of everything but the value of none. The old republic had been a creaking house, and corruption, that termite, had brought it crashing down. With society descending into anarchy, people quickly recognised the error of their ways. Now corruption was as evil as treason, and all who practised it were treated as heretics. But it lurked in the shadows, in the stomachs of evil men, and in dark, smoky chambers, feeding, growing, and maturing. People would be led astray by evil when they saw fit. Most people are idle, and unoccupied people are but tools to those with a plan.

Harlequin and Merceides, my older twin brothers, are identical in almost all aspects of life, except how they differ in degree as to the amount of love and respect they have for me and the regard they hold my opinions in. Harlequin is cool-headed and rational, but Merceides is an impulsive creature, and these animals have the tendency to be put down inconveniently. Luckily, I had found his leash.

Denise was in love with Merceides. Their affair had taken time to grow and deepen. With a prod in the right direction, she had found that love was a gift, free to all who believed they had the capacity to share it with those who truly desired to have it. I didn't believe that nonsense when I said it to her. But a straight face and some sad days went far to embolden my act. But it didn't stop her from stealing into my room on some cold nights to warm my sheets. I wouldn't readily judge this act as good or evil, seeing that we never reached complete intimacy, even though there was a lot of sexual interaction. My brother satisfied her body, and I was forbidden desire. Yes, it was wrong of me to keep the act going, but all I did was agree to be objectified by my brother's betrothed. It was a dangerous arch that could tip me into hell. They say love is blind, but I know that rage and jealousy are cataracts in the mind's eye. I hope the day never comes when he finds out that I have always been plucking at the apple of his eye. How he would be glad when he sees me, his foe, outstretched beneath that tree.

Emerson and I had become acquaintances. You know the saying, "Keep your friends close and your enemies at home."

He dropped by sometimes, not at the Quinns' residence, of course. I had an apartment in the rich and quiet part of town. That countryside, where your neighbours lived in Dubai and their maids kept the house clean until they came back for Christmas. The Sultan had insisted I take the reward money, but I declined and only asked for a phone. He wouldn't give it to me if I didn't ask for more, so I asked that he give Machiavelli some money to get a car. Boy! Had Machiavelli been overjoyed! Cairo was the one who drove it around town.

When the Sultan asked his daughter about the kidnapper, we were shocked to hear that it was singular. We couldn't believe that one man pulled it off without any help. But dying men had nothing to lose. We agreed on that possibility.

She told us that Levine had died in the fire, which was confirmed soon enough by the police. The plot thickened when the Sultan discovered that Levine had been a former employee of his company, but under the branch operated by his brother. That was something I had not anticipated.

He couldn't understand why the man then insisted that he had worked for him, unless he was covering up for someone else — his brother, for example.

The fact that his daughter had been held in a location known only to them heightened his suspicions. It was a thrilling sensation to observe the distrust in his eyes. I felt bad for my new friend. I know he would have confided in me, but he's a secretive man. That, I understand.

Nadia didn't show up most of the time when we went to the Sultan's palace. She would come by sometimes, greet us, and go her way — or not come out at all. Machiavelli didn't mind, and I kept my opinions to myself. I had slipped her journal away among the things we cleared off the sub, erasing all traces of where the main event had taken place.

Contrary to folk expectations, I didn't get the girl after becoming her knight in shining armour. And now that Denise was the cherry on my brother's cake, I didn't get the chance to take the other sister to prom. I was alone, as always, while the other butterflies fluttered in pairs, but I didn't mind. I wouldn't know what to do even if I had someone.

Concerning Harlequin, the bullet he used had been a blank, and our Secret Service had already arrived moments after the shot. It all happened so fast, and they were out before Navina could get herself. A clone was what we had buried because our enemies would see to it that they waited until the body was lowered, and they did.

The plan had gone well, and Harlequin sometimes went to visit Navina disguised as Merceides. He was to tell her that it was part of his preparation for the next games, and she would understand and cease asking him questions. He went out only at night, and both twins never left the house at the same time. Navina was all too pleased to have him around, and like the smart secretary she was, she never spilt the truth.

By now, all was well and good; the country was functioning fine without a president in the seat. And I was wondering if I should join the games, but, most importantly, if I needed to make some extra eggs and eat some more when there was a knock on my door.

Nothing stays buried, and certainly not the consequences of our actions, which always find their way to becoming our nemesis, no matter how good or bad they may be. And sometimes, if your bad has some luck attached to it, they come bearing gifts.

"Come in."

I was just finishing breakfast, and it was a little after 10 a.m. The person hadn't heard me. I ran over and pulled the door ajar. Honestly, I didn't know what to do from there.

It was Nadia, and I hoped things would not be a little bit awkward, considering the part of our history that she didn't know about.

"Hi," she said.

***

Sarki had not found it pleasing that his brother was conspiring behind his back. The rift caused by Nadia's revelation was gutter-deep. And now that trouble was in our enemy's house, all we had to do was decide how best to move forward.

So, "I don't think he should go back in, Father."

"Are you nuts?"

You already know which of my brothers talks like that.

"Let him talk," Harlequin said.

"It will set a bad precedent. He should run next term. If he stays dead, our adversaries will be relaxed, focused on running next term, and choosing who to install, rather than being bent on destroying the plans of a dead man. With him out of the picture, our power is solidified. As we have made it clear that we don't want Merceides in office for his own sake. They will be shaken when Harlequin returns."

"So, what are you saying?"

"Let him wait, Father. I assure you, the Sultan isn't done with us. Once things are right in his family, he will be back for us, and we must be prepared for any kind of warfare. The only advantage we have is Harlequin's death. He can only come back alive as a last resort.

Quinn sighed. "You sound sure, almost as if you plan to aid his plans."

"Frankly, yes, I do."

"No one is listening to me. He is nuts!"

"So, you've got a better idea, then? Because I'm tired of hearing nuts in sequence."

"Father…"

"Son…" Quinn folded his hands and looked at Elzaiya, who grudgingly apologised.

"So then, what is the plan?" Harlequin asked.

"Emerson is an acquaintance, a very good one at that. It is in the nature of men like him to want to mentor people like me. In the process of mentoring me, I will learn some truth."

"Would you do what he tells you? You know, if you don't, he might suspect something."

"I would do what he tells me to."

There was silence in the room. "We would have another meeting." Quinn was about to dismiss them when he halted. "Not a word leaves this room." They all nodded and left, but Elzaiya stayed behind.

Quinn was bothered. It was not just that Elzaiya was becoming entwined with Emerson; it was the fact that Denise was going out with one of his sons while she visited the other secretly. At first, he turned a blind eye. Elzaiya was smart; he knew what he was doing, he had told himself. But the thing had eaten him up until he couldn't hold it in any longer.

"Emerson is one of the most dangerous men I have come across," he began. Elzaiya observed him closely; his father was like an onion. Just when you are sure you know him, you discover that there is more to him.

"I would be careful."

"That isn't good enough. He isn't just any smart-arse; he's a brilliant psychopath. He has no remorse; he is ruthless, unemotional, and makes no mistakes. If he has a plan, he will achieve it."

"I know that, Father."

Quinn paused and looked at his son. "What do you think about his daughter staying with us?" Elzaiya's eyes narrowed.

"I think it's safer to have her closer than distant. It makes it easier to watch her. By the way, she hasn't tried to contact him, or he her."

"How would you be so sure?"

"I have my ways."

"Do they include objectification?" Elzaiya didn't appear shocked; normally, he anticipated all these things, but he wasn't ready for this, and his father knew that. He swallowed and held his breath. It was the strangest thing when he discovered that his heart hadn't skipped a beat.

That was why I left home, and now things had gotten a little bit more complicated.

***

"Wouldn't you invite me in?"

"Oh!" I came back to the door. "Come on in. I totally forgot... I naturally assumed you would just... I said, 'Come in...' I figure you missed that?"

"You are ruffled," she smiled. I looked at my body. Christ! I was putting on a long-sleeved T-shirt, and my jeans were unbelted. Thank God it wasn't falling off. "I was just finishing breakfast," I said.

"That's fine," she looked around the living room as I closed the door. "May I?"

"Oh! Please sit down. Where are my manners?"

"I guess you're not a morning person?" She sat down and looked at me. Particularly at my slipping jeans.

"I'm not a waking-up person. Sometimes I'm just generally disorganised." I was lying.

"I came to wish you Barka da Salah," she raised the package she was carrying.

"Oh! Ummm... yeah... yeah... ummm..."

"You mean to say you forgot that it's Salah, but you want to say thank you?"

"Yes. Exactly in that order. Thank you. I'm very grateful." I proceeded to buckle my belt, so I turned around.

"Did I interrupt something, apart from breakfast?" She peered at my back.

"You mean like…?"

She nodded.

"No! No… Good God, no. No."

"It's not like it's a terrible thing. Guys your age usually find it exhilarating."

"They do?" I turned and placed my arms on the table.

"Most of them, yes."

"Well…"

"You're not most of them."

I smiled. "Can I get you anything? I have some pizza. doughnuts, noodles and…"

I was reeling, trying to recall the things I had. It wasn't like I could. I wasn't the one who had gone shopping.

She was silent; I could see from the glassware that she was staring at me. Was she checking me out?

"I would like a drink."

"Water?"

"No, a real drink."

"I have some wine, but you're…"

"A Muslim and the Sultan's daughter," she stood up and adjusted her gown. It was big and loose on her body, intended to hide everything underneath. She pulled it around her so that it was instantly tight. Her figure popped out. She wanted me to check her out.

"Where do you keep the wine?"

"In the kitchen."

She dropped the paper bag on the table and walked to where I stood. She had brown eyes, and her light face glowed under the ray of sunlight that stole in from the curtain, making it seem as if she was emanating the light back like a…

"Are you freckled?" She asked suddenly.

"You're the one with freckles." I pointed toward the kitchen.

She led the way. "Don't be shy; it fits you. It's a good match for your eyes. Let me see."

"No," I retorted.

"Please?"

"No."

"What if I command you?"

"You're crazy…" I paused and gritted my teeth. She was the Sultan's daughter after all.

"To think I can command someone like you," she completed.

By now, my head was in the cupboard looking for stuff I did not keep.

"Are you sure you have whatever you're looking for?"

The fridge! How did I even forget that wine would be in the fridge?

I edged past her to the refrigerator; my arm grazed her breast. I pretended not to have noticed. Apologising makes things awkward.

She said nothing.

Bang! I found the wine and turned with a smile of victory. "You look as if you've discovered the origin of science."

I laughed. She had no idea how hard it was to search for things I hadn't arranged.

Machiavelli had insisted that he go shopping for me, and Cairo had changed my design; now the place looked like a woman's lodge.

I had just poured the wine when a car horn interrupted our sipping. She did not, like hypocrites, pour the wine away or drop the glass. She brought it with her to the living room and raised the curtain to look outside the window. "It seems you have some company."

Cairo opened the door like it was her house and flew onto my body like she was my wife, then she kissed me on the cheek and asked how I found the place.

"Splendid," I said. I just wanted her to feel happy.

I felt like a single shoe on a racetrack. I didn't know that Nadia was observing the whole thing from the kitchen corridor.

"We miss you," Cairo said.

I was hoping she never said anything about the Quinn residence. It was too early to lie.

"What's good, Dad?" Machiavelli came dragging a bike.

"I'm good, son, but hold it. Tell me you're giving that thing out tomorrow. I don't have space for trash."

Nadia smiled and disappeared into the kitchen, where she could hear them without being seen.

"I thought you would find cycling in your neighbourhood and throwing stones at your neighbours fun. But it's for me."

"Avelli, what part of 'this is my house' don't you understand?"

"You love having me around," he pushed the bike past me to the end of the corridor. I smiled.

"Oh, oh!" Machiavelli came around. "I know that look. You intend to hurt my bike."

"You're welcome to leave it inside."

"I will park it outside, at the corner of the house," he said, 'On second thought.'

"Oh! Please leave it. I love seeing its cushioned butt hanging on useless steel rims. It kind of reminds me of how it feels having your worthless ass around."

"Don't be like that, darling."

My heart nearly skipped; I did not know they had come with Denise.

She came in, hugged me, and kissed me on the cheek. Machiavelli was just coming in from outside; I motioned him toward the corridor and met him there after disentangling myself.

"Why did you bring her along?"

"She insisted."

"You know as well as I do that she's part of the reason I left the house."

"Forgive me, but how do you intend for me to silence a Chevrolet?"

"How is that my concern? You'd have changed your course. She shouldn't be here."

Nadia overheard bits of the conversation. She stood in the kitchen sipping the wine. She wasn't one to make herself known. She waited for them to finish talking, and then Machiavelli went to the living room.

I thought she was in another part of the house and was surprised to see her standing in the kitchen.

"You seem to love the solitude. Little wonder some crazy maniac kidnapped you," I said to her back.

"It seems saving people from fires and taking bullets isn't the only thing you do," she turned.

"Life gets complicated along the line." I looked at her lips and filled my glass.

"You look complicated; I don't expect other parts of you to be simple."

"Barka da Salah." I toasted. She raised her glass.

"Hey ya…" A female voice said, coming from the corridor.

Shit! I looked at Nadia and turned around.

Denise stormed into the kitchen with the undeniable resolution of someone with very sexual intentions. "I've missed your…" She noticed that I wasn't alone.

Nadia wasn't popular until her kidnapping, after which she didn't have to introduce herself anymore.

"Cocktail..." She trailed off. She looked at Nadia, and I could swear I saw a blazing furnace in her eyes.

"Hi, Nadia," she said, brushing past me to assert dominance. "I am your cousin, Emerson's daughter."

Okay, I might be mixing things up. Let's start from the beginning, after I saved the princess from the burning thingy.

10

WHAT IS OUR FUTURE?

Emerson hated all forms of religious inclination. It made people judgmental, easily manipulated, biased, and, worst of all, plainly stupid. How do people not pause to figure these things out?

In the beginning, God created the world. He had no problems with God. You must be insane not to believe that this universe was designed by a mastermind. He agreed that there was a God who had lovingly given up on mankind, as in, come on, look. There had been a time when God cared about this world, and it was evident. No climate change, no heat, no fucking flies buzzing in your ears, and no goddamned mosquitoes! Seriously, what did man do to deserve mosquitoes? But the worst off among these pests was man. Men fought over land, food, drinking holes, and maize, as well as fire, sticks, and stones; men fought over tinder and dates, the edible and the artificial, but it was all good.

If Peter stole Paul's wife, they fought to the death, and one problem ended that day. It was reasonable and understandable, even manly. But then the religious men grew beards, picked up a stick, and decided it was time to take the lead. Early prophets were shepherds, no? Sheep and goats were not enough, so these alpha males called on the puppies for backup. They set up sects and became elite. Following the death of the third generation, the story and ideals became misplaced, as is typical of men, and religion became the world's greatest source of pain. It wasn't the only thing that annoyed him. The prodigy morphed into a brain-dead generation that lauded those who were slightly above average as geniuses. Seriously, aside from social media and digitising the world, the jet age had no other purpose but to fly into its inevitable demise.

"Allah ya biya."

Then there were beggars, a plague worse than locusts. This man had two good hands and complete feet, yet he sat on the ground because he believed it was his right to be given alms. He dropped a bitcoin slip on the man's plate.

"Nagode maigida," the beggar said.

The man's voice was craggy; he didn't like beggars who weren't grateful. If you would sit on the road to beg, why have the pride and the audacity to choose?

He checked his wallet and found a five-hundred-naira note. He retraced his steps and was about to take the slip back when he noticed that the man was blind. He had already come back, and the money was out. He dropped the money and continued walking. The beggar was lucky. Not lucky to be blind, just that some things were beneath him.

"Maigida," he scoffed as he found the right angle in the park.

He sat down and observed the children playing. How ludicrous! Parks were now complete with a full five miles of plain sand where children could come and have a good time, rolling around like dogs. Who would not appreciate being born in the 2000s?

But the sand was not his problem today, so long as he kept his head above it. His brother had had it out for him since he found out Levine was a former staff member of his. Former, for god's sake. It wasn't like he should be held accountable for what the man did with his spare time. If his hobby was kidnapping people, how was he to know? His brother did not believe that he wasn't the architect of that plan. How he wished he were; the little thing would not have had the nerve to come out of that hole.

The heat had better be dealt with; if not, people might need to start walking around with rain-umbrellas.

A man came to sit beside him. He had on a hat and sunglasses and looked like a harmless father among the crowd. He held a sweet in his hand, which he used to lure a toddler over as they spoke.

"Baby steps towards achieving our plans, are we?"

"They are all gone." The man said. "The Sultan has no more heirs except for Nadia." The toddler came over and took the sweet from the man's hand.

"Keep me informed," Emerson said. The man nodded and, after some time, left. Emerson went on thinking his thoughts. Would it not, in the end, be best if the country had an atheist president? But that was taking it too far. What if the country had an ideal president just like him? Like him… There was someone like him. If he could pull this off, it would be the perfect plan to put everyone in their place.

***

Sarki knew enough not to trust his brother. Since Emerson arrived, his plans had been put aside, and his brother had pursued his agenda. He had thought Emerson would be wooed by the need for vengeance, but it seemed that he despised the Quinns too much to waste his time hurting them.

He had received a rather unsettling message today. There had been news that he had children outside. The ones he knew, he provided for until they had died, but most of these children were born to Christian women who did not want to be found, while others were prostitutes. As it is with that profession, the matter was kept secret. Some women had literally disappeared with their children, only surfacing with the news that they were dead.

When they were younger, he had been with countless women. All of them eager to be the wife of the next sultan. When he had received the title, the wives came as tribute, and he could not satisfy his gluttony.

He hungered for those other girls; they knew how to give him what he wanted. His wives were boring; merely for show. He was bothered now because, in desperation, he had sent one of his councillors to find out if he had any children left outside, and yes, he did. He had been elated until they, too, started to die. He would have blamed it on God again, but he knew better. His brother would do almost anything for him, but it seemed he had plans of his own, and as secretive as they were, they did not favour him.

After digging deep into the Levine matter, he found what he was looking for. There was an anonymous donation coming in from an offshore account to the dead man's child. He tried to get more information, but it was a dead end. Who else but his brother could pull off something so authentic? Enough with the games; it was time he played his hand.

He sent a text and reclined on his throne. How beautiful it felt to have power and amass more. What could he do now but find a suitor for his daughter so there would be an heir when it was time to pass the crown?

Nadia! She had changed after the incident. She seemed to have had a turnaround. She had become more Western and radical in her Islamism. And now, she stayed out late, telling him not to worry about her being abducted a second time. And she was seeing that boy—what was that name again? Elzaiya, yes.

The boy reminded him of his brother in his early years: smart, intelligent, and full of ambition, pride, and vision. He had come to the house the next day to get his phone, as requested. He had caught his daughter peeping from behind the curtains. She had said she wanted to know who it was, but he knew it was a lie. She carried a torch for the boy. He, on the other hand, preferred the friend. He was witty and made a lot of funny jokes. It was not often that he had the time to laugh. He just hoped they wouldn't get themselves into trouble like kids do.

When he asked about their origin, they said they were foster brothers who had grown up together. They didn't know who their parents were, and they thought it best if they never knew. Sometimes the truth was prevented from people for a reason. He couldn't agree more.

Since he couldn't harm the Quinns' remaining son, he had resorted to more diplomatic methods. He had called up a friend, who had a friend, who knew a guy that had a friend in the police department and another in the press. Before long, Merceides' picture was on CNN, calling for a murder trial. He was proud of himself. Hadn't the Quinns said they didn't want their son involved in politics? Now he would forever be tainted.

But what was up with this heat? Even the air conditioner was not as effective as it was supposed to be. He turned. The damned thing wasn't even on. These servants deserved to be flogged. He stood up and left for the balcony.

He passed the maid on the way, the one who always delivered the bad news. He pitied her. She had watched so many children grow, only to watch them die. All of them, except for Nadia, whose mother never let go. They had said she was mad. She kept saying she would be the one to take care of her child because someone was coming to steal the souls of the other children in the night. But had she not been accurate? She took care of her child until the girl was 19, and then one day, she shared a dream where she died. He had laughed it away, but she had died that afternoon on her bed, in a peaceful sleep. They had said it was suicide; he had not objected.

He had just crossed onto the balcony when his mind reminded him to get back into the house. It was not often that he had this aura, but recently, he was suspicious and careful.

He went in; everywhere was silent, and everything was fine. It was a big house anyway. He was just about to get back outside when he noticed that the door to his room was ajar. He never left it that way. He swung the door open and found the maid bending over his medicine chest. In shock, the contents of her hands spilt, and little blue pills poured all over the floor.

***

We are oblivious of the future for a reason. Sometimes it's denied us, because we might misuse what we have gleaned or change our course and in doing so change the course of another man's destiny. Sometimes it's because we are too surprised when the future happens. Most times, it is to save us the pain that might come our way. Either way, the future is shielded from us for whatever reason the gods have willed. But when it is revealed, it is so that we may be warned. So that we can change what we can, if we are wise enough to heed true prophecy from the rattlings of common deceitful folk. But the future holds for each man a plan, and these plans take time to unfold.

I was lying on my bed when I received a text. Father didn't waste words in messages; he was direct: "2 a.m., take the tunnel. Rest. Meeting by 9."

What could have gone wrong now?

But it wasn't long before I would come to find out. I was just digesting the news about Merceides when one of my sources, in a note of concern, told me that the press was gathered around Harlequin's grave and that his body was missing. I thought the whole thing through before putting another call through. "Avelli," he sounded creaky, like I had woken him from wood, "I was asleep. "What's the matter?"

"Sandstorm," I said. There was a four-second pause before he replied calmly, "I'll close the windows."

I sprang out of bed and went to my secret compartment. There was the bulletproof vest, which I always wished not to use. This thing was too dangerous for me and Avelli. I closed the wardrobe and made another call.

It was around 11:24 when Avelli came over in a black bulletproof Rover. "I figure we'll need the big dog," he spoke as I got in. My source had told me that the body was being kept in the general hospital, and if I was right, it was being guarded, but by whose security? We wouldn't be able to tell who worked for whom.

We parked under a tree in the dark; we had driven with the lights off so no one would see us coming. If we were going to steal a body, we needed a plan. Twenty minutes later, we were running towards the car, bullets whizzing past our ears.

"I thought you said they would be unaware," Machiavelli cursed.

"They were supposed to be." I jumped over the wire mesh.

"Someone must have told them we were coming; these guys were waiting for us."

"Did they see your face?"

"I never took my mask off. Did you?"

"I'm not stupid." I ducked.

"Who do you think set this thing up?"

"Let's make it to the car first. Damn it!"

We had no weapons, and I, for one, was not interested in spilling blood. I never have, as much as I wanted to, but a gun wasn't my weapon, and these men were just doing their jobs.

"Now."

We both sprang to the car and jumped in on time before a bullet nicked the door. Machiavelli threw a canister of tear gas and revved out of the driveway with bullets tapping on the glass.

"Whose men do you think they were?"

"I think this is Emerson trying to make things up to his brother by proving to him that Harlequin is alive. In the case that he is, it means we have been playing them all along, which, i.e., you see, makes him innocent and others guilty."

"I.e., the family."

"Hide the car and meet me in the house. We have some work to do."

"Will we make it out of this mess?" Machiavelli was worried, and this was the second in a long time.

"You'll make it out," I said.

I knew he had more to worry about now than he did before. It was evident he wanted to build a life with Cairo, and that meant being careful and slowly pulling out of the danger we had come to love so much.

"You would both be alright," I said.

He nodded; he was now assured.

"That was no coincidence," Quinn said. "You assured me everything would be fine."

I admired how Father was calm. We shared that in common.

"I did, Father."

"What went wrong?" Everyone was now looking at me, which was just great.

"I think it was Emerson; we know what he's capable of, and we know that he is topmost on the list of those crazy enough to disrespect the dead. But I have a suggestion: I think we should wait."

"Wait? Should we wait? For them to come and ask why we told the nation that their president was dead? And why isn't his body rotting?"

"If we wait, we will know who got the body."

"What do you mean, 'got?'"

"My source told me that the body was at the general hospital, but if not for precautionary measures, we would not be alive."

Quinn was more concerned now. "What happened?"

"They were waiting for us, that's what," Machiavelli said.

"And the body?" Harlequin asked.

"There was no body."

"I don't understand."

"I put a proximity GPS device in the body. If I were three miles away, it would send a signal. We went in and scouted the whole hospital down to the mortuary, but there was no signal."

"Maybe they tampered with it," Harlequin said.

"Only a laser beam can damage that device."

Merceides had been silent throughout the discussion. He seemed lost in thought. "What did Emerson talk to you about when you met him last?" He finally asked.

"How does that fit into our current problems?" Harlequin asked. He seemed to be on edge, which was unusual.

"He said I should consider the presidential games."

"And?"

"I told him I wasn't interested."

"But you are."

There was silence in the room.

"No, I am not."

"I think you should go in," Merceides said.

"What!" Harlequin stood up and looked at his twin brother with disbelief. "He's inexperienced. By the way, he has never been the political type."

"I think they should both run the challenge." Quinn agreed with Merceides.

"Both?" Machiavelli was surprised.

"Yes, you and your brother." It was the first time Quinn called them brothers.

"But none of us are interested," Machiavelli said.

"Power is best given to those who don't want it," Quinn said.

"And what about me? Do I remain dead and end my tenure that way?"

"You would come to light once everything is settled. I think you have done well enough. If we were to develop the Northern region without friction, we would need to be backed by one or more of our enemies, and they would never back any of my sons."

"So, what do we do now?" Harlequin seemed to have succumbed.

Everyone looked at Merceides.

"I think you'll make a fine president, both you and Avelli," he grinned.

11

WHAT IS DECEIT?

As expected, things went awkwardly that day. What with Nadia, her sister, and her cousin around. It took adeptness on my and Avelli's parts to play the role of unencumbered men. We ate the Kilishi and Suya that Nadia brought and got to talking.

I asked Nadia how it felt to have been kidnapped. *Yes, I know I sound like an ass right now. But what was I supposed to have asked?* The whole place was as tense as rubber bands.

"It was an eerie feeling," her eyes twinkled as if she missed it.

"I wouldn't use 'eerie' to describe being kidnapped," Cairo said.

"It wasn't bad," Nadia tried to explain. "It was as if it was meant for me to be comfortable. The kidnapper went out of his way to make sure I didn't get nostalgic.

"Creepy," Machiavelli looked heavenward to avoid my gaze.

I looked at him and then back at Nadia. Denise stared at me with her expression closed. *All these relationships could get mixed up.*

"The room was an exact copy of my room. And when I woke up, thinking I was home, I did the stupidest thing and asked for my maid."

We all laughed.

"The guy must be a crack addict," I said.

"Some expensive crack," Nadia conferred. "But I don't think he was the brain behind it."

"How so?" Machiavelli probed.

"Something didn't feel right, and when my father investigated the matter…"

"Oh yeah!" I cut her short. I didn't want her to mistakenly slip the fact that Denise's father was the bad guy in my plans. I didn't need smarts to tell me it was a bad idea.

"Aren't you scared that maybe the psycho would come back to finish what he started? With intelligence like that, the person could be someone close to you. Perhaps the kidnapping was only a small part of the bigger picture." Denise sighed and pursed her lips.

I found that my thought tempo raced. I didn't make the mistake of turning to Avelli.

"It could be someone close for sure," Nadia said, her voice trailing. "But I'm not scared."

"What would you say if you had the chance to meet this person? Say if they were at your mercy?" Denise asked again.

She kept pushing, pressing for where it would hurt.

Machiavelli's smile had slipped. He had been tapping his foot on the rug, but now he stopped and looked down at where I sat with the rest of the girls.

I continued to stare at Nadia. Cairo shifted closer to where I was and put her head on my lap. I started to caress her hair. It was a force of habit; I had restless hands.

"I haven't thought about that," Nadia said.

Cairo looked up at her with dilated pupils. She hadn't mentioned the fact that she was her sister or even Denise's cousin. I think Cairo was wiser than she let on.

"I think some stones are better left unturned."

There was an uncomfortable silence. It was mindful retrospection.

I looked at Denise's face reflected on my watch. She was looking at my face, waiting for me to look up at her. She knew something, and that gave her an advantage. She wanted me to know that she knew. My laptop! Had she seen Nadia on my laptop? I caressed Cairo's hair and looked up at Machiavelli. He was stabbing his phone with ferocity. He was thinking.

My glance caught Nadia's, who was staring at me and Cairo. She looked beautiful. I wonder what she looked like underneath that… The oven's ping made us turn toward the kitchen.

I caught Nadia and Denise staring intensely at me. I just hope that things don't get messed up over time.

Merceides was thinking about proposing to Denise, and I was fully in support. It's not being evil, selfish, or whatever moral code you want to slander me with. I just wanted them both to be happy, and for Denise to get out of my life.

It was past 6 p.m. when Nadia told me that she was leaving. Cairo was sitting in front of me. She had this silly habit where she lay on you like a puppy. I used it as an excuse to wave Nadia goodbye.

I didn't know she expected more. I didn't have more; I had reasons. And Denise seemed to be content with my actions.

When it was just the four of us left and Cairo was swinging Avelli like a door with loose hinges – seriously, how could two people make such a racket? It was only sex.

I was in the kitchen making dinner when Denise slipped in and held me from behind. My hands were occupied, and honestly, I loved the way she was—sweet, in a depraved way.

Her hands found their way to my belt. I could have dropped the things in my hands and resisted, but I didn't mind a last fling.

"Your brother is going to ask me to marry him," she whispered.

Her hands were in my jeans, but it was funny how my mind was thinking of something else. I guess some men truly are not to be ruled by their passions.

"Will you say yes?"

She stroked, and I kept my mind in check.

"I love some parts of him," she unzipped the jeans. I suddenly felt jabbed by a bad feeling.

I knew I should stop the slicing and tell her to stop, but it's been so calm for a while that I couldn't help wanting to lust after some chaos.

"You two will make a happy couple." I smiled and reached for a plate.

She increased the rhythm to keep up with the sounds that came from the other room. It was clear what she wanted.

"Do you think I will so easily forget about you?"

I was suddenly breathing hard with anticipation. It was hard to resist temptation when the aura of sex was all around the house.

"I don't think it will be a good idea to add me to the food."

She laughed. "Are you scared you wouldn't be able to hold back? Can't you allow yourself to be vulnerable for a change?"

"What do you think about Nadia's kidnapper?" I asked and noticed how her pace slackened. Now I was sure.

"You have to stop doing that," she said.

"What?"

"Stop grilling me when we're like this. You only ask questions when the moment is sensual; you think I'm desperate."

"Are you?" I turned to face her.

She moved in and kissed me. There, those crimson lips that looked like lambs' flesh. She wanted my teeth in her, and it was hard to resist. Somehow, I felt that my brother had the better end of this ordeal.

"You'll never be mine, and I can't say I'm content with that. I'm caught in limbo, feeling things that will never be satisfied. I love you, but I'm starting to hate how you make me feel. I shouldn't ever have let this happen in the first place," her hand was moving rapidly, and I could tell she was in an emotional place. I was trying my best not to explode. What was wrong with me? I should make her stop.

"You are a child in some ways. In many ways, you are yet to become wise. And I don't know how I fell for you, knowing who you are and the things you'd rather want. Maybe I am just my father's daughter, after all, falling in love with dangerous men. Monsters…"

Okay, that was enough. I wanted to drop the things in my hand and push her away, but she pushed me to the centre of the kitchen and increased the pace. I could hear my heart pounding. I could feel everything and everyone, and right now, it felt like the whole house was one big sex machine.

"I'm sorry I made you feel that way. I…"

She kissed me again, and I relaxed and gave in. She became all that I desired. And as our lips intertwined, I could feel the burning water from her eyes and the pain in the tears that she cried, which almost stung my eyes.

I wanted to ask her why she felt that way when all I felt was ineffable, and the deepest part of it was, "Why?" And then she did something with her hands and…

She didn't let me go. She kept moving her hand while holding me close to her with the other. It was warm on me and, by the sound of it, slurpy on her hands. And I was caught wondering what emotion 'why' was.

When she let me go, there were still tears in her eyes. I took a deep breath, like I'd been resuscitated from the deep end. Her dress was ruined by my ejaculation, which dripped all over the front. *What have I done?*

"I know you kidnapped Nadia," she said. "You have to forgive me, I'm sorry," she ran out, with tears still in her eyes, and I could hear the exclamation from Cairo as she ran into them in the corridor.

I buckled my belt and waited for them to reach me.

"Oh, my God! How could you?" Cairo was more confused than concerned. "She's going to be your brother's wife."

I looked at Avelli. He took a deep breath and folded his hands. "I'm disappointed in you, man," he managed to say with as much shock as he could muster.

That was good acting, but I had a pressing matter. "Where is she?"

***

"But Harlequin, it's the right thing to do, or one of them. At least it's politically correct."

"It doesn't help me at all."

"Maybe not, but as long as it works and is flawless, why not? Elzaiya and Machiavelli should run for political offices. Elzaiya isn't popular yet, but he would win because, by your description, there is no way he loses the game. Machiavelli has a 90% chance of winning as well. When one of them wins, the other becomes an ambassador and represents all your interests. Isn't that what you've always wanted?"

"Yes, but…"

"But someone else will get the fame, and that's not what you want?" He was silent.

"You should let it work for the greater good," she said.

He smirked and was about to get a drink from the freezer when he heard sounds outside—a commotion. They both went to the window to see.

It was Denise talking to Merceides, telling him to calm down about something.

"I wonder what she's done."

"Your brother seems angry; wouldn't you go check it out?"

"I'm dead, remember?" He sat down. "By the way, he deserves whatever's happened. He's the one who brought up a plan that doesn't favour me."

***

Merceides was blinded by rage. He felt like a fire was being pumped into his chest, and soon he would explode. He would kill Elzaiya; it was long overdue.

"Don't hurt him, please. He's just jealous." Denise pleaded tearfully.

"He's psychologically sick!" Merceides yelled.

"It's my fault; I slept on his bed and the gown was short…"

"It doesn't justify anything."

"Please, don't hurt him, I beg you."

"How could he do this to you, knowing what you mean to me?"

"He has urges; maybe he thought it was normal."

"Normal? Enough of this!" He strode past her to his Rover and drove off, nearly knocking the guard out of the way.

"What happened?" Aaira asked her husband, who was looking down from the tower at Denise. There was something about her that he didn't find fitting.

"She said Elzaiya assaulted her. He tried to sleep with her. Rape, perhaps. Apparently, he ejaculated on her dress while she was asleep in his room."

"No way!"

"No way, what?"

"You know he didn't, right?"

"When it comes to our youngest, I'm not sure what I know."

"He would never assault a girl," She began to cry.

"Most probably not," he held her.

Aaira wasn't emotionally fragile, but tears just came naturally to her. He wondered how she coped with crying that much, whether happy or sad.

"What if they fight? He has fragile bones. What if…"

"We would not always be around to look out for them," Quinn said.

Harlequin waited until everything was calm before he and Navina snuck out of the compound. He had promised that he would take her to a club for her birthday, and with Merceides at Elzaiya's place, it was perfect timing.

Merceides drove the car furiously, occasionally turning to look at the baseball bat on the passenger seat for comfort. He would become the murderer the news had made him out to be.

Denise didn't know what to feel. She had not thought about the consequences of her actions. It had been impulsive. She needed him out of her system, and if her husband could get him out of the family, she would feel better. She had hoped.

***

He had told them to leave. Machiavelli wanted to stay, but he would not have it.

"When have I not been okay?"

Machiavelli reminded him that nothing like this had happened before. But he insisted that it would be fine.

"Zaiya, did you?" Cairo had finally asked. She was in shock, seemingly from being unable to correlate the person to the event.

"Whatever Denise said was the truth."

Machiavelli looked at him and, from years of being his brother, knew that he was lying. It was not a case of honour. He just wasn't one to defend himself or explain his actions.

"I don't believe what she said. You're not that kind of person."

"You don't know me," he said coldly. It was one of his truest statements.

There was a flash in his eyes that reminded her of the man who had come to check on her before she had left home. She kept silent and stormed out. Machiavelli nodded, and after a while, Elzaiya heard them drive away.

There was a bracelet hidden in his wardrobe that he never wore. It had been given to him after he fractured two ribs and injured his knee. It had been more of a parting gift after the doctor had said he might not make it through the night. He had held on to it until morning, and the beads had carved their marks in his palm, leaving impressions on his skin. It was an artefact he treasured, along with his family ties. The beads and their scars together symbolised loyalty.

He took it out of the case along with a knife he had never used. He usually joked that it should be used to cut his parts when the family needed a sacrificial lamb.

He dropped the knife on the floor and knelt in front of it. He took his shirt off, held the bracelet in his hands like one in prayer, and waited.

He heard the car pull into the driveway and then nothing, until his door swung open.

Merceides walked over to him in anger. He raised the bat and approached him cautiously. He was about to swing it when his brother raised his hands with the beads for him to see. The scars remained, faint but red, on his palm.

Right there, Merceides remembered the promise he had made to his brother.

***

The club had been fun, and Harlequin was having a blast. He did not see the man in the corner sipping a drink, taking his time to observe him microscopically.

When he stood up to pee, the man followed him to the bathroom. They bumped into each other, and Harlequin was about to apologise when he froze.

"I see you are surprised to see me in a place of inebriation."

"No, I'm not," Harlequin said, free of glee.

"Merceides, right?"

"Yeah," he extended his hand.

"Then what are you doing, sneaking around with your brother's girlfriend?"

"She was bored." Harlequin was getting worried.

"Spare me the speech. Nice job you did digging your body back up."

"My brother is dead." Harlequin headed for the bathroom.

"Where is your precious Navina?"

Harlequin turned to look but couldn't find her. "What have you done to her?" He demanded.

His voice was drowned out by the noise in the club.

"I have an offer you should consider. It's not like you have an option. The good news is that I would assist you in regaining the power you seek."

"I thought you didn't want a Kafir as president?"

"You have no idea what I want," he leaned in. "We are two men getting back what we deserve. In a way, I'm doing you a favour. All I'm asking for is a little something in return. You will find that I can be a very resourceful friend."

12

MY FAMILY. MY LOYALTY

When they were kids, Merceides had been very fond of his younger brother. He still was when he acted like a normal human being.

On that day, they had been playing in the garden when Merceides decided that they should play a pretend robbery. In the process, he stole a car. His brother had told him that the plan wasn't a good one, but he wouldn't listen, so he crawled into a van and, after experimenting as they did in the movies, found the ignition wires and jump-started the car. He had no idea how to drive, but it did not occur to him that a car could start its movement in reverse. When the car moved, it hit something, and he got scared, so he pulled the wires apart and jumped down, elated and happy that he was safe. That's when he saw his brother in a pool of blood.

No one had seen it happen, and he was too scared to admit that he was the perpetrator of the gimmick. His mother would lose her mind. When they were found out and taken to the hospital, he had prayed that his brother would not sell him out.

When Elzaiya regained consciousness, he said he couldn't remember what had happened. Merceides knew it was a lie. So, he had promised not to allow anything to hurt him so long as he was alive.

And now, staring at the beads he had used to seal that promise, he was unsure what to do.

"I wouldn't answer your questions because I know the answers might hurt," Elzaiya said. "You know what I can and can't do. But what happened here today was a lady trying to prove that she was right in choosing who she loves. I think you deserve to be with her. I think she made the right choice, and I think she will make a good wife. I'm sorry for allowing it to happen. Maybe it was because I was envious of what you had. I don't feel things, so I'm not sure what drives passions in the human mind. I'm sorry for being who I am."

"Get up."

Elzaiya stood up and looked at his brother.

"Do you love her?"

"She is very attractive in many senses, but I don't think love in context should be…"

"Do you love her?" Merceides dropped the bat.

"I don't think I am capable of so great a feat."

"I know what you would do, brother. But I also know that you love to stretch the limits of what you can't or wouldn't do. It makes it hard to know you. Sometimes I wonder who you are."

"She loves you, and she is willing to do dangerous things to prove it."

"I know." Merceides walked around his brother to the wine cabinet. "I see you have some good stuff."

"I had visitors. Isolation is a good thing. See what happens when I let people in."

Merceides poured himself some wine and filled up another glass. "Here."

"Thanks!" Elzaiya accepted it. "Please make yourself at home. There's a bottle of expensive wine in the cabinet. Pour yourself a drink."

"You were at my mercy some minutes ago."

"You're violating my good stuff; we're almost even."

Merceides stared at him for a while.

He was cool as usual, unbothered as if nothing had happened.

"I knew you guys had something."

Elzaiya nodded.

"Why am I not surprised? I assume you were the one who told Dad to tell me about it?"

He nodded again.

"Oh, devils! You knew this would happen."

"I needed what we had to end; she would soon become your wife."

"And if we were not getting married soon, what would you have done?"

You remember that part about a man's rage and my brother finding out that I was the one plucking at the apple of his eye? Well, sometimes it's a man's humility that can quell him.

"I desired her, but I knew I couldn't have her. She wanted a distraction, and I did what I did out of lust. But then, I knew she would choose you. You were always a better man than I."

He looked me dead in the eyes, and I didn't flinch. Sometimes it is an antidote of generously cultivated lies that breeds the trust we need for our relationships to thrive.

"You are the best of us, brother, just not yet," he said.

I gave a smile of relief, doing my best to lace it with a little shame and sadness. I was almost starting to think he could see through me.

***

"I don't understand. He isn't that type of person. He won't…"

"He's not," Machiavelli was tired of hearing the same thing over again. "He's not that type of person, okay. You know it, I know it, everybody knows it."

"So how come he…"

"Because he wanted it to happen! Whatever happens to him, he wanted it to happen. He knows things. How he sees them and how he knows them, I don't know. It's like he has the universe in his mind, and just like a book, he can flip it to any page he wants to find out whatever he wants."

"Stop yelling at me."

"I'm not yelling at you."

"Yes, you are."

He took a deep breath. "Okay, okay, I'm sorry. Do I sound less yelly now?"

"You're doing that thing."

"What thing?"

"That thing that he does when he's making fun of you."

"No, I'm not."

"Yes, you are."

"I'm not."

"You're yelling again."

"You're the one making me yell!"

"What is wrong with you?"

"What?"

"I mean, apart from the fact that I'm pestering you about what happened and all that, what is wrong with you?"

"I don't know," he sat on the hood of the car and looked at his feet. They were some yards from their house. They too had moved from the Quinns' residence. He didn't tell her why. He only told her that they should stay on their own like grown-ups.

"I think I'm afraid."

She hugged him. "It's normal to be afraid. Just don't let the fear control you," she looked up at him. "What are you even afraid of? I thought you were invincible."

"I'm scared for him."

"Elzaiya?"

He nodded.

"He seems fine. I don't think his brother will harm him."

"That's what I'm scared of. He keeps crossing lines and keeps pushing people to their limits. He keeps falling into trouble so he can get out, all for the thrill of it. He's addicted to living on the edge because it makes his mind sharp, but sometimes the cost is high. If Merceides forgives him today, what of the person who would hold a grudge tomorrow? He's the most intelligent person I know, but I worry that he's on the path to self-destruction. He'll be the one who'll release the hounds that will tear him apart."

"You are concerned; super concerned. I'm almost jealous. Hell, if he were a girl, we would have broken up right now."

"Don't be like that. It's just that he's a good person. But in the long run, I doubt anyone would see it that way."

"If Denise can love someone like Elzaiya, then turn around on him to that degree. I think she's lethal. I hope she never finds out who I am."

"You don't want her to know she's your cousin?"

"Sister, to be exact. And I'd love for that information never to spill. Her vibe doesn't resonate with mine. I prefer Nadia."

***

Merceides parked his car and breezed into the house. His mother watched from the window of her room.

"Sit down and quit worrying. Do you think he would harm his brother?" Quinn said.

"They are my children. You talk as if you don't even care for them."

"I do care. But if we keep watching over them, they will never learn to co-exist. The world is cruel, and as bad as it may be, I think our youngest is the bravest of his brothers and, in his way, the strongest. He would be fine; at least of that I am certain."

"We should have had a girl."

"We would have. You were the one who didn't want another broken child, remember?"

"I was scared he was going to die."

"All the more reason why you should have had a girl."

"Then give me one."

He smiled and continued reading his book.

"Come give me a baby."

"Did you know that the anus develops early in humans?"

"Are you driving to the point where you explain why you're an ass?"

"That was a blow to my ego, ma'am."

"It better be a big blow."

"Bigger than your arse, I'm sure."

"Are you saying…?" She turned from the window where she'd been looking out with her hands on the sill to wipe him. He ducked and covered his face with a pillow.

"You know, from this angle, your ass looks like a wine cork."

"You'll know about wine corks; you invented them."

"Don't be a killjoy; I was hoping to riddle you with teases tonight."

"You've lost your mind?"

He laughed and dropped the book. She was smiling at him, eyes gleaming. "I didn't know a time would come when I would hear you speak like a Nigerian."

"The fact that I am only a quarter Nigerian and half African doesn't mean I can't learn stuff. Thank God my sons are not as dumb as their dad."

"That didn't hurt. If only their mother had not fallen in love with the right half-wit," he laughed and pulled her away from the window.

"Don't touch me. I hate you."

"No, you don't."

"Yes, I do."

He parted her hair. "You're beautiful."

"I am?"

"You are beautiful," he said connivingly.

She sat astride him and kissed him. "Now give me that baby."

***

"Merceides, I'm sorry." Denise started when he walked in. She hadn't thought it through until now. What if Elzaiya had told him how it played out? Then it was left for him to decide whom to choose: his future wife or his brother.

"Why are you apologising? He's the one who should apologise," he came to hold her.

She felt an immense sense of relief. She was right. Elzaiya would never tell.

"Please don't be mad at him; it was my fault for going there."

"It's his fault, and he said he's sorry. He said that he was jealous of what we had. He'd never had something like it, and because he is covetous, he desired you for himself, and he hopes you find a place in your heart to forgive him."

She nodded and then kissed him. "So, don't you want to know if I want to be your wife or not?"

"Now? I thought I needed a table and candles and all the classical stuff."

"You are always too late to the party, my love."

***

Harlequin looked at Navina as she slept peacefully. His life was a mess. When he had asked for the body to be dug back up, he hadn't anticipated that his brother would attempt to retrieve it. He had only hoped that the news would propel his family to put him back in the seat to save face. But they seemed to have other plans, all of which did not involve him.

His brother and Machiavelli would be running for office. If they won, his brother would no doubt outshine him. If Elzaiya were president, he would have unimaginable accomplishments.

He looked at the card in his hands. If he called Emerson, he would be in league with the devil, and that meant he would come near the brink of betraying his family. Was that an option worth considering? But Emerson had used Navina as leverage. He had been forced to listen.

He would be back in power, but then he would undermine the Sultan's power after announcing that he was the one who had set up the murder his brother was accused of. It almost seemed like a giveaway, so harmless.

When he asked what Emerson wanted, he said he just wanted to have political power on his side when the time came.

"Do not think about double-crossing me, or she dies," Emerson had said with a warm smile, which sent a cold chill through his body.

The man was the older version of his younger brother. No wonder they made great acquaintances. Did he know that, too? He dialled the number; it rang once.

"I knew you would come around," Emerson said on the other end.

Machiavelli was still listening to Cairo as she explained what had happened.

"They each slept with the Sultan's wives."

"So, why did your mother not marry one of them?"

"Emerson was in love with Aaira; he was never going to have another woman but her. Sarki was looking for an heir, and my mom was caught in the middle. She loved them both; Emerson more. But she had no future with him, so when she got pregnant, she disappeared and stayed that way."

"Shouldn't you tell him?"

"No, I don't think he cares. Look at Denise. I'm better off without any of them."

"You've had quite the adventurous life."

"Until you showed up with your sweet talk and stuff."

"Stuff?"

"You know what I'm talking about."

"Why did you have sex with me that day?"

"You want to know if I have sex with strangers all the time."

"Well…"

"You were my first. I guess I just believed all the things you said, and I fell for you. I thought you were one of those men who stay after sex, but you had better things to do."

"I don't know when I fell in love with you; it was between the bus and now. It must be true what they say: no one knows when love happens."

I disagree with Avelli. I think we all know when love happens, just as we know when it starts fading. Love is like a seed. When you share the first smile, after you've had the first thought, it starts to grow. But it makes you dumb and illogical along the way, so that you don't notice all the little things that lead to it becoming a tree. But it's always there. If we are conscious of the falling seed, I think we can primarily watch love grow to become a big tree. But that's me. I see and feel differently from most other people.

Putting love aside, I need a plan to get us all saved. This family drama was becoming worse than I had planned. I lied when I said I didn't know whose men those were at the hospital. I had seen a face there before.

Once, two years ago, I had walked into Harlequin's room. He was talking to a man and had waved me away. The man did not turn, but I saw his face on the glass panel of the shelf. A little bit distorted, but I would not forget any face. What game was he playing? And who could I trust? Now that everyone wants something right on their terms?

I and Denise were done; we would never cross paths. I would make sure of that. I needed a new plan.

"Dirige nos domine ad augusta per angusta, sic itur ad astra excelsior."

God would hear me, somehow. But first, I must visit an old friend.

13

THERE'S A BISHOP

The trip to California was essential to the plan. He felt something coming, so he had best be prepared. There were those nightmares again that threatened to drive him mad. Emerson had told him to consider running for office, but he had refused. He said it was a headache he didn't want. When he asked Emerson why he didn't go for it, he said it was because he would soon be over the participating age. When Elzaiya reminded him that he had at least ten more years, he said leadership wasn't his thing. They had laughed it off.

Emerson had told him that he had nightmares, too. They had talked about a lot of things and had toasted to many more nightmarish years.

When they talked about children, Elzaiya said he hadn't given it much thought. But in his opinion, they were a pain in the arse. Then they toasted to their parents not having the same opinion about them. Emerson had told him he had a girl, a daughter he wasn't certain was his. But if she believed he was her father, why deny her such a horrible relationship? If a father was what she desired, then heim! He'd tried.

Elzaiya told him that he sucked at the "daddy" part. "I absolutely think I would have been a better father if I had a son like you," Emerson had laughed.

"Cheers to absolutism!" They toasted again.

They usually met at bars or parks. Sometimes they went to attractions to take pictures, and at other times, they'd take a spin in Emerson's car to the beautiful places in town to critique. Emerson had said it was essential to the development of civilisation. Sometimes they left the keepers of attractions and galleries in tears. But the people on the streets loved them and always hoped they would come their way.

Elzaiya seemed to make Emerson a better man. They made a jolly pair, but they had things they didn't talk about and lines they didn't cross. They just had a good time because they seemed to understand each other in ways most people couldn't.

Looking down, everything was exactly how it was supposed to be: small. He remembered some words from his journal: *Small. Everything starts to become so small. You tend not to stop stepping on people if you're standing on the world.*

"Let me not fall," Elzaiya prayed.

***

Sarki found the maid's silence inconvenient. He had asked what she was doing in his room. She'd said she was searching for something.

What? She refused to explain why she was holding his pills. He had asked twice before he lost his temper and kicked her in the face. She had hit her head on the bed and fainted.

He called his guards to take her to his private prison, resuscitate her, and chain her up. He'd then called his doctor to have the pills sampled.

The doctor had said that the pills were the normal medication he took for stress, but the capsules he would examine.

"Rai'n ka ya da'de'. Amma kowa na so ya zama sarki," he spat.

Things had started to fall apart because of his brother. When has Emerson not made everything about himself? Narcissist.

He had told him that he couldn't have heirs, and he had suggested help. And then there was Nadia. If not for the affection he had developed for her over the years, he would have despised her now that he was unsure if she was his child or just another seed in his brother's twisted plan.

The news on TV stated that Harlequin's body was discovered by vandals looking to steal body parts, but the national surprise was that the body was not decomposed in any way.

"They have played me for a fool," he left the room and locked the door.

His doctor was waiting for him at the entrance to the living room.

"Sarki…" he started. He meant it in terms of "king", not his name.

"Ka kaskanta?"

"I met our young pharmacist. He helped me cross-check the pills with the ones the maid used to buy. He wondered why she was getting it but…"

"Get to the point."

"The capsules are a decoy; they are filled with sugar. But the pills, which even I mistook for your normal pills, are infertility pills, sir." Sarki felt his blood run cold. This man has been their family doctor since he was a teenager. He had replaced the other doctor, who had died of old age. He was bound by loyalty to the Sultan.

"Nagode."

The doctor bowed and was about to leave when he called him back.

"How did Doctor Usman die?"

The doctor paused. He wasn't ready for that question.

"They said he died of old age."

"Just like my father?"

"Yes, my lord."

"You were young and curious at the time. Did you go through their files?"

"I did, sir."

"Was there anything strange?"

"Nothing strange, sir, except…"

"Except what?"

"There was a night when your brother was brought in to the doctor's lodge. I think he had been punished by your father. He was covered in blood and animal dung. He had blacked out, and after we treated him, he woke up with no memory of what had happened."

"That's strange."

"That's not the strangest part, my lord. When I was cleaning him up, I had to remove dead flies from his hair, mouth, ears, and other places. I went to sleep before he awoke, so I don't think he knew I was a part of the cleaning process. When he woke up, the doctor asked him if he was alright; he smiled and said he felt perfect. After the examination, the doctor kept his file hidden, which I went through. When your father and the doctor died, it was natural, except for a similarity. They both died on the same date, years later, that the event happened, and according to their times of death, they both died within a three-hour gap. Your father first, at the time he would have used to start the punishment, and the doctor next, at the exact time your brother was brought in unconscious. The most bizarre part is that they both had a single splash of blood with a dead fly on it near the heads of their bed."

"Where is the file?"

"The original copy is missing, my lord. I couldn't find it after the doctor died. But I have a copy, and can make it available anytime you want."

***

"Does this dress look a little too big on me?"

"Nadia, you'll look lovely in anything you wear. But what's the occasion?"

"Nothing, I just want to go for a visit."

"You want to go see him again," Mariam said disapprovingly.

"Last time I just went to give him a Salah gift."

"A Salah gift that you wanted to deliver days before Salah. You spent weeks talking about him, wondering where he lived and everything. You wouldn't rest until your father invited him over for dinner, and then you wouldn't go out and eat with them because you didn't want it to feel as if you were too forward. What's with you?"

"Nothing... I just I like him."

"Like noodles and cakes?"

"What! No..."

"Debino and Arakke?"

"No... and stop comparing him to food; he's sweeter than that."

"La ila! Have you tasted him, kuma? Dadi' kamar sugar kenan."

"No... I wouldn't do that... gross. Go away!"

"Tau, how did you know he's sweet?"

"You can just tell. He's nice, he looks romantic, and all the other girls like him. I think Denise does too."

"Denise, your cousin? Emerson's daughter?"

"Yes, she was jealous when she saw us in the kitchen together. I think they had something."

"And you want to put yourself in the middle of it?"

"Ba haka ne fa."

"Tau yaya abin din yake?"

"I feel something when he's looking at me. Kamar yana jawo zuchiya ta."

"Ki bi shi kadan kadan. Men cannot be trusted."

"Ai na sa'ni."

Mariam knotted her hair and smiled at Nadia in the mirror. She had been her maid since they were kids, and they were the same age. She had grown to become her sister over time. She was a bit jealous because it was the first time Nadia had developed feelings for someone else.

"So, what will you tell him you came to do?"

"Ummm… I don't know. I came to see him?"

"That would sound desperate. You have to make him want you."

"So, what will I do?"

"Tell him that you came to see if Denise was around and if he could help you with her contact."

Nadia said it was the worst excuse ever, but Mariam insisted she use it.

Nadia smiled and caught Mariam staring at her in the mirror. She would go see him today and find out what kind of person he was. She really liked him. He was the first person she had such raging emotions for. Other people sickened her.

She remembered the day before she left. Denise had asked if she liked him. She had lied because she didn't know what relationship the two had. She had said he was a good guy, and she liked him as a person.

Denise had laughed and told her it was obvious she was lying. She said nothing after that. Elzaiya had been cold to her through it all. She could see that they respected him; even when he joked and played, there was a class halo that made you fall in line when relating to him. She had been sad, almost angry, that day when he had waved her away like she was insignificant. Could he not tell that she liked him?

California had been resourceful, and Elzaiya was certain, as the plane flew back to Nigeria, that things would turn around. Not soon, but they will. He hoped things would not get worse, but when they did, he had a failsafe. The country would not suffer because people wanted to satisfy themselves.

He opened the diary that lay on his lap.

During her kidnapping, Nadia had spent more than half her days writing out her mind, expressing herself, and regretting the things she hadn't done. He had kept it for himself. He knew he should get rid of it, but he enjoyed reading it.

He didn't want to admit how he felt; it wouldn't help him. He had to focus and get things done. He thought about her on his worst nights, when his nightmares wouldn't let him sleep. She had become the place he went to when he wanted to find peace. He would get her out of his head; she was making him…

***

Harlequin didn't sleep well. But why bother? What was wrong with a father wanting to reconnect with his daughter? Emerson had said he wanted to make amends with the family. If, in the end, his daughter, whom he had not acknowledged, would want to marry into the Quinn family, would it not just be the right thing for them all to be on good terms? It was a reasonable fallacy coming from Emerson. But he had to play his cards with sincerity.

"You don't look present. You've been drifting out of conversations since last night. Are you alright?"

"What?"

Navina sighed. "What's on your mind?"

"Nothing," he kissed her cheek. "I'm just wondering how to save face over this whole thing."

"Leave the people who planned it to end it."

"Wise counsel as always."

He stood at the edge of the bed and gazed out of the window. It was midday, and the sun would soon be scorching.

"I'll be back in a sec; I want to meet with my brother."

"Take your time," she said that and covered herself with the sheets. He smiled. She didn't know what he was doing to keep her safe. That was the problem with falling in love.

Denise was walking in the gardens as usual. She had made it a habit to walk the entire garden before going back in to hide from the sun. She was about to leave the grounds when he met her on the path to Elzaiya's apartment.

"Hi..." She seemed flustered.

"Sorry to scare you, I didn't know..."

"It's fine," she continued walking.

"Actually, I was hoping to bump into you."

"Me?" He removed his face cap and looked at her. "Oh, silly, you nearly..." She stopped dead in her tracks. "You're not..." She gasped. "Harlequin."

"Yes, I am." "It's a pleasure to meet you, Denise," he stretched his hand. She smiled and took it. The card was in his palm. He dropped his hand. "Don't read the card yet."

"What's..."

"Your dad wants to talk."

Quinn and Merceides watched from the window of the study.

Elzaiya had told Merceides to watch Denise. But Harlequin was also behaving strangely now.

"This picture was taken in the club by one of our observers," Quinn said. There was no mistaking Emerson and Harlequin shaking hands.

***

Sarki had just returned from another meeting in Borno; he was exhausted. His mind was fuzzy about the recent happenings. He didn't know who to trust. The maid was refusing to talk, a sign that his contender was powerful.

He had read Emerson's file. If his brother was indeed as damaged as the file said, he had to be put down. He had concluded, logically, that it was his brother who had killed their father and the doctor, but why? What reason did he have to commit a crime so abominable as patricide?

He had asked the doctor if there was any place he knew or any information he could find about what had happened that night, but the doctor had said he couldn't help. He had nothing more to offer, and it would be best if he did not let it be known that he was looking into it.

After much contemplation, he resorted to the librarian. The man was old — dead was the right word, but he still functioned effectively. It was a miracle.

The man's apprentice sat down on a mat with his prayer beads in his hand. They both bowed when they saw him, and after that, looked him dead in the eyes. Knowledge, he had come to know, was more valued than power down here. Except when you had both, and he had not been coming here since he became powerful.

"Ina nima wani litafi."

"Wace' iri?" The apprentice stood.

He explained that he needed something about the old rites and customs of the Sultans.

The librarian told him to be more specific. So, he asked if they had something about a punishment that involved blood, dung, and flies. The librarian looked at him for a very long time, and when he was starting to wonder if the man was deaf, he called the boy to his side and whispered something to him.

The boy asked the Sultan to follow him, and he led him to a crypt. A different section of the library that he did not know existed. And there he saw a glass cage, beautifully carved and curved like an hourglass, big enough to hold a man. It had chains to hold the hands and feet, and it was visible that the glass was soundproof. He was still staring at the glass when the boy came back with a book. They left the crypt, and he was about to leave when the librarian called him back and whispered something in his ear.

Emerson came in and did not find his brother around. That was a good thing. He was just getting comfortable when he got a text telling him that the maid had been caught. He sent a text to ask if she had talked. She hadn't, which was fortunate. He sent a reply and reclined to enjoy the silence.

It was getting dark when Sarki started shuffling around. He had given his men an order due today. He hid the book in his room and made sure the door was securely locked.

He was about to sit down for dinner when he was told that the maid was dead. No one seemed to be able to say how.

Emerson joined him at the dinner table. He seemed to be in a good mood.

Sarki smiled at him as he sat down to eat.

They were halfway through the meal when Emerson, without warning, flipped his plate over with such anger that it broke before touching the floor.

"What happened?" Sarki asked, standing up, shocked.

"There was a fly in my food."

"That was why you broke the plate?" Sarki asked unbelievably.

"What sort of cook..." His phone had been ringing. He shushed his brother and picked the call.

"What?" His face went pale, he dropped the phone and sat down.

"What's wrong?" Sarki asked, concerned.

"Someone blew up one of my oil wells."

Sarki was about to say something when he felt his phone vibrate. He excused himself while ordering the cook to change his brother's food. He checked his phone and saw a text from an unknown number. "Mission complete," it said, whatever that meant.

He deleted the text and joined his brother at the table.

Elzaiya had just come in from the airport, and Machiavelli was waiting for him. He came with Cairo.

"Of course," Elzaiya sighed.

Machiavelli seemed to be in very high spirits.

"What's tickling your Elmo?" Elzaiya asked as he got into the car.

"We had the best sex ever," Cairo giggled.

"You know, in some religions, you two will make it to specific chambers in hell. But sharing that biased knowledge is wasted, seeing as you both belong to one of those religions. I want to make one thing clear. I never want to know how your sex went. Ever!"

"It was dirty."

"Mean."

"Grubby."

"Please! Would you two just stop? Drop me off along the way so I can die in peace."

"We're kidding," Cairo laughed. "Come on, Avelli, give the guy a break. It's not his fault he's not getting some."

"I swear I would jump out of this car, and my death would be on you."

"I dare…"

"Don't," Machiavelli locked the car doors.

"So, he would have?" Cairo asked.

"There's no telling what he would do. This fellow here is a psycho."

They drove while talking. No one asked what he had travelled out to do. They decided to stop to buy some ice cream, chicken, and chips to take home.

Elzaiya saw the black BMW parked in front of the supermarket but didn't think much of it. He was tired.

They had finished at the chicken part, and he had gone to the other side to get some groceries. He was forgetting something. Grapes! Yes. That was it. He reached for it, and his hand covered someone else's.

"I'm sorry I didn't..." He looked up. "Nadia?"

14

NOT HOW IT SOUNDS

Before you judge, let me explain. Nadia is incredibly beautiful. Fairytale kind of beautiful. And the only reason I hadn't emphasised that was because I didn't see us being intimate. The whole thing was strictly business. I kidnap her, save her, take the credit, and take the secret to my grave. It wasn't that hard.

But then I spent nights watching over her. You don't spend your days watching someone without feeling something. And you know what Bismarck said about your enemy. *You know, you love, and then you destroy.* Now I knew her, and this whole thing was messed up because I couldn't bring myself to destroy whatever was there.

I'd watched her dance and read her diary; I knew what she was like in the dark. I'd seen her crazy and messed up. I'd tempted her, played with her psyche, and tried to see who she was underneath. But she was just human, a very simple person with soft, rosy skin, and I couldn't get my hand off hers.

"What are you doing here?" She asked.

I snapped back to reality and cringed.

"I was going back home with Avelli and Cairo. We stopped for some chow and groceries."

"Oh!" She looked up at the row of cans like she was wondering about something. "You want the grapes?"

"Oh… No! I mean, yes. Sorry. I mean, do you want them?"

I realised my hand was still on hers. I pulled it away, embarrassed. *Oh shit! Now she suspects that I like her. Great!* I have to rectify this immediately. She must be thinking, "Oh, my God! He likes me. He stutters whenever he sees me."

"It's the last pack of grapes," she said. "Would you have them?"

"You should take them."

"Maybe we could share?"

"I could just get some at another…"

Oh! It crossed my mind that she was flirting with me, grape-wise.

"Sure, we could… or you could come to my place."

Now it was as if I wanted her to come over. Great! Just freaking dandy. Soon I'll start sounding needy, and she'll be thinking, "Oh my! It's obvious he wants me."

Coincidentally, that was the thought on Nadia's mind. It was a relief to be invited, so she wasn't going to need some silly excuse like, "*Hey, sorry to bother you, but I wanted to know if I could get Denise's contact information from you so we can reconnect.*" How stupid that would have sounded.

Now she just needed to get some real groceries. "I want to get some chocolate if that's fine," she said, her admired gaze fixed on him.

He had a light blue hue around him. Did he have a halo? But chocolate... Chocolate? How was chocolate real food? Please don't let him look into your cart.

"You like chocolate?"

"I love it. It's absurd not to love chocolate."

"Right? It shouldn't even be confectionery; it should be a feeling."

"You're funny," she laughed. It's good to know they felt the same way about something. But what about their differences?

He was glad he made her laugh; it was so easy. She has very beautiful lips; no harm if they were parted in a laugh or... *Shit*! What was he thinking?

"Thank you," he said, looking at her cart. "Are you throwing a party?"

"No!" She pulled it back. She was fretting.

This was no coincidence; she was thinking of coming over. He thought. Ah! And I was beating myself up.

"I was just stocking up on..."

"All that."

"Yeah. You know, in case something comes up."

"You'll survive on Pringles, orange juice, and all that other stuff?"

Her face turned a shade, or it must have been the sun. "I love Pringles and these other things."

It was a lie; she didn't like Pringles. She disliked the taste after the first ten to fifteen slices. That was on the 14th page of her diary. And she liked funny guys, too. She also didn't want a husband who grew a moustache.

"Well, I can make you something better at the house."

She loved fruits, and I knew how to make an amazing salad. I was going to give her a fruit-gasm. *Okay, that was stupid.*

"Shall we get the chocolate first, then?"

"After you."

Now I know what she must be thinking. *He wants to stay behind me so he can access me from behind. What if this dress isn't the right one? I should have…*

I was correct. She missed the chocolate spot.

"The chocolates are here," I called her back.

She is distracted. I think she's falling for me.

She smiled and joined me, flipping her hair in the process.

Nadia, Nadia, you can't help nature, can you? You know when I said that we know when the first seeds of love are sown? Mine were sown on those nights when I watched her on my laptop screen repeatedly; hers began to grow after I saved her from the fire, her knight in shining armour.

I hope the day never comes when she discovers the rust hidden inside of me. She had been vulnerable to this bird of prey, and now that I was loving the lamb, I could already taste its blood in my mouth. Would it not be best if I stopped playing this game now that it was safe? I looked at her and smiled.

She was eager to know me, my darling lamb.

***

Emerson was irked. It had to be Sarki. No one else would attack his company with such gusto. See the way he had sneaked off to check his phone, and then he had deleted a text immediately. He thought he was smart; he didn't know he kept tabs on all he did.

When he was in this mood, he always had a conversation with Emerson – Emerson and Omar – Omar. It was a fallback neurological pathway that his mind had created, or so he convinced himself, to avoid the fact that he had multiple personality disorder.

Ah! You always say that. Shut up! Shut up! You're stalling the inevitable. He doesn't deserve a chance. What have you done but help? Kill him! Kill him!!! Look what he did; he wants what you have. He will never be content until you're dead. You're smarter and better. Everyone loves you! It's your right. He still sees you as competition. Oh! Just kill him already!

"Shut up! Let me think. What do I know that my brother doesn't?"

He knows you have a daughter. But he doesn't know that she's dating one of the Quinns. You must tell him so he will trust you. A gesture of good faith. Tell him that you're working with Harlequin and that you're doing it for him.

Why did he even summon you to begin with? Revenge? No, it's an excuse too shallow for a man like him. What will he gain? His motivation… "Power!"

Emerson sprang from the couch, nearly spilling his wine. He wants to be president. All this while, he's thrown me off with another form of longing. There was something else Emerson knew that Sarki didn't.

Years ago, when they were young, their father had been selecting wives for his brother. A young woman had arrived from Arabia. She was betrothed to a prince, but there had been a political affair that had to be sealed by marriage. She had been given as a wife to his brother. Except that she hadn't taken it well and had refused to accept that she was his wife. Nadia's mother had consistently run away from the palace to meet her lover, and that was where the rumours started that she was mad. Their father had passed away just before their wedding.

In a bid to keep the alliance intact, Sarki had slept with his wife. But he did not remember the events of that night because Emerson had drugged him. Sarki had slept the whole night, and when he awoke among sleeping women, he assumed that all had gone well. The only woman missing was Nadia's mother.

Nine months later, just like the other women, she had given birth but had insisted on taking care of her child. Not because she was scared the child would die, but because she wanted the memory of the prince to be forgotten before anyone would associate him with her child.

Staying with people made you look like them, and as Nadia looked like her mother, it was only fair to assume that her qualities came from the maternal side of the family. That was why Emerson had spared her life. Nadia was not a threat. She was not the Sultan's child. But he needed to be sure.

***

Sarki turned the other page. The things he saw were horrible. The process was disgusting. He could feel goosebumps on his skin as he imagined going through with it. What did the librarian mean by "do not repeat the mistakes of your father"? What mistakes had his father made?

The punishments in the book were for people who refused to change their ways, but for whom the Sultan also had mercy. He was tired of reading the book. Yet, he could not seem to drop it. The punishments were gruesome and ritualistic, each with its own technique. Customs seemed to extend beyond marriage ceremonies and burial rites. He flipped to the end and was about to close it when he stumbled on another section, ISKOKI. So, there were punishments for demons? Or was it for those possessed? And then there were the blood rituals… Sarki didn't have a degree in psychology, but he knew that what they referred to as demons were shadows.

It seemed the Hausa people knew a bit about psychology. That was a middle finger to the Western world. What do we have here? He found a page neatly folded, with Arabic letters lining the edge. A warning. He unfolded it with his eyes widening.

***

The first part of his daily routine, after the early morning prayer, was to be examined by his doctor. It was a family tradition, and there was no neglecting what was good. Today, he had questions.

"Tell me, Sani…" He asked after explaining the ritual in detail. "What are the worst consequences this could have on a person?"

"Apart from the shallow diagnosis provided by science, each patient, as a biometrically different human, would exhibit unique traits. If your brother is the cause of your father's and Dr Usman's deaths, then I would say he utterly hates all forms of religious authority and seeks to liberate men from the shackles of religion."

"He says that a lot."

"It goes deeper than that. He suffers from a messiah complex deeply rooted in his royal-religious background. He will find it a calling to a higher purpose. He is not drawing away from God; instead, he is a light showing men the things they need to sacrifice to become gods, even if it is their lives. Because of what has happened to him, according to the ritual, as you've explained. He would want to exact justice on the people who did this evil to him. It would be immediate at first. Directly on those who have wronged him. But because of his messiah complex, he would want to save others from the kind of torment he went through, and that means severing the weed from the roots. Which could mean your bloodline, his included, and in the worst case, bring down the whole caliphate system."

Sarki wiped his face. "Is there more?"

"He has multiple personalities, which could naturally be striving for different things. We don't know what he wants, but there is a tendency for him to inflict harm on himself and others unconsciously, even on people that he loves. He would tend toward self-persecution, self-sabotage, and violence. Since it hasn't been taken care of, he would be lost in the chaos he feels. He will be at the mercy of the person or persons he has become.

"Do you notice how he cleans himself up? It's because he seems unable to be clean, and he doesn't know why. He'd be lonely, looking for a kindred spirit to help him on his quest—someone who understands him, someone who thinks like him. As we know, he would have no respect for the dead and would constantly have nightmares, maybe forever, coupled with insomnia and temporary amnesia. Contrary to other people with DID, I don't think he would have suicidal tendencies. He is projected outward, and other people are the ones who will suffer for it. He has never truly been loved, so he does not fully understand the concept, making it difficult for him to see flaws in his actions. He is a self-loathing narcissist, and that combination doesn't get close. He would have, over time, developed a ritual—a symbol. This is, as we see, represented by the splash of blood and the dead fly. He is hanging between a psychopathic, religion-focused serial killer with messianic tendencies and something yet unidentified."

Sarki sighed. "And there is nothing we can do for him?" He asked with pity.

"I don't think you can help him. You could only try to save him from himself or take any precautionary measures to save yourself from him."

"My poor brother." Sarki swallowed. He understood now what the librarian meant. He had been the one who provided the book. But the person was to be killed, sent to war, or kept in prison after that kind of torture, as the book prescribed. The thing haunted his mind.

"You are in excellent shape, my lord."

"Thank you, Sani. You have been very helpful."

The doctor bowed himself away. Sarki felt sad for his brother. It was cruel what their father had done, but their father was ignorant and rigid. Would it not have been a better world if he had just allowed his brother to do what he wanted? He had been such a loving child; now he was a monster. Deadly, even to himself, and there was no room for monsters in this world. He was not going to make his father's mistakes.

***

Denise didn't know what to do. She had hoped that someday her father would notice her, but now that he had asked to be united with her, it felt strange. Why was that?

"Hey, Love, what's wrong?"

"Nothing," she was staring blankly at her phone again.

"Something on your mind you want to share?"

She laughed. "If I can remember it, I'll let you know."

"That's reassuring." Merceides wished she'd open up so he could gain her trust. Now, she has only proved his brother right.

"Sure," she was lost again.

He sighed and left. He was going toward the courtyard when he saw Harlequin walking back to his lodge. He paced over to meet him.

"What's up, Harley?"

"Don't 'what's up' me, dude."

"Why the mood?" He stood in his way.

"You didn't take my side when I was politicking to be put back in office."

"That's what this is about?" Merceides was disappointed. Harlequin hissed and walked past him. Merceides stared at his receding frame and, for no reason, recalled the prophecy.

***

Emerson was in the clinic again. He usually came once a year, but he wanted to make sure there was enough of what he needed in the event that things didn't go as planned.

"Mr Emerson?" The nurse called out.

"That's me," he smiled and stood up.

He loved hospitals; they provided a feeling of sanctuary. He went into the doctor's office and closed the door behind him.

"Mr Emerson." The doctor was surprised. "We really appreciate you coming, but we already have your blood in store."

"I just want to add some more; it's a precautionary measure. I might be the one in need of it."

***

Elzaiya and Nadia drove Nadia's car to the house, while Machiavelli and Cairo raced behind them.

"You people have lost your minds; I was holding my breath all the way," Nadia exclaimed, panting.

"We get bored," Machiavelli laughed.

The house was cool when Elzaiya unlocked the door. He pulled his bag from the back of the car.

"He's coming back from a trip?" Nadia asked.

"Yes," Machiavelli replied.

"Where did he go?"

"It would be better if you didn't ask," Cairo said. Machiavelli beamed. He was proud of her. She learnt fast.

"Why?"

"Because there are so many more things you would want to be asking," Elzaiya said behind her.

"You tend to sneak up on people." Nadia turned to face him.

"You're not supposed to see me coming."

There was a momentary silence that lasted too long, and then she shrugged.

They closed the trunks and packed the bags into the house. The girls went into the kitchen while Elzaiya and Avelli went to his room to discuss the trip.

Machiavelli told him everything, up to when Harlequin and Emerson partnered. He wanted the whole thing to end; the suspense was killing him.

Elzaiya laughed. He found it funny that anyone would want something like that to end. He loved it. The danger, the thrill of playing on your enemy's back and pulling the disappearing act. He reassured Machiavelli, who finally left him to unpack, and soon he could hear them giggling. They'd soon scatter to the other room, leaving him tortured by their sounds, as usual. Seriously, how did his house become Casa Avelli?

He finished unpacking and sat on the bed, directly beneath the fan, staring at the blades as they chased each other, like the fates. He must have closed his eyes and drifted off to sleep.

The dream had been the ideal erotic fantasy until it switched from the woman to the spider. The spider in the glass ran frantically looking for a way out. It needed to breathe. How did he know what the spider wanted? It was big, hairy, and strong. Very strong, because it cracked the glass any time it hit it. When the glass broke, it came out, with red blood dropping from the places where the glass tore at it. It looked around and saw him staring. He knew what it was going to do. No... No... It wasn't listening. It sprang up, and he could feel the goosebumps on his body when it jumped high up to the ceiling, about to land on his face. He jumped out of bed and threw something down in his path. He fell too, and the spider disappeared into the roof.

He had landed on something soft. It had a pleasant scent and…

"Oh, my God! Are you alright?" He was on top of Nadia.

"What made you jump out of bed like a springbok?"

"Spider," he said.

"What?"

"Nothing," he shook my head. Then it occurred to him.

"You're…"

The problem with a hard-on is that you're not the only one who feels it.

"You're squeezing my hand."

"Oh!" *Thank God.* "I'm so sorry." I helped her up.

Nadia wondered what kind of dream he was having to have a hard-on and a nightmare at the same time. "I was alone," she said.

"How rude of me; I'm coming right away," he said while turning his back on her.

"You'd better."

"What?" There was a double entendre in there somewhere.

"I mean, you'd better hurry; I don't want to eat my chocolates alone."

I smiled. "Let's go on then." Personally, I'd really hate for her to eat her chocolates alone.

15

CRIME AND MOTIVE

The first attack was on a church in southern Kaduna, followed by two more in Yola. The second was at a mosque in Zaria and then a school in Kano. After that, not a month had gone by without an explosion razing down some Northern institution.

The news had started by calling it a coordinated attack against religious organisations. But there was no pattern to it; no one could be apprehended for the attacks. They were carefully organised random acts of violence, classified as "institutional vandalism".

That was when Sarki came into the picture. He believed that to have control, you needed orchestrated chaos. He aimed to spearhead the affairs of the Boko Haram members. Being the Sultan, no one would see the wrong in his volunteering to pacify these anarchists. He had spoken with them and had held meetings in public and behind closed doors with their leaders. And then had come the long-lasting peace that the people had so hoped for. He had received two peace awards and had been celebrated as a national hero. It had been perfect, and he was about to commence the real crux of his plan when the brothers had come to offset all that he had worked for, stealing his glory overnight, rising out of the senate, donating and building, performing wonders, and bringing new meaning to community development.

The attacks had started immediately after Harlequin stepped into office, and the peace had been disrupted. But Harlequin had cleverly directed his energy to other places where their influence would not be felt. He gained his reputation as the youngest, smartest, and most cunning president the country has ever had.

The problem was that the game chose you. First, you needed a certain amount of intelligence to figure out the code that came with the invite link. After which, you had to play your way through the game, not knowing who was part of the board monitoring you. Each person had a personalised test designed by the system. There was no point reviewing past games. You did not know who to bribe or where to meet them. They, in turn, did not know if they were being watched. Campaigning was against the rules, so there was no means of gaining popularity.

The game was crazy, just like those who had designed it and those who had the nerve to see it through. Out of the 100 people chosen to play the games, only about 47 made it to the next day. It went to show how only a few were real leaders. Truly patient, smart, selfless, courageous and all the other non-cognitive skills it took to be great.

Sarki wondered what he would do now. Should he divert his attention from his brother and focus on running for office again? Or should he find a way to put his house in order? Was it not only a living man who could run for office?

"Hello, brother."

Emerson! The man was becoming a pain in his arse.

He shifted on the chair. "Brother?" He turned to see him beaming.

Emerson stood with a young lady beside him. In some confusing way, she looked like him. Oh dear! It was the daughter, they say, he had.

"I know I should have told you this sooner, but this is Denise, my daughter."

"Hello, sir," she said.

This one would be as disrespectful as her father.

He plastered a smile on his face. "Denise, you look so much like your dad. I guess you picked your good graces from your mum."

They all laughed.

"I should have told you earlier, but you know what I'm like with children. Recently, though, I've evolved. Hence the change of heart."

"It's fine; I guess Nadia would be overjoyed to know she has a cousin."

"Oh, she knows. We met already." Denise said.

"Girls, huh!" Emerson seemed to be having the time of his life.

"Well, we are going out on a date; we will get to know each other as adults, and I'll see how much of my daughter she has been without my influence."

"I doubt you will be disappointed," Sarki said, his mouth twitching. He bade them farewell and watched them leave.

After their car drove away, he made a call.

"It will soon be ready." The receiver said.

Honestly, he couldn't wait.

***

"You have nightmares like this all the time?" Nadia was walking behind him to the kitchen.

He led the way in a majestic procession. "Not all the time," he replied.

"So?"

"So what?"

"I see you don't want to talk about it."

"Good thinking."

"Isn't that supposed to signify a sort of mental imbalance? Considering how violently you reacted when waking up from your sleep. Aren't you supposed to be seeing a doctor, a therapist, or someone?"

"What sort of confocal reasoning is that? I thought we weren't talking about it."

"We aren't; I am," he imagined her batting her lashes. "You seem not to want to talk about anything."

"I apologise for that."

It occurred to him that he had been wandering on and off in his mind. He didn't know what it was about. She must think I'm a wowser.

"I was tired; I must have drifted off to sleep. Sometimes the nightmares come in the afternoons. But they come on most nights, I end up waking up, working through till morning."

"Most nights?" She asked with obtrusive concern.

"Yeah, on some nights I just sleep regardless."

They got to the kitchen, and he started opening cupboards and peeping into shelves, while she balanced herself by leaning on the door frame.

"So, you never have normal dreams?"

"What's a normal dream?" The concept of a normal dream sounded absurd. There was nothing like a normal dream.

"You know, eating your way out of a castle of chewing gum and then blowing the world up into one big bubble?"

He laughed and sliced an apple. "Who has that kind of sick dream?"

"I, for one, among many other ordinary children who had always wanted to meet Santa for Christmas. By the look of things, you aren't Santa inclined," she went to the shelf and picked some ceramic plates.

She started sorting through them; she seemed to be looking for a favourite.

"By the look of which things?"

"Your things," she looked him up and down.

He was wearing a white long-sleeved shirt and blue trousers. What was the obsession with white and blue?

"You're looking at my things?" He asked when he caught her eyes.

"You don't want me looking at your things? How private."

He laughed and kept silent. He didn't want to say anything. Especially not the truth. He didn't want her looking at his things. His body, he was fine with. But what of his other things? His plans… his mind.

"You have very beautiful legs," he said and continued slicing.

"What?" The plate in her hand slipped. It smashed on the floor, breaking into pieces at her feet. She didn't know whether to continue listening or to pick up the pieces and apologise.

He smiled to himself. She wasn't the only one who knew how to talk. He made the decision easier for her.

"You have the most gorgeous eyes I've ever seen."

"You're messing with me," she said, looking around for something to clear the ground with.

"Your voice is the most amazing musical sound my ears have heard."

"Stop doing that to me," she said.

He stepped over the broken pieces. Skilfully avoiding them as he moved closer. She picked up the knife he had been using and held it firmly in her left hand.

"Your beauty is like a variety of perfumes. You make me giddy and nostalgic. Your scent fills my body with every breath that I take; you grow flowers for the butterflies in my stomach."

"You mock me."

"I would walk through any kind of fire for you. I would take bullets to get to you. I would demolish anything that stood in my way of you. I will kill my way to get to you."

"Stop," she raised the knife and pointed it at him. She was leaning against the kitchen counter, with only the space between the knife and the tip pointed at his chest separating them.

He moved in and walked into the knife, pressing his chest against it. She did not flinch. He walked on as the knife pressed into his shirt, tearing through the fabric. Slowly, with the force of his body behind him, he pushed her hand back while the knife tore into his body. When he stood in front of her, her hands were down at her sides, the knife still in her grasp. She saw how it had wounded him, cutting an impression into his chest, from which a trail of blood followed.

"Your affections are to be earned. And I am willing to walk through knives and spears, horses and men to get to feelings worthy of being deserved. My ties to you will be as thick as thieves. And we will always reunite like strangers' kisses on an amnesiac night in which lost memories have spilt. You are not an ordinary woman, and I don't think you deserve anything but someone worthy enough not to be an ordinary man."

He paused. "So, how do you want it?"

"I…"

"The salad," he turned to the bowl.

She was looking at the cut on his chest. She feared it was deep. But she feared far more for what she wanted from him. He was too close for comfort; she wanted to vanish… but she wanted to vanish with him. What had she done? No! What had he?

"I'll serve myself; thanks for the innuendos."

"It wasn't meant to be."

"Really? You were just…"

"I wasn't doing just, Nadia," he looked into her eyes. Her pupils were dilated, and her breathing was shallow. If he listened closely, he knew he would hear her heart beating. He looked at her lips and took some steps back.

"Would you eat my salad with me?" She asked.

"Is that an innuendo?"

"You're flirting with me," she threw her hair back.

Biology was rewarding if you paid attention. He turned to get a spoon. "You're just realising that?"

"I'm shy around you; you unnerve me."

"Powerless people have no options but to be meek and patient. They then accept them as good virtues learnt over time, oblivious to the fact that it was imposed by necessity. Where do I take your nerves to?"

She laughed. "A Comedy of Errors. Why do I have the feeling you want more than my salad?"

"Nadia, if I ever have the privilege of eating your salad…" She picked up a piece of pineapple with a fork and shoved it into his mouth.

"Do you want me to be quiet?" He asked after chewing.

She found herself hapless. "I don't want you to be quiet. I want to hear what's on your mind, no matter how it sounds. I want you to be honest, say something real. Say something concerning how you really feel — not just innuendos and words attached to strings."

The space between them was two knife slices thick. He stared into her eyes. She could feel the intensity of his gaze as it nearly seared her flesh. She could smell him; she could almost feel him. She stared at him breathlessly.

"Let's go watch something on Netflix," he said, picking up the bowl of fruit salad from behind her.

Shit!!!

Machiavelli and Cairo joined them halfway through the movie. They seemed to have enjoyed their hours of the day.

"Let's play truth or dare," Cairo suggested.

"Elza wouldn't play; it's not his type of thing," Nadia said straightly.

"How did you know what I wanted to say?" Machiavelli said.

"He'll play; he'll do it for me. Wouldn't you, sweetheart?"

"I know you think I'll say yes," Elzaiya sat back in his chair, "but no."

"Please, don't let the fun pass; it wouldn't be that much fun with just the three of us," Nadia said.

"You haven't tried."

"Please."

He thought it through and then agreed.

"WOW! You convinced him? I think we need to marry you two up ASAP."

"Shut up, Avelli."

Elzaiya came down to join them on the floor, folding his legs between Cairo and Machiavelli. Cairo ran them through the rules of the game.

"Rule number one: no backing out…"

They had been playing for about 30 minutes when the turn passed to Elzaiya.

"Tell us the worst thing you've done that you don't want anyone to know about."

"Dare. I'll take a dare."

Machiavelli wondered if it was the same truth he harboured in his mind.

"You will make out intensely with a girl," Cairo read from the back of the card.

"Then let's start," he said as he moved to where Cairo sat.

"Whoa! Whoa! Whoa! Get your hands off my woman, bruh," Machiavelli pushed him away.

"So, I can't do the dare?" Elzaiya jested.

"There's more than one girl here, bruh," Cairo said, mimicking her boyfriend.

"Her? You want me to make out with her?"

"Why not?"

I knew I had a bad feeling about this.

"Can't he drop some money instead? Cut his thumb, clean the house, or do something else?" Nadia said.

"No. You guys have to make out, or forever be branded as those who broke the rules of truth or dare."

"I'm good with being branded," Elaiya said.

"There are no exits, son; you both gave your solemn word," Cairo reminded them.

"I don't think I..." Nadia started to say something when Elzaiya stretched and kissed her before she could finish.

It felt like time had stopped. He didn't stop the kiss, and she didn't fight him. The lights went off, and he knew that they were alone. His fingers found hers on the ground, and the only thing he could hear was the sound of atoms in his body screaming. He wanted to take everything from her.

It was past 7. He knew that she might say she would leave soon. The thought was unpleasant, so he stopped the kiss. "It's late; I think I should leave," she said, as if she'd read his thoughts. Maybe she had.

"Yeah, I think you should," he said coldly.

"Do you want me to?" She could not believe that he was the same person who had just been so hot.

He nodded. "You don't ever admit what you feel, do you?" She said.

He stood up. "I'll make you a take-home pack, in case you want to have some more," he went to the kitchen and left her sitting in the dark.

When he came back to the living room, she was not on the ground.

"Nadia?" The house was silent except for the chuckles that had become the tone of his environment. He called again, but there was no reply.

She had not left; he would have known. He could scent her out wherever she was. Yes, he could. He followed his nose, and it led him to his room.

He saw her sitting on his bed, her feet on the edge, her chin on her knees. He stood by the door, observing her. He didn't say anything; the feelings were too strong.

He moved to where she placed her feet and knelt. She didn't move. He stroked her feet, and she placed her hand on his head.

"I don't…" He started.

"You don't have to," she cut him short. He stood, and she looked up at him.

He stretched his hand and helped her up.

"I'll be on my way," she said.

In that instant, it felt like both their hearts would break.

16

SINS OF THE FATHER

Emerson would have dropped Denise off at the Quinns' residence, but she insisted otherwise.

"I should have reached out earlier, but I didn't want to bring any more of my inadequacies into the world. Now I'm glad I have you and am proud of you."

Denise beamed with pride as she heard the words she's been longing for all her life.

"I see the Quinns are treating you well," he added as they walked toward the car.

"They are very nice people," she said jokingly.

"I wonder how they'll react when they know you're my daughter," he muttered almost to himself.

"They do know about that," she said.

"They do?" He acted surprised. Even though he knew nothing got past the Quinns.

"I'm happy for you," he said, and went on to tell her about better days when he was in love with Aaira. "It was young love and all, and then it passed," he waved it off as irrelevant.

Denise begged him to go on. He smiled. Communication was bait.

"She was every guy's dream, and we were getting somewhere when Quinn came from nowhere and swept her away. They deserve each other."

"We don't always get what we want," Denise said with sadness.

They got to the car, and he relaxed on the frame, careful not to let the dust smear his suit.

"How is that?"

"I had a mild crush on Merceides; then we went to the house, and I met this guy. He was different, which is the best description of him. He was almost out-human; superior in his own way. I was drawn to him. But it was a phase; it passed."

Emerson had since lost interest but had to keep up appearances. "He's still in the house?" He asked with a fazed look on his face.

She shook her head in the negative.

"He sounds like a reasonable fellow to me. As if he understood that his absence would make you happier."

"He understands a lot of things. But he's in love with someone else now, so that's in the past."

How sad. Emerson said in his head. "He loved you. In his own way."

She smiled.

"That's more than most people ever get, trust me."

She laughed aloud, a cackling noise that reminded him of the chicken he had just had.

"You sound like you're speaking from an unpleasant experience."

"That's Daddy's history class for another day," he mused.

She wanted to ask if he thought he would ever fall in love again, but as she was dismissing the thought, he answered her as if he knew what was on her mind.

"But it's never too late to try again," he said, opening the door for her.

Her father was a rude gentleman.

"Coming from you, it's weird optimism," she settled in behind the wheel and started the engine.

He laughed, keeping his hand on the door. "You're my daughter, alright."

"Take care of yourself, Dad," she said. She didn't have to be told that he wasn't the type for hugs.

"I will. Send my regards to Aaira."

She nodded, and he closed the car door and waved. He noticed a dust stain on the side of his trousers. He resisted the urge to clean it off immediately. He started thinking as he walked to his car. The sound of it unlocking as he pressed on the control brought him back to the present. He threw his handkerchief on the passenger seat and started the engine.

It was when the cool air started to blow that he looked down and saw that the stain had cleaned off. Strange! He couldn't recollect bringing his handkerchief out of his pocket.

***

"How was the date?" Maryam asked for the fourth time.

Nadia decided to spill it out. "It was the most unusual day of my life."

"Ya ya-zama haka?"

"Ban sani ba! Abin mamaki ne."

"Tau, fada' min; me' ya faru?" Maryam twisted her braids with jittery anticipation.

"I didn't go to the house directly; I stopped on the way to get some snacks and other stuff, and then out of nowhere he materialises in the supermarket."

For a servant, Maryam was well-educated. Nadia had made sure of that. "Yana bin ki?"

"Ae' I mean, 'ah-ah'. He wasn't following me. He was coming back from a journey."

"Tau! Sai mei?"

"I was disoriented, so I bought chocolate and we went to his house and then his son came over…"

"Yana da yara?" Maryam bent to make sure she had heard correctly.

"Abokin shi ne; Machiavelli." Nadia laughed.

"Tau! Ki chigaba."

"So, we talked, and then he went to his room and fell asleep. I was alone in the living room, so I went to look for him. I saw him on the bed, lying down. He was…"

Maryam paused the plaiting. "He was what?"

Nadia skipped over what was on her mind. She didn't know how appropriate it would sound, even to Maryam. She had been drawn to him as he lay there, helpless in his dreams — an antithesis of what reality was to him. She had wanted to…

Maryam pulled her hair. "Continue fa."

Oh! She had drifted off again. What was wrong with her that she couldn't concentrate? A thousand curses on this love spell.

"He was dreaming," she continued. "I was about to touch him when he sprang up and landed me on the ground. He's heavy and strong for a guy his size."

"Yana da aljenu?"

"Ah ah! He was having a nightmare. Kamar yana hira a ciki."

"Sai mai ya faru?"

"He stood up and apologised. I could tell he was having some weird dream. He said he was dreaming of spiders, but how does that make you…"

"La ila!" Maryam burst into laughter.

"Tau, Amar bai yi komai fa."

"Maybe he was having two dreams at once," she concluded.

"Is it normal?" Nadia asked, concerned. How does someone have two dreams at the same time and feel both equally in the same mind? Will it not break?

"You don't describe him as normal."

"Gaskiya." At least Maryam had provided useful insight.

"So, nothing happened?"

"Well, he made me a fruit salad. A very amazing one, and then we played truth or dare, and we kissed."

"Ba haram ba ne?"

"Haba Maryam, it's not haram fa. We have an attraction, and I couldn't help myself."

"Is he a Muslim?" She asked, catching Nadia's eyes in the mirror.

"Does it matter? I know he is not, but when the time comes, we will cross that bridge."

"You are the Sultan's daughter. Some bridges, you can never annexe."

"Maybe not; I could be like my uncle and stay in the middle. I thought you would be happy for me," she turned to look at Maryam full in the face to see if she could read any emotion.

"Ina jin dadin ki, amar, but some things are just not meant to be."

"So, what is meant to be, Maryam? What should I do?"

"Ai kin sani."

"I don't know, ki fada min." Maryam dropped the brush and, patting her hair, kissed her on the head.

Nadia found her cheeks burning. Maryam loved her; she knew that, but it was true what she had said: some things were not meant to be. She found herself suddenly disturbed. What if it didn't work out? Would she now not get the one thing she had really wanted? Maybe she had inherited that from her mother.

"What will be, will be," Maryam said in consolation, seeing as her mood had changed.

"Ai na sani," she answered.

***

Emerson returned in high spirits. After taking a shower, he took a stroll to Dr Sani's lodge. He knew how the doctor regarded him: with the utmost level of respect associated with the highest class of disdain. It made him feel peaky.

The doctor was an educated Muslim who did not have regard for one who condescended so low as not to believe in a God. Be it that of any religion, but a god nonetheless. That was how Emerson perceived him; that was how he treated him.

Dr Sani, however, saw Emerson in a different light: as an interesting psychological test subject. That if the day came when he ventured into that field, he would have a befitting case study.

"Assalamu aleikum."

"Amin aleikum salam." The doctor opened his door and gave a lopsided smile when he saw Emerson.

Here was one human who could chew his own cord. "Ya zan taimake ka, rai'n ka ya da'de?"

Emerson felt elated. This man had just used the highest form of diplomacy by literally praising him as he would the king. Here was a man who knew his worth. If he had come to kill this man, he changed his thought.

"There has been something troubling me, Sani," he said. "May I come in?"

"E' mana, you are always welcome."

I know; we own the place. "Nagode," he went in and allowed the doctor to close the door behind him.

The house was, in a word, scanty. It seemed the good doctor believed in space, even in his personal life, seeing that he was still alone. That was one good trait they shared.

"I am worried about my family." Emerson started when he had taken his seat. The chair creaked, and he hoped it wouldn't cave.

"How so?" Dr Sani was not one to dispel his curiosity.

Emerson wondered which one made him more curious. The desire to know the problem, or the conniving fact that it was coming from him. Curiosity was a necessary mental bacteria, essential for the survival of the human species.

"There has always been the issue of an heir in our family right from my grandfather's time. It seems nature decided to make the males few and the children fewer as time went on. And now, in my brother's and my time, thin them out totally."

"Allah will be merciful." The doctor sat and crossed his legs. This man marvelled at him.

"Insha Allah, good will come our way, but what if it doesn't? Will our generation then die out, and to whom will the title of Sultan fall, seeing as we are all that remain of our bloodline?"

"Then you should try procreating through other means."

"Procreation is my brother's problem, and it is because of my brother that I have come here."

"What's wrong with him?" Dr Sani was now more attentive.

"Oh! Nothing at all; the problem is with his heir."

"Nadia?" Emerson nodded and cleared his throat.

He had planted the seed in his brother's mind that the girl might most probably be his daughter, but that has not worked to sever their ties. What if he learnt the truth?

"You know, quite recently, a maid was caught changing his pills. It means my brother has been infertile for a long time. That woman has been here since before Nadia was born. I need you to perform a DNA test. I want to know if she is indeed my brother's daughter."

"She's the Sultan's daughter." The doctor uncrossed his legs and placed his palms on his thighs.

Emerson tried not to read the man's body language.

"I know she is. I just want us to be sure before the time comes and our dynasty becomes entangled in a scandal we could have avoided." Dr Sani said he understood.

Emerson told him to keep it a secret and then requested that he keep him updated about his findings. The doctor agreed, and he left.

Dr Sani closed the door and, without wasting time, called a friend to see how fast he could perform the test. After the date had been scheduled for that night, he called on Maryam to help him with a comb that contained Nadia's hair and one of Sarki's toothbrushes. His doctor friend came to pick him up when everything was ready, and they went to the hospital to seal the fate of the dynasty.

It was the next evening that Dr Sani came to meet Sarki. That was where his loyalties lay, and that was where Emerson wanted him to go.

He didn't hear his brother react, and he didn't know how the conversation went. But when he asked Dr Sani about the result, Sani told him that Nadia was the Sultan's daughter. He thanked him and left. The result he'd seen spoke for itself.

***

Quinn was bothered. Both he and the doctor looked like they could use some rest. "He has to know. I know that was the only reason you apprehended him about Denise."

"I still think he needs more time."

"You will always want to give him more time. But he needs to know."

"Know what?" Aaira entered the study with a tray of juice and snacks.

"The truth." Dr Kendrick insisted. She dropped the tray and sat down.

"Our problem is that this transcends family. In a way, it is a political issue. We can't just tell him the truth out of the blue. Have you considered the consequences? That boy is volatile in ways we don't understand. He battles with things that he wouldn't share, but that I know go way deep. He is smart; he knows that something is wrong, and he might discover it on his own someday. But he is my son, and I will do what's best for him. That means telling him the truth, only when I think he can't handle it."

"And when is that? If we don't tell him soon, he could feel used when we do. There are a thousand ways it could go wrong, but you raised a perfect human being..."

"Perfect, but human. And humans are unpredictable." Quinn interrupted Kendrick. "We will find the right time, not too early or too late."

"Let's hope he doesn't find it out himself, then," the doctor said. "And what about Nadia? What is this newfound affection he feels for her? Are we not going to do anything about it?"

"You keep on bringing up problems to back your reason," Aaira said.

"I think it's the right time."

"Where would I start? Where, really, is the ethical line?"

"Anywhere. Begin wherever you want, but tell him, Aaira, for his sake. Let him at least find peace when he understands."

Aaira disagreed by shaking her head and sipping some juice. "So what do we do about Nadia?" Kendrick asked again.

"We have to tell him that it cannot work," Quinn said.

"He is a human being, and as you said, he cannot be controlled."

"We will tell him that he cannot be vulnerable to the enemy's daughter until things are settled."

"Does that even sound like something he would listen to?"

"We should only tell him to take it gently," Aaira said.

"I don't think that should be our concern. We should decide on who best to tell him, when and how." Quinn said.

"How is mistakenly sleeping with Nadia not our concern? Or do you have no moral values left?" Aaira probed.

"If we know him well enough, I don't think he'd allow that to happen. It would take time for him to let her in and more before he would get physical with her after the event with Denise."

"How long do you think we have before we can tell him?"

"Maybe three weeks," Quinn said.

"So, who will tell him?" Kendrick asked.

"Machiavelli. We should tell Machiavelli."

"No! I'll tell him." Aaira said.

There was silence, after which Quinn sighed and started to sip his glass of juice in silence.

***

Nadia couldn't sleep, and neither could he. It was past 1 a.m. He wondered what she was doing. He missed watching her at night. She had his contact, but they had never talked. He hadn't exactly known what to say or how. He flipped his phone and stared at the screen as she floated in his mind.

The same sleep evaded her, and forcing it was like trying to force her feelings away. Both were broken pencils; pointless. She tapped her screen awake and sent a text.

"Hi..."

17

BURNING HANDS

Elzaiya had all the information he needed to know about the terrorists that plagued their country. But he was only willing to give it to him if he accepted the invitation. "Why not give it to one of your brothers?" He asked.

"My brother Harlequin has been corrupted by power, and Merceides is too emotionally fused to see a cause through," Elzaiya had said as they played chess. Synai always had the upper hand at the beginning. Elzaiya had a flaw; he could never use his bishops effectively.

"So why not do it yourself?" Another pawn went off the board.

"It has to be you because no one would see you coming," Elzaiya cleared his rook off with a knight.

"I can't do it; I am too ambitious to be in power," Synai said. There was more to it. Elzaiya smiled.

"The Quinns are at war with the Sultan. He wants to take over the Quinn borderland, and the Quinns can't allow it," he moved a pawn to the end of the board. "knight".

He continued. "If the Sultan gets to be president, he would abuse power to unimaginable extents. And make the country a Muslim state, plunging us back into the era of jihads and civil wars. You were a veteran of the last war; you know what I mean. If the Quinns seize power again, things would be at a stalemate. The Sultan would not allow any progress to occur. And if I go into office, I could lose myself; I can't afford the risk."

"Why are you sure I can make a difference? Would the Sultan not undermine my tenure, too?" Synai used his bishop to take Elzaiya's knight off the board.

Elzaiya laughed. The move was too symbolic. "All you have done is prove people wrong. The Sultan and the Quinns would burn themselves out. All you must do is put out the sparks for tomorrow's sake. I know this would come out wrong, but I'm not just asking that you use the army to rid us of those terrorists. I'm asking for total annihilation. We have learnt from the first of our civil wars. We allowed a second. If this country is to survive, we must get it right this time."

"Why do I still feel that there's more?" Synai took away another pawn.

"It's because I might burn out with the fire. The country needs some air; we have inhaled smoke for so long that the young ones are being born with the lung cancer their parents have. How long will it be before anarchy takes over?"

"I will think about it," he said, taking away Elzaiya's queen. "Check!"

Vivian could see that he was worried, and he didn't get worried often.

"Obim! Are you okay?" He had not touched the food either. This was indeed a very big problem.

"I'm fine," he turned from the window, which looked down at the city, to focus his attention on her. Believe it or not, women were the most intelligent of the species. They could tell when you were not focusing all your attention on them.

"You look worried. Is it because of the wedding? It's still far off."

He laughed. "Why do you think the wedding is bothering me?"

"So, you're saying our wedding isn't important enough to bother you?"

"I didn't say that," he frowned.

She smiled. "You implied it."

"I did not."

"So, it's not the wedding. Then what is it?"

"You love Scrabble, right?" He brought out the bag of letters and scattered them on the table, shifting the food away from the letter mess.

"Yes, I do, but you don't play. You say you find it hard to focus."

"How does it feel when the letters connect to make a word?"

"It makes me feel like I'm going somewhere with the game."

"What about chess? Do you still think the queen is the most dangerous piece?"

"Why yes. Which one do you think it should be?"

"I might be biased, but I think it should be the Bishop. People are used to dynamism, which makes them watch out for the Queen because of how she moves. They focus on taking out the queen, and the pawn that is closest to power is the one they try to take out because they don't want it to amount to anything, especially not another queen. Elzaiya used to find it hard to use his bishop in a chess game. He couldn't move diagonally; it seemed not to make sense in his mind. But after a while, something changed; he started to use both bishops as effectively as he used his queen. When I asked what changed, he said, 'You can't be that close to power without wanting it for yourself.' It is the nature of things to want to be corrupted, so they become corruptible.' He said that each piece can be replaced by a hard-working pawn, except for the king, of course. The king is weakest because his power makes him so. The king is beset by enemies. He has no friends."

"You're not talking chess, are you?" She asked, arranging some letters in a row on the table.

He shook his head.

"So, the bishops, are they for you?"

"No! They're for Elzaiya. He wouldn't have come if he wasn't in trouble. It's not about the country. With him, it's always personal."

"Then you should find out who his bishops are," she raised her hands from the letters, and he looked at them.

He smiled, and she kissed him.

Scrabble was her game; there was no doubt about it; she knew how to send a message. "Eat your food before it gets cold."

***

He was awake, staring at the ceiling. Today was one of those days when he was amazed that he woke up. Today was his birthday.

One uneventful month had passed. Early December was when all the good stuff happened. He didn't know if he would see Nadia again. The thing about private messaging was that the person didn't know if you'd read their message or not.

She had typed and deleted a "hi". He didn't want to overthink anything. But he knew that eventually, he had to wake up. Avelli would soon be here with his theories of enjoyment and good living. He hoped he wouldn't break today's code by bringing his girlfriend over. That would be…

The doorbell was ringing. "Oh, God! Where did I drop my phone?" He couldn't hear his voice. Strange!

Last night had been wild. He had been with Emerson till 2 a.m., and every second of it was mad. They had tasted wines and eaten meats, fish, sushi, and other French and Italian dishes that sounded gloomy.

After that, they raced each other to the lower part of town and bought some helium from a guy who was missing four teeth and an arm. 20 minutes later, they were laughing their asses off and throwing stones in a sleeping neighbourhood.

After much yelling from the people, they started to sing and dance, and that was when the dogs were released. He didn't know how they had managed it, laughing and running at the same time, but they had been the two maddest men on the streets. The doorbell was still ringing.

"I'm coming." It just occurred to him that he couldn't move. Oh no! What else happened yesterday?

After the dogs stopped chasing them, they had torn their shirts from jumping off a few fences into their cars. They had gone to another bar and had some shots, and then there had been the shisha competition. Who had won at that stuff? It was Emerson. He had brought out a haze from his ears. How did he even do that? He had to teach him that stuff. Did it mean he could breathe through his ears like a fish, too? Or… the doorbell, for heaven's sake!

"I'm coming," he tried to sit up.

Who could be coming here so early? It was just 4:10 a.m. He could make it out correctly even though the clock was a little dizzy — or was it him?

He heard the door open. The sound of it shutting gave him a small headache. He heard feet shuffling and then heard the door to his room open. He would have turned, but he couldn't move his head, and his eyes seemed to have been closed all along.

"Oh, my God!" It was a female voice.

So Avelli brought Cairo over. How sacrilegious!

"Are you okay?" A hand was touching his head. It felt cold.

"Go away. Niertz… ditzch…" Did he just speak German? He smiled.

He was getting pretty good at a lot of things. He heard Cairo saying something; she was talking to someone on the phone. He was about to go back to his comfortable sleep when she pulled the sheets from his body and turned on the air conditioner.

What sort of wicked person would do that with the kind of cold the morning brought? This year's harmattan seemed to last longer. He was groping for the sheets when a pack of ice was dropped on his head. It seemed to cover his entire body.

"Tu edes… idiota…" He swore in Spanish.

He heard the door open again and then felt the prick of an injection on his skin.

"Harlequin…" Why was he calling his brother's name? He could remember something, but he couldn't place what it was.

The cold was becoming unbearable. He reached down for the sheets, but they were gone. "Stay steady," the voice was saying. He hissed and heard a male voice laugh.

Very funny, Avelli.

"He has a very high fever, which is causing the hallucinations, but he should be getting better by evening," another voice said.

"Who is sick?" He asked, partly to himself.

"You are sick, very sick," Cairo said. Why did she not smell like Cairo?

"What is today's date?" He asked.

Why was he even bothered about the date when he should be asking why they thought he was sick? "It's February 12." The male voice answered.

Yesterday, he should have accepted the invite to the game. "Where is my phone?" He reached out, but the bed felt like a desert.

"There is no phone," Cairo said. He was trying hard to open his eyes, but they were so heavy it felt like mountains were placed on them. Why couldn't he remember what had happened yesterday?

"You're such a pain in the ass." That was Avelli.

He raised his hand to wave him over. He thought he did. He couldn't seem to move or even speak. His German gibberish was getting better as his English was getting worse.

He heard Cairo ask Machiavelli what he was saying.

"I don't know. Why are you asking me what goes on in his head?"

"You're closest to him; you should know."

"You said you came in and found him like this?"

"Yes. I knocked and rang the doorbell, but I didn't hear anything."

"I was coming," I said. No one was paying me any attention; so much for being the sick person in the room.

"And the door was open?"

"Yes. I came in, and the house was quiet. So, I walked into the room, and that's when I found him like this."

"He doesn't allow himself to get this sick. And he wouldn't leave the door open under any circumstances. He hates insects, especially mosquitoes."

"The doctor said it was a very serious case of malaria."

"Yes, which is quite normal. Except that he doesn't get sick, especially not with malaria. Not since he worked his ass off to prevent it from happening again."

"Has he been this sick before?"

"It happened once, about 9 years ago."

I didn't hear them say anything again. I figured they might be thinking about what to do next.

"Did the doctor examine his body?" Machiavelli asked.

"No, he just checked for symptoms and acted fast before the illness got to his brain."

"So, he has been like this for approximately 10 hours or more?"

"Yes."

"It means the malaria was not caused by a mosquito bite."

"How?"

"If a mosquito bit him, which it didn't. He would treat it so this wouldn't happen. But malaria is a communicable disease, and diseases can be manipulated. If the malaria was cultured in a lab and an agent was added to increase its potency and then injected into the bloodstream, it's only natural for the subject to display the heightened symptoms of malaria on a level equal to the potency of that agent."

"You're saying he was poisoned with malaria?"

It seems Machiavelli nodded.

"Do you even know how insane that sounds?"

"I do. Now, help me roll him over to his other side so I can see if he has any needle marks."

I could feel myself turning, and my headache along with it. There was a moment of peace before hands started raising my limbs and tracing places on my body.

"Nothing," Cairo said.

"I wouldn't say so," Machiavelli was holding up my elbow or left leg; I didn't know which.

"It's so tiny, you would miss it," she said. "But why would anyone want to infect him with malaria?"

"To slow him down..."

"For what?"

Machiavelli seemed to be thinking. "Did he say anything to you while you were here that made any sense?"

"He asked for his phone," the female said.

"It should be on..."

I knew what the silence meant. My phone was missing. There was another momentary silence, and then we heard a phone vibrate. I kind of felt it.

"It's coming from underneath the pillow." Somebody raised my head while they scouted for the phone.

"Oh no!" I heard Machiavelli say.

"What's wrong?"

"It's the invitation. The link expired this morning. Someone doesn't want him running for president."

"But he said he didn't want to run."

"They were threatened. Maybe they thought he'd change his mind."

"Is he in danger?" Cairo was concerned for me. That was cool!

I could feel Machiavelli's teeth on edge. I knew what I would say if I were in his shoes.

"No. He wouldn't be in any further danger."

I was proud of him.

"Would you stay with him while I prepare some food?"

It seems she nodded.

Machiavelli was already at the door. "Thanks for taking care of him and for calling me. He can be a pain in the ass, but there's a special place in his mind where he holds you dear."

"Isn't it supposed to be in his heart?"

"The heart will always be nothing more than a blood-pumping machine to him." But you know as well as I do that he feels something for you; honestly, he's never felt anything like that for anyone else before."

"Anyone else but who?"

"Me."

Nadia! I felt my temperature flare as her hands shifted the towel that held the ice from my head to my chest. It would be the most beautiful feeling if I could just die right now.

***

Harlequin waited underneath the bridge for a full half hour before Emerson arrived. The man lacked punctuality for someone so formal.

"Where in God's name have you been?"

"I apologise for my misconduct, young man, but it's for your good, so don't you dare direct that fit at me."

Harlequin apologised.

Emerson loved pushing people to the extreme. He had been in a taxi at the other end of the bridge, observing Harlequin and all he did. He had not talked to anyone, but he had made two calls, both to Emerson. He had concluded that he was desperate.

"I was dealing with a threat. I have a list of people, friends, who I believe should rule. But seeing as some of them have time and I've made you a promise, I had to make sure they don't get in the way."

"At what cost? At least I'm stupid enough to know it isn't for free."

"Oh yes! Thanks for reminding me. I need you to put this card in your mother's journal." Emerson gave him a card. It felt heavy, like lead. But it was paper.

"How do you know she has a journal?"

"It's ocean blue, and the pages are lined with gold. It has a golden pen beside it. I bought it for her. Didn't she tell you? We had some cosy nights together."

Harlequin gritted his teeth and clenched his fists.

"Oh! And she knew how to get what she wanted. Man, was she a banshee!"

"Thanks for sharing. I'll ask her when I'm unoccupied," Harlequin hissed.

Emerson smiled and left, heading toward the bridge on foot. Sarki watched, satisfied with what he saw. He had suspected it all along, but what was Emerson's endgame? That he couldn't figure out, and it was causing an ulcer in his mind.

***

Synai looked at the map. That was the whole story, as Elzaiya had narrated it to him. Sarki and Emerson were in a shadow fight but maintained brotherly civility while suspicions escalated.

Harlequin was dead to the public but roamed about as his twin. He wanted to get back into power, and it looked as if, with the proper motivation, he would be driven to get it at all costs, thinking he was doing it for the common good.

Merceides was on Elzaiya's side. Which was a wonder considering the kind of strained relationship they had. Denise was neutral. Now that she was reuniting with her father and keeping it from her boyfriend, it meant she had chosen her side. She was a door waiting to be passed through. Machiavelli was their ally. He would be loyal to the end because he trusted the force he was working with. There was no cause for suspicion.

Cairo had come into their lives at a convenient time. She had fallen in love with the person who could make Elzaiya vulnerable; she didn't seem like a danger, and somehow, she was too smart for herself, but she still wasn't vindicated. It was safe if she didn't know the politics behind everything.

Quinn had everything to lose with Elzaiya's demise. He was the most favoured of his sons, and he would not want to harm the boy. Not consciously, of course. Aaira was his mother, but she had a reputation for wanting to rise in power. She was the one who had put her sons in place for the future. Could there be more to her plan?

Now the question was: who stands to benefit with Elzaiya out of the picture?

"Machiavelli is the queen; he would do everything to protect the king. He moves in all directions and is connected to everyone. He moves only at the bidding of the king. He will lose everything if anything happens to the king. Harlequin is stepping out of line. He's moving like a knight. I think he would find a way to do the right thing when the time comes. Merceides and Quinn are rooks. Quinn has no interest in politics, except in how the person in power would affect his economic interests; he is a businessman. Merceides is watching over his brother in a strange, ineffable way. Cairo is a pawn; once she discovers how she connects, she can be a queen, but she is doing what she can not to be seen. She knows a game is being played; she's avoiding everything. Denise was in love with Elzaiya. When love turns to poison, it can be a very potent evil. She is moving toward Emerson, and she doesn't want any of the Quinns to know. She's a bishop."

"Emerson doesn't know that Elzaiya is a Quinn. What if when he does?" Vivian asked.

"He's an enemy on the other side of the line. We know where he stands."

"But who can tell him and use it to their advantage?"

"Denise and Harlequin. But I don't think Harlequin will."

"So, which one of them will be the second bishop?"

"I don't know. Maybe the person isn't doing anything, or maybe they are smarter than we think. Either way, for this person not to have been seen, I think we are dealing with a more dangerous piece. We should consider the possibility that there's another bishop masquerading as another piece."

"So, what would you do now?" She sat in front of him and placed her hands on his shoulders. "You have less than an hour before your link expires."

"I'm still thinking about it."

18

WE HAVE AN ENEMY

"When you walked through the fire to get me. You were like a phoenix—fierce and brave, that even bullets couldn't stop you. Yet look what malaria has done to you. Mummy should have named you Alexander."

The fever was down, and she just kept the towel damp, occasionally adding a block of ice.

"Quit your whining; I'm starving."

She smiled as he opened his eyes.

He would have slept till she left, but something told him that she wasn't going anywhere. He was angry at how he had let some fool mess him up like this.

"It wouldn't kill you to be polite."

"We don't know that; little things kill big people."

"You, Elzaiya, have a very big problem."

He groaned and covered his head with the pillow. "This isn't the right time for something like this."

She pulled the pillow off his head. He let her have it. For a royal, she was aggressive.

"Oh really?" She threw the pillow at the foot of the bed. "And when would that right time come? "When will we have time to talk if you keep avoiding me when kana ta yawo a garin kamar jaki?"

"I'm not avoiding you," he said, looking longingly at the door and hoping Machiavelli would come in. "How did I? And did you just call me a donkey?"

"I will call you far worse if you don't start being reasonable and stop behaving like an ass."

"An ass? You're the one being unreasonable," he faced her to dump it on her and see her reaction. "I'm sick, which is by no fault of mine, by the way, and then I wake up, and the first thing you tell me is that I have a problem. You're the one who stayed in your house, chorusing that I'm avoiding you."

"Would it kill your ego if you came for a visit?"

"Oh yeah! My vain ego aside, you never know what the Sultan is thinking. One stupid unscheduled visit on his worst day could be my last."

She gasped. "I don't believe you... how would... My dad is not a threat."

"You know nothing about that. And you judge me for not visiting; well then, why did you stop?"

"You made it obvious that you were not interested in me."

"How did…? How…?" This girl was frustrating him, and his fuse was short right now.

"Avelli!!!"

He was starving. He had not eaten for a whole day, and here he was spending his first waking moments exchanging words with a woman. Some risks were not worth taking. Relapsing into illness didn't sound like a suitable relaxation right now.

Machiavelli came in with a tray of orange juice, water, and a whole set of fruits. As colourful as they seemed, monkey food wasn't going to satisfy him. "I should have hired a chef."

"You should have hired a lot of things." Nadia hissed.

He mimicked her and played puppeteer with his fingers. Her face burned, and he felt better.

"Please, people, ease up on the squabbling," Machiavelli said.

Elzaiya looked toward the drawn blinds. It looked like evening. "What's the time?"

"It's past 6."

"Aren't you going home?" He asked Nadia. She opened her mouth to say something when Machiavelli stepped in as an intermediary.

"Please! Before you guys go back to that, let's round up, so I'll leave you both to your… stuff."

"Okay, out with it, zipper."

"I see the humour is back," he hissed.

"Fortunately."

"What do you remember?"

Elzaiya told him all that he remembered about going out with Emerson and how he had come back home around 1:33 a.m. after all the fun and was about to turn on the lights when he noticed that something wasn't right.

"What was that?"

"It sounds irrelevant, but the handle of the front door wasn't cold. It was chilly outside, but the handle was warm. It didn't occur to me until I was in the house. When the realisation struck me, it was too late. Two men held me, and someone else covered my nose with an oxygen mask. I passed out, and that's all I can remember."

"They didn't steal anything," Machiavelli said. "Everything is intact. Meaning they only came to make sure you wouldn't accept the invitation."

"I'm not sure that's all they did," Nadia said.

"How so?" Elzaiya asked. Curious as to what she knew about their backyard activities.

"That's because I'm quite certain you're not the one who sent this text."

Hey... Ummm, it's been a while. Can we talk sometime? Say tomorrow morning?

"You know me so well."

"Okay then," Machiavelli said. "I think you guys have things to 'talk' about."

He left the room with an angry Nadia blazing a glare. Elzaiya ate slowly to avoid a conversation.

***

He was the lesser of two evils. Sarki finally admitted this fact. The Quinns were a problem he had created for himself; if he left them alone, the problem would solve itself. Haven't they been on defence the whole time?

But he had to set up certain measures for the sake of the future. If the situation worsened and, God forbid, he died without an heir, would his name and dynasty not be lost forever? That was it! Emerson wanted it to end.

He had chosen a path so subtle that it seemed like a natural occurrence. They were the sole heirs, the only branches left on their family tree. Allah ya ṭsare! He concluded. He would sleep with his wives and have them well protected. But that was not good enough. He needed a more rewarding plan, something secure. His face brightened.

Dr Sani was in his laboratory when Sarki came in to meet him. "Assalamualaikum."

"Amin alaikum salam."

"Rai'n kay a dade'. Mei ya kawo ka nan?"

"Aboki na, walahi I am troubled. Zuchiya na baya kwana."

"Should I get you something to drink?" Dr Sani pulled his gloves off and waited.

"Anything that would steady the nerves. You don't by chance have any chemicals in here that can whip up a good drink, do you?"

Dr Sani laughed. "Haba Sarki! I am a doctor, not a chemist. It is not true that men of science know how to combine everything."

"I will take a soft drink then, or anything you have."

The doctor went to the small freezer in the corner of the lab and produced two cans of Malt.

"Isn't that where you keep the cadaver?"

"Just their insides," Dr Sani said casually.

Sarki refused the drink. "I am just kidding; I don't do that work here. The cadavers are in the other lab."

"Pardon me, I am jittery these days," Sarki said, accepting the drink.

"I understand. If I were in your shoes, I would be far more nervous."

"Well, my people don't need a scared leader. Which is why I'm here. I have a favour to ask."

"Anything, rai'n ka ya dade'."

"With the way things are playing out, I am starting to consider the possibility of artificial insemination."

Dr Sani had thought about it too. "It is a wise decision, my lord."

"Thank you, Sani. I've decided to entrust it to you so that when the time comes, if I have no heirs left, it will be our last hope. What do you think?"

"It is an excellent choice, my lord. I would have brought it to you for consideration, but I did not want to make it seem as if I was considering your death. I think you should prepare it as soon as you can, and I would keep it safe. And best, test it on a woman to see if she can get pregnant."

"You said, 'If she can get pregnant'?"

"The results of your test came in yesterday." The doctor said, standing up to run through the scattered files and envelopes on his desk.

"What test?"

"I ran samples on the infertility pills you've been taking. They do not just leave the system for a very long time. They are designed to prevent the person taking them from ever being potent."

"So, you mean I can't have any children?"

"I mean to say, let us hope for a miracle." Dr Sani passed him the test results, and even though he was not well-grounded in the sciences, he agreed with the doctor that he needed a miracle. Emerson had crossed a very dangerous line.

***

It was past 8 p.m., and Cairo had come to assist Machiavelli in the house. Nadia had refused to go. It wasn't like he didn't want her around. He just didn't think it was the best time to be sharing vulnerabilities. For some strange reason, the injection he was given seemed to have made him feel more alive. Maybe this is how heroin feels?

"What are you smiling to yourself about?" Nadia asked.

Machiavelli and Cairo were in the living room. This time, they weren't having sex. It seemed adulthood had finally dawned on them, and their relationship had come to that stage where they ate popcorn and cuddled off to sleep like raccoons on the rug. They shouldn't break apart. They were his model couple, and he'd come to like them together. These were words that would never escape my mouth.

"I am?"

"You would stay a while, smile and then stay for some time again and smile. What's with you?"

"Must be the effect of the drug. Some of them have these weird 'if they persist, call your doctor' kind of reactions."

"Uh-huh! So, this one is making you smile? Maybe you should fall sick more often."

"I thought if you liked someone, you were supposed to say nice things to them all the time, even if that presupposes more than a one-time white lie."

"I haven't heard you say nice stuff to the people you care about; why should I?"

"Maybe I don't care about them."

She snickered, and I took a turn. "Aren't you supposed to be in your house by now?"

"You're chasing me away again?"

"Yes. And that's because I haven't had the angry dad experience before; I wouldn't want to have it now."

"My dad wouldn't harass you."

"Right… So, what would you wear? Wouldn't you go home and at least get some clothes or maybe just come over tomorrow?"

"I ordered what I would need from my shop already. They are in the living room," he didn't want to ask about her shop. "So, you would share the guest room with Cairo?"

"She insisted she wanted privacy with her boyfriend."

"Ewww… that's gross," he said.

She laughed. "Hypocrite."

He was amused. "I'm fine with name-calling."

"I know; nothing seems to get to you in your world of steel."

"Seeing as I'm sick and I can't do the grand thing and stay in the living room, you know that's where you'll sleep, right?"

"You're not sick. The doctor combined your drug with an agent that will triple the potency of your healing drug. You were cured hours ago. And, I would have loved to stay in the living room, but for health purposes, Cairo said she'll flit that zone before going in to sleep, so that leaves me here."

Damn! There were things I tried my best to avoid. "Would you stay on the couch or the floor? There's a spare mattress in the guest room."

"I am the Sultan's daughter, Zaiya. I have never slept on the floor."

"And this is my house," he said with equal pride. "I don't intend to leave this bed for you."

"I'm not asking you to leave the bed. I'm just telling you that I'm going to bathe in your bathroom and change my clothes in this room, and you would have to excuse me unless you belong to that group of naive men who strongly uphold the statutes of patriarchy, in which case you will reduce the amount of respect I have for you."

This was why he avoided relationships. They were full of concessions that a man was not supposed to win.

"I would sleep on the floor," he said.

She looked at him for a while. Cairo must have told her that he wouldn't stoop low enough to sleep on the floor. No kidding, he was surprised at himself.

"Okay then. I would get my things."

He smiled and felt very satisfied. He began to wonder why people did bad things and found it difficult to sleep at night. Maybe they didn't do their bad things right.

It was past 10 p.m. when she finally lay down on the bed. He had been nice enough to change the sheets while she bathed.

Cairo didn't give him the mattress. She didn't even allow him into the room. She locked the door and told him to share the bed with his girlfriend, to whom he had spent 12 minutes trying to explain the concept of a 'girlfriend.'

Cairo had turned on the radio, blasting him out of the passage. In his own house!

But he wouldn't jeopardise himself because of a little tussle. Most women were crackheads, if not all. He wasn't in the mood to ask her what kind of pot she smoked.

"I bet you're comfortable," Nadia said.

"I never knew sleeping on the floor could be this rejuvenating. It feels like an earth massage." Earth massage? He was losing it.

"You should wait until the cold comes. It drives out the ants and cockroaches. You would think you have none, but those things always find a way to walk into every room in a house."

Cockroaches! No! He tried to close his eyes, but he was becoming paranoid. What kept him on the floor was his pride and stubbornness.

"Goodnight, Zaiya," she turned her back to him and went off to sleep.

"Goodnight, Nadia," he said, staring at the ceiling fan. It had a ray of light from the moon that danced with the blades. He stared until he drifted off to sleep.

The smell of roasting meat woke him up. He saw one of his old acquaintances, though he had changed a lot. He was the one with the meat. He handed him a big slice and pointed him toward a grill. He was turning it over when he looked up to see some people pointing at him. It seemed he had offended them somehow.

"What's up with those guys?" He asked his friend, who looked back at them.

When he turned to look at him again, he noticed that he was missing half his face. He didn't appear to be scared.

"We killed one of their people," he said. His tongue was literally in his cheek.

"They should have known better," Elzaiya said. He was surprised that he knew the history of what had been happening.

He took out his knife and sliced off a piece of meat. He started to chew through, but it was uncooked. He swallowed it anyway. We stayed there until it was dark, and then he tried to stand, but his stomach was giving him hell.

"What's wrong with you?" his friend asked.

"It must have been the meat."

"We can't stay here. We can't let them find us here."

He was still talking when an axe whirred and took his head off. It landed at Elzaiya's feet. He was still trying to move, but his stomach was killing him. That's when he saw a hand stretched toward him, pulling him up, trying to save him.

"Help me... Help me... HELP ME!!!" When he sprang up, one hand was on his stomach, and the other was raised to cover his face from the torchlight that had been pointing at him. So, it had all been a dream.

"It's alright... It's alright. You're okay." It was Nadia, and he was too scared to feel ashamed.

"Come with me to the bed," her voice was soothing and comforting.

It was the only sound he wanted to hear at night. When he looked at the clock, the LED light read 2:11 a.m. The only thing she had on was a short black nightgown.

He wasn't sure he was fully awake. She pushed and cooed him into bed before kneeling on the floor. "What are you doing?"

"I thought Christians pray when things like this happen."

For the first time in his life, he was shocked. "Most of them do; I just go back to sleep."

"You should pray," she said.

So, for the first time in a long while, he knelt on the bed and prayed. When he opened his eyes, she was kneeling there, staring at him; willing, waiting, but defiant.

"Would you not go back to sleep?"

"Is that what you want?"

"What I want is none of your business," he said mindfully.

She stood up and went to lie on the blanket he had kept on the floor. He didn't let her head reach the pillow before bending over her on all fours. "I want everything; nothing seems to be enough."

"Then take my everything," she said. "And if it's not enough, I promise, I will give you a lot more."

For a long moment that felt like the time between dusk and dawn, he stared at her, unsure of his resolution. But it was not just her body that called to him. As much as his hands were roaming her thighs while his mind thought about right and wrong, he didn't know which one pushed him on. The things he felt or what he knew he could.

His legs were parting hers. Had that been unconscious, too? Just like he was pulling her pants off. What was he doing… He would have begged himself to stop! But who was talking; who was listening?

He held her up, and she looked down and noticed that they were feeling the same thing. She came closer and kissed him and felt him harden on her.

Was she a part of his dreams, she wondered? He was not the person who slept, nor was he the one who dreamt, nor the soul that awoke. Who was he?

She put her hand in the middle of their embrace and stroked. His hands ran through her hair, and he kissed her neck. He was being gentle, covering up his violence. Without warning, she rose and pulled him to the bed. He was surprised, and she laughed.

She went to the curtains and pulled them apart so the moonlight flooded into the room, and there, like the queen of all silhouettes, took everything off. She stood there, silent, fingers on her lips, luring and daring.

He stood up to meet her, but she pushed him away. He held out his hand; she slapped it away. He understood. He took his clothes off and stared at her, the moonlight glowing in his eyes, his beard flashing, and his body burning. She meant to see everything, and he stood like a king, daring the world to come fight him. She came close, like a curious animal, inspecting his body. The freckles that ran down the left side of his body, making him look like a leopard in wolfskin. She leaned in and kissed him, their bodies touching, their souls acclimatising. She could feel the heat, and it felt like he would burn her through. And just when she thought the shivers in her soul would break her down, he threw her on the bed, intent on devouring her.

She fought him, but he was no ordinary predator. She felt the translation of his love for her in the mutual understanding of his kisses. This was beyond all ordinary bonds, and they knew that the cost would be higher than they would be willing to pay. But they were in it for the gamble, and they would fight the odds together.

When they started to echo in rhythmic patterns, they forgot everything else. She gave him a sense of magic, a sense of beingness that only the most enlightened and inexperienced could comprehend. "Love at first sight", some call it. But there was more to it than the feeling. Only the courageous could give everything, and only the bravest of them had the power to take it all. She was art, and he appreciated her.

'Thank you' came in different ways, in all forms, in indistinguishable paints. He was evil, a creature of the night. Something misunderstood by most. She knew that. But she hadn't come to give him light. Peace, maybe, but sometimes. She was going to be his moonlight, as he wanted it. His soul did not long for redemption, not for saving or for the sun, but for chaos. She would be his disaster, his beautiful hurricane.

When he indulged himself in her, he threatened to break her apart. She knew she would love him for as long as he was this natural force. She would be his sea, and him, he could be all he wanted to be with her when he wanted to lose control.

19

AAIRA HAS NO MOTIVE

The card slipped out when Aaira opened her journal as she did every night since Emerson had given it to her on her 20th birthday. She immediately recognised the logo.

"I saw the edge sticking out." Quinn said, turning back to his book.

"Someone must have placed it there," she muttered.

"The room was secure when I came in. Should we be concerned?"

Aaira had a sharp mind. "No."

Even though Quinn didn't tell her most of what he and the boys did, she knew that Emerson would find a way to get to her—through family.

"I think he wants to talk," she said.

"About what?" Quinn shifted uneasily. "That man is a law-abiding psychopath."

"Maybe I should listen to what he has to say before we end up on the losing side of this war."

"I don't even think we are at war anymore. We just have a problem, and it's Emerson; the man is everybody's headache."

Aaira sighed.

Quinn wondered why he was beating himself up. She would contact Emerson.

She sensed what he was thinking. "Are you jealous?"

"I am cautious. No good would come of this meeting."

"What if he wants to wave a white flag?"

"The flag could be transparent for all I care. It doesn't make me trust him more or despise him less."

"What if he's found out about our son?"

Quinn paused and dropped the book. "What if he hasn't? I'd rather call his bluff."

Aaira was silent for a while before picking up the phone.

"There she goes." Quinn sulked.

She dialled and waited, but there was no reply. When she tried it again, she was told that the number didn't exist.

"Do you feel better now?" She asked her husband.

He gave a fake smile and lay down.

Some twenty minutes later, he was asleep with his back turned to her. She was just about to sleep when the phone vibrated. She picked it up and slid down to view the notification. There was no reaction on her face as she scrolled through the pictures on the phone. She took up her earpiece and inserted it so as not to let the sound wake her husband up.

The scene was one that she was familiar with. The year before her son was born, she had gone on a delegated visit to France as an emissary. There she had met Emerson, and they had talked in-depth. Then he wasn't the enemy; he had never been her enemy.

After their talk, they found themselves in a hotel room, drunk and out of their minds. They had made love and it had gone on until she was done with her duty. It was during that time that she learnt of his hospital habit.

Harlequin was about to join Navina in bed when he received a text. Coming from Emerson, he felt dread. However, upon opening the text, he was overjoyed.

When Nadia awoke, she was struck by the sunlight. She turned to the window and gazed outside. The light was bright, a sharp contrast to the blunt chill in the air. But deep within, she felt like spring.

She could hear voices from the kitchen. Eventually, she would have to leave the room; she had to face what had happened. But she couldn't leave the bed; she was spent.

She just wanted to lie there forever, if that was possible.

The door opened, and she slid under the covers. She felt ashamed, having just realised that she was naked.

"Hail Mary! What mother of disasters happened here?" It was Cairo.

"Nothing… Cairo, please go away." Nadia shooed her.

"So, if nothing happened, where did all this blood come from?"

"What? "No…" Nadia brought out her head to check. Truly, there were traces of blood all over the sheets. She couldn't look at Cairo. "Yesterday was…"

"Deep?" Cairo smiled.

"Please don't say anything more," Nadia said shyly, her cheeks burning.

"People like this won't tell you they love you." Cairo picked a pillow up from the floor and sat on the side of the bed. "They keep their feelings to themselves because they don't want to be vulnerable."

"And yet, isn't vulnerability essential to love?"

"Not for everyone, darling. Not for everyone," Cairo stroked Nadia's hair affectionately.

She was her younger sister, and she was fond of her, even though she wouldn't tell her now. The girl radiated joy. She was beautiful. God!

"Is that how you are with Avelli?" Nadia asked, curling her knees under the sheets.

"Well, when I and Avelli met, he was a total jackass," Cairo laughed.

"And now?"

"Now he's lost the jack," Elzaiya said, leaning by the door.

"I'll leave you two alone," Cairo said. "Take it easy on this one."

"Ewwww…" Nadia said, submerging herself.

Elzaiya and Cairo chuckled. Cairo stopped to whisper to him that he owed her. This would not have happened if she hadn't insisted they sleep together. He was about to swear when she told him to take care.

He understood and nodded. He closed the door and sat on the bed.

"Get dressed; we're going to a mall."

"For what?" Her voice was muffled.

"We want to taste their food."

"Like you…"

"Like I tasted you," he pulled the sheets away slowly. She knew there was no point in telling him no. He had bathed and was dressed in a white shirt and blue trousers. His black shoes complemented his belt.

He kissed her and played with her hair. "Why do you always wear a white shirt and blue trousers?"

"Well, that's because you can easily recognise when your white is stained. But most importantly, you will be conscious enough not to get it dirty. The blue to me is a symbol of honour, humility, loyalty, faith, trust, confidence and…"

"Royalty," she said.

"And royalty."

"And they tell you who to be when you tend to forget what you're bound to represent."

"You want to be who you want to be, never who you are," he said, looking deep into her eyes. Her skin glowed. He bent as if to kiss her, and she closed her eyes. He sat back and smiled at her when she opened them.

She frowned. "Does making love make you this beautiful?" He asked.

"I don't know. I've never made love before now." She returned his gaze. "You wanted to kiss me."

"I did?"

She nodded. He kissed her and then left her to take a bath. She wouldn't stand up if he were in the room with her.

When he came back, she was dressed. She had on a pair of jeans and a denim jacket. She didn't cover her hair, which made her overwhelmingly beautiful, and he let her know.

They went to the mall in Avelli's convertible. Cairo did the driving while they shot middle fingers at anyone who complained. They had finished window shopping and had examined all the nooks of the mall when they finally went to the restaurant to eat. They made their orders and had been served, except for the ice cream.

When the woman came with the bowl of ice cream, she took one look at Elzaiya, and the bowl slipped from her hands. They could see that she was visibly shaken, but not from fear; more like surprise.

The manager started to shout at her, but Elzaiya told him it was enough. Mistakes were bound to happen. He paid for it and ordered another bowl.

The people there, including the girls, were surprised, except for Machiavelli. He knew how his friend understood the poor.

The woman had stared like she recognised him from somewhere, and she too looked familiar, but he couldn't place the face.

While they ate, she stared at him. After they finished, he took the bowl to the counter and was about to say something when she gave him a piece of paper. He nodded and left with the others.

The CCTV on the far end of the wall captured everything.

***

Merceides had been trailing Harlequin for days. He hadn't missed the meeting under the bridge. He had also been watching Sarki, who trailed Emerson.

It seemed the issue of distrust was riven deep on both sides. He had given thought to Denise's changed behaviour. Their wedding was coming up sometime in June, but he had not decided on the exact date yet.

If she kept on this path, he might need to stall until things were settled. He didn't want to be sleeping with the enemy. He would have asked for advice, but he knew what Elzaiya would say. His brother was a bastard to his emotions.

It had been a year now, and the terrorists had not attacked. They were waiting for their leader's action. But with this politics in the background, Merceides could bet Sarki didn't have their time.

"I'll be going out this evening; want to come with?"

Denise had a certain aura whenever she was going to meet her dad. He was not going to interfere. The sooner she chose a side, the better.

"No, I'll be going out today for a meeting," he said. *When did stalking an enemy become a meeting?* He judged her for being a less qualified liar.

"Should I come?" She asked.

He told her what she wanted to hear. "No need; go do your thing."

"I intend to visit Elzaiya, if that's okay; I heard he was ill."

"I would have gone with you but…" He waved it away like he still bore some malice.

"It's fine, I understand," she started to fold her clothes.

It was 2 p.m. Sometimes the days were so slow that you started to wonder if the world was still spinning. He fell asleep with that thought.

When he woke up, it was past four, and Denise had gone out. She left a note on the bed with a P.S. on it.

My love life has been reduced to "post scriptum".

He took his bath and deliberately wasted his time. It was past 5 when he got ready. When he arrived at his brother's place, he heard their laughter. This lot seemed to be having the best time. Of course, Denise wasn't here.

He knocked, and someone said they were coming. Cairo was the one who opened the door.

"Hey yo… Benz…" She said.

Cairo insisted he should have used Benz as a moniker, and he always corrected her that he was not named after the brand.

"Hey Cairo, I could hear you guys laughing clownishly a mile away."

"We are playing games," she whispered, allowing him to pass.

He smiled, went in and closed the door. He was surprised to see Nadia in the house. They exchanged greetings and talked for a bit before he excused himself and Elzaiya. They went to his room to talk.

Merceides told him about Harlequin and Emerson. And they agreed it was best they let the Sultan and his brother self-destruct their relationship, but they had to find a way to handle Emerson.

Elzaiya asked after Denise, and Merceides waved it away. He didn't bring it up again.

"I was going to check up on someone. Want to come?"

Merceides said it would be nice. It's been a while since they've done anything together.

Elzaiya waved to his people and left with Merceides. Telling them that something had come up in the department. Machiavelli understood.

They got to the location that the woman in the mall had given him, but she was not there. She had told him to be there by 8 p.m. They waited for twenty more minutes and gave up.

But instead of going back home, they went back to the mall. They met the manager and asked him for the woman's home address, which he wrote down on a card, and they appreciated him for his effort.

The house was in a small neighbourhood; it was wedged, just like Israel, between a church and a school. They knocked, but there was no reply. When they turned the lock, the door swung open.

They were both surprised at how someone in this neighbourhood would leave their door unlocked.

The house gave off an eerie vibe. It felt like the inside of a cave: dark, stuffy and gloomy. Elzaiya brought out his phone to look for his feet and the damn light switch. He was about to turn it on when Merceides called to him. He went to meet him where he stood behind the couch.

He was standing over a body; the woman's dead body. Her wrists had been slit, and it appeared like suicide.

Elzaiya frowned. "Now we'll never get to find out what she wanted to say."

Merceides was still inspecting the body. Suddenly, he bent and pulled up her right sleeve. There was a birthmark on it that looked like a patch of oil burn.

"What's wrong?" Elzaiya asked. "You're not supposed to touch the body. We're not even supposed to be here."

"This woman was the person who raised you until you were three years old."

Elzaiya's curiosity returned. He looked at the body for a while longer, but his memory wouldn't aid him.

"We have to go," he suddenly said. "Someone could be framing us for murder."

Merceides hadn't thought about it that way. He agreed, and they were about to leave when Elzaiya pulled him back. "Listen."

Merceides paused. "I don't hear anything."

"Just listen." There were more ways than one in which Merceides concluded that their brother was more animal than he was human. His ears twitched, and Merceides could swear that they stood like those of a wild animal during a hunt.

They crouched and waited in silence for about 70 seconds before the door creaked open.

They had parked their car at the end of the street, so whoever it was probably didn't know anyone was in.

The silhouette of a man blocked the door; they held their breath and waited. There was a curtain at the side where they hid. After about 4 minutes, the man didn't move; they started to crawl to the door and prayed they wouldn't hit anything.

Merceides had been framed for murder before. Twice would make him a serial suspect.

They crawled into the bedroom and waited. All the lights in the house were turned off, and they could not risk putting on a light when they didn't know who was watching. It seemed like forever as they waited until they heard the shuffling of feet. More people, at least two more, had joined the man at the door.

The room they hid in was dark, and the air was coming in through a vent.

Merceides put his phone screen on the rug and turned it on. The light automatically dimmed. He then turned off the automatic brightness and the blue light. In the dark, they could make out that there was a window, big enough for them to escape from.

They opened the window gently. Luckily, it made no sound. The people in the living room were preoccupied. They managed to slip out of the house and landed in the back of the church. It was quiet there.

"Should we call the police?" Merceides asked.

"And tell them what?"

"We should report it. It's murder."

"A murder linked to our family, linked to me. It's too convenient. We can't take the risk now."

The church had a low fence, which they climbed across to the street where they had parked the car. They hadn't gone far when they heard an explosion and saw the rising of smoke. Great that they had thought about escaping.

Merceides had unlocked the car from about a yard away. They got to the car and were about to get in when Elzaiya touched the handle; it was warm. Merceides was about to open his. "Wait!" Elzaiya yelled.

"What? We have to go."

"Don't open the door," Elzaiya said. He had been bitten before; now he was coy.

"What's wrong?"

"I don't know yet," he bent to look underneath the car. As he suspected, there was a bomb attached to it, and the timing was desperate.

"Run!"

They were both at a safe distance when the car exploded into an unrecognisable mechanical wreck.

"Oh, my God!" Merceides exclaimed. He couldn't believe it.

"You needed a new car anyway," Elzaiya teased. Somehow, he found these things funny.

"Why aren't you taking any of these seriously?"

"I am. Someone is trying to get to me, and now you."

Merceides didn't get it. "How?"

"I was made to fall ill so I wouldn't be able to participate in the games."

"I thought it was malaria?" Merceides asked.

"Crazy, right? But yeah. Anyway, both you and Machiavelli are now in the game, and someone isn't finding it funny. Sarki has been on defence since he learnt about Emerson conniving with Harlequin, and now, we can assume he's playing offence again."

"What if he's not the one?" Merceides was breathless. It was the second time he had evaded death in a short while.

"Denise, where is she?" Elzaiya asked.

"She went out. Why, what's wrong?"

"I fear that Denise is now in league with our enemies. You have to be careful."

Merceides did not want to agree, but he knew that the statement was not out of spite. He may be right, as usual.

***

Harlequin went through the constitution and saw the clause he was looking for. "*In the case that the president faked his death in a bid to save himself from those who would see him dead. He has the right to return to office and participate in the games, which provides him with the chance to serve the country for an extra term. Wherewith the...*"

Emerson was a genius, he thought. He was the only person whom he knew could outwit Elzaiya.

20

INSTIGATING WAR

Sarki felt better knowing that Nadia was far from Emerson. The palace wasn't safe, but that was something to think about after all other business had been properly conducted. There were murmurs in the living room. He left the tranquillity of the study to investigate the rousing.

Breaking news: "It is no wonder that the bandits know when to strike and whom to attack. Formerly, we thought their ties were limited to the military. But a new insight has resurfaced, which could only have been accomplished by my playing dead. I have discovered that there are members of the elite class who are involved in this pathetic attempt at undermining our government." Harlequin was saying.

"Could you reveal them to the public, seeing that you promised the citizens a truly transparent government?" A reporter asked.

"Why, yes."

Just a bluff. Sarki thought.

"The Sultan, for one."

A wave of shock emanated from the TV, reaching everyone watching.

Sarki felt the nation vibrate, and a crippling pain in his chest left him unable to move. Those watching did not make the mistake of turning to look at him.

"Are you saying he supports these acts of terrorism?"

"I'm saying he sponsors them. All of this with solid evidence to back it up."

"Leave," Sarki ordered. Everyone quietly left the room. He should have seen this coming.

"He was the one who framed my brother for a murder in Palestine so he would be too preoccupied to run for office."

"And what of his brother, Mr Omar? Are they in on this together?"

Harlequin was well prepared. "I very much doubt that. I have not been able to find any correlation between Mr Emerson and his brother's activities. As we know, Mr Emerson made his disinterest in politics very clear."

There was one reporter at the back who had been silent all through the discussion. Now he edged his way forward. "Mr President," he adjusted his tie.

"Yes."

"There were leaked photos released on our site this morning. Of someone who facially could only be you or your brother. Going into a building with someone else. Shortly after, the building was engulfed in flames with a woman inside, whose body was recovered from the ruins. Is it safe to say that the person in the picture is your brother, seeing that he has a habit of ending up in questionable situations?"

Harlequin recognised the reporter. Emerson had told him that he would send someone to shift the spotlight onto his brother, and that bit was important.

"It's safe to say it wasn't me. Whatever my brother does when I am not around is none of my business. He is answerable for his actions."

"And what of the person accompanying him?"

"As I said, it is none of my business. Whatever it is, they are answerable for their actions according to the law and constitution of the Federal Republic of Nigeria."

The reporters kept throwing their questions, but the deed had been done. Harlequin would take his rightful place today until the games began the selection process. As a bonus, he would have a chance to play again.

The whole country was watching the news, as was the rest of the world.

Synai turned the TV off and looked at Vivian. The game had just taken itself to a whole new dimension.

"Bishop?" she asked.

He nodded.

Elzaiya, Machiavelli, and Merceides stood watching the news. The girls sat behind them, and Nadia, strangely enough, wasn't flustered. She hadn't asked what had happened last night. She knew better.

"What is he doing?" Merceides was mad with rage.

The question wasn't in the context of what Harlequin was doing. It was rhetoric as to why he had not consulted the family.

"He's reclaiming power," Machiavelli said.

Cairo tapped Nadia, and they both left for the kitchen.

"Who set the fire?" Elzaiya had been trying to figure it out since last night.

"It would be Sarki. He's desperate to get back to a position of strength," Machiavelli said in a whisper. The whole conversation followed suit.

"If Sarki killed the woman and set the fire, who planted the bomb?" Merceides asked.

"It should still be him."

"What if it was Harlequin that arranged the killing and the fire?" Elzaiya asked.

"He is our brother; he can't…"

"Maybe he just did, Merceides. We don't know what Harlequin is capable of anymore. Emerson has gotten into his head."

"Why would he try to kill us?"

"It wasn't meant to kill us. It was a threat. You didn't take his side when he needed you to, and it was my idea for him to stay dead."

"So, our suspects are Sarki and Harlequin?" Machiavelli asked.

"Emerson," Elzaiya said.

Merceides was exasperated. "Pick someone, dammit!"

"We don't know what else he promised Harlequin apart from restoring him to office. But what did Harlequin batter in return? Most likely, information that we are unaware of. I was conveniently taken out by someone, and now, you were framed. Emerson doesn't care if we are alive or dead, so long as he keeps his word to Harlequin. If the cost is a brother, it makes it more interesting. Harlequin gets the power and regrets it for life."

There was a vibration, followed by another. Merceides and Machiavelli both checked their phones to see the red line that had never been followed with a smile. It simply read: *We are sorry; you are no longer a participant in the games.*

The top three contenders had just been eliminated.

***

"A church!" Aaira looked around the citadel and didn't feel anything.

She wasn't much of a religious person. Sacrilege was not a term she understood well. She turned 360 to make sure there was no one else around. Her Arabian eyes dimmed a bit when she turned to look back at him.

"I want to see if faith is tied to belief in the supernatural."

"But you alone are supernatural, aren't you?" She bowed, raising the edges of her gown to genuflect. "The almighty Emerson, maker and

destroyer of all that is holy. So divine, he can't let go of human vanity."
She laughed and dropped her bag on the bench in front of him.

"What I feel for you, Aaira, isn't vanity."

"You are too refined to understand the stupidity encased in love,
Emerson," she said and started to dance. In many ways, she was still a
child.

"Is that why you chose Quinn, because he understands stupidity?"

"Why did you want to see me?"

He pulled her from her twirling. "I've missed you."

"Is that what all the fuss has been about? You miss me?" She pulled
away. She hadn't aged, and it baffled Emerson.

"You pretended not to notice that I was around."

"You could have visited. That's if your intentions were pure."

"Would you have that? Teenage drama all over again?"

"So, you'd rather play with a whole country?"

"And you still wouldn't notice me," he said as he moved to meet her;
she shifted back.

"Why should I? You seem to forget that I am married and have sons to
be responsible for."

"You have nothing to be responsible for, Aaira. You are not bound to
anything. Why are you giving excuses? Have I not done what I can to
please you?"

"You tried to kill my son."

"I tried to get your attention."

"Go deal with some other woman, Emerson. I have no time for this," she raised her hands to twirl on her toes again, and he caught her by the waist.

She didn't refuse him. Instead, she started to lead in a waltz, and he followed. If it was a dance she wanted, he would.

"I'm giving you another chance. You can rule this country as you've always wanted. You can set things right and make women respectable. You can have the power to do what you want. That was what I gave you by attacking your sons. Something you wouldn't do yourself."

"I don't want power. My sons should have it. They'll do better than I will, anyway."

"I can take Harlequin out just like this." He snapped his fingers.

She shook her head. "He is my son, Emerson. I know it means nothing to you, but he is my son. If you love me, you will protect him for me."

"I love you."

She looked into his blue eyes. The sun reflected on his face from the glass roof that showered light down on where they stood. "I know," she said.

"Then just…"

She kissed him. She pressed into him and pushed him back into the chair, kissing him recklessly. She took her heels off and held him down on the chair. She could feel his need for her, and it was strong. She laughed, unzipped him, and then turned as if to go. He dragged her down and ripped away at her underwear. She sighed when she felt him in her. She could feel his hand on her back, pushing her closer to him, and she wanted to come. It was not like she wanted to stop herself. She loved her husband, but she loved him too; he pleasured her in a completely different way.

***

Quinn watched the news with utter dissatisfaction. He could not believe that Harlequin was his son.

"I should have disowned that boy. No! That will not do. I should take him to the central market and have him salted and flogged for a week and then…"

"Calm down… he's doing what politicians do," Dr Kendrick said. He would have laughed, but he knew that outside the visual descriptions, Quinn was not joking.

"He has broken our code. Our family lives by a code. Whatever we do, we do together! He has gone against every single ethic I raised him by."

"It is what men do; he is no longer a child."

"No longer a child? Better if he were still a child. He's behaving like a damned fool. In league with Emerson?"

"He would come around."

"He'd better not come anytime soon."

Dr Kendrick sighed.

Quinn had a bad habit of making people laugh at his innuendos whenever he was upset.

"Have you heard from the other boys?"

"They are in the living room with their girlfriends. Merceides is strangely cool-headed about everything these days."

"He's keeping company with his younger brother; maybe it's rubbing off on him."

"One goes astray, and the other comes home."

"Better one than both. At least you have one you can always rely on."

Quinn sighed and sat down. "Has Aaira told him yet?"

"She wanted to, but then that accident happened with the fire thing. The woman is dead; she doesn't think it's the best time."

"She won't find the perfect time."

"Let's hope she knows what she's doing."

Quinn watched the boys on the monitor and smiled. Machiavelli appealed to him as a son. He was in a corner of the house kissing Cairo; they were both laughing. On the other screen, Elzaiya was in the kitchen, slicing up some fruit. It was rare to see him eat real food.

Denise, who had been in the living room with Merceides and Nadia, excused herself and went to the kitchen. Quinn watched this new development intently. Denise interested him.

"I would be on my way now," Dr Kendrick said.

"Take care of yourself, too, doctor," Quinn said in farewell.

Dr Kendrick left, and Quinn focused his attention on the screen.

"I see you've recovered back to your full self. Is that thanks to the fruits or Nadia? Which have you been eating recently?" Denise asked naughtily.

"Why the sudden interest in my choice of nutrition, Denise? Are you looking to adopt a diet yourself?"

She laughed. "Poor girl, she'll give all of herself to you, only for you to hurt her in the end. Does she know how apathetic you really are? Or does she have the sad belief that somehow you would turn out to be that loving gentleman, her knight in shining armour? Does she know you like I do?" He kept silent and continued slicing the fruits with a sly smile on his face.

"You're a fox," she said.

He did not reply.

"Maybe I should tell her about the clip on your laptop. about how, by chance, you were able to save her. How you became her hero. Or should I tell her about all those nights we had when you went deep into my soul, satisfying your exuberance? Or share with her a taste of you? Should I tell her in detail about all the marks on your body? I bet she can cry rivers of pearls with those beautiful eyes. What was she like? Or are you just torturing her as you did me? You want her to lose her mind and beg for you. Oh yes, that's what you want, isn't it? Because you like to be the one with power. It's always about power for you. You want her to break apart and fall helplessly for you so you can do to her as you please. I bet you've thought about this for months now, wondering how she would be when you start your games. It's not just about the pleasure, is it? For you, it's about the anticipation, the scheming, and seeing those scenes play out. You like playing god in other people's lives."

He dropped the knife and shook the bowl of fruit so that they could mix properly. And then he moved toward her with the bowl in his hand. She wore a light gown that stopped just above her knees. She stood with her hips apart and her hands on the counter. He used a fork to select one piece of each fruit: apple, watermelon, pineapple, and grape.

"Open your mouth," he said.

She opened, and he put the fruits in her mouth.

"I'm sorry if that's how it appeared to you. It was never my intention to use you. In some twisted way, I was in love with you. But after what you did, I think we are even. So, if you come at Nadia, I'll be coming for you. And believe me when I tell you this: there'll be nothing left of you when I'm done." He left her in the kitchen with a taste she could not savour.

***

It was evening, and Elzaiya had taken Nadia to his apartment. Machiavelli would stay in his old room in the house. She had insisted on staying here with him, oblivious to their cold war.

What she didn't get was what Elzaiya was to the family. She had only just learnt that he worked in IT, and she didn't believe it at all.

"Why not?" Elzaiya said, producing his ID.

"You work in IT, and they pay you this much?"

"It's a rich family; they like me."

"Everyone likes you; that's the problem. Even Denise is still in love with you."

"That isn't true."

"It is. I see how she looks at you."

"Nothing would come up between me and Denise."

"But you have history."

"Yes."

She asked him to share, but he said he found it inappropriate, but he'd tell her later. His mind told him it was bad timing. She insisted, but he declined, so she said she'll go ask Denise herself. He laughed and shook his head as she sulked and left the house, banging the door behind her.

She'll come around, he thought to himself.

Nadia wasn't going to meet Denise; she intended to walk the estate until she got lost, and he had to find her. The garden looked appealing.

She was ten minutes into the garden when she heard feet rustling behind her. She turned to see Denise walking with a headset on.

When Denise saw her, she took it off. "Hey…"

"Hi…" Nadia said. Denise made her feel uneasy.

"I come here every day to have some quiet time," Denise said.

"Yeah, it's lovely," Nadia said, looking around at the trees and rose bushes. Denise studied the girl and made up her mind about why Elzaiya found her so fascinating. She was simple.

There was an awkward silence that made them both know they were beating around the bush. Nadia decided to catch the rabbit.

"What happened between you and Elzaiya?"

Denise pretended to be taken aback. "He didn't tell you?"

"No," Nadia said.

"That's true; he keeps things to himself."

Nadia agreed.

"The truth is, it was more of an infatuation on both sides. I mean, who wouldn't fall for him? But then he became cold after I saw a recording on his laptop, and things just died between us."

"A recording?"

"Yeah, it was a recording of you in a pink gown in your room. I asked what it was, and he just closed the laptop and chased me off. Since then, he's been treating me like the enemy."

Nadia felt the world tumble, and then it stood still. That was when she had been kidnapped. That was the only time she had worn a pink gown. How could he have it if…

"I'd better go," Denise said. "He gets angry seeing me around you. I'm sorry I told you all of that, but I think you have a right to know; he's a dangerous person."

Nadia found that she was about to cry. She thanked Denise, who put on her headset and was soon out of sight.

It was past 9 p.m., and Nadia had not come back. He went to the house to look for her, but she wasn't around; even Denise said she didn't know where she was. He checked the whole compound and then went to the garden. He didn't go with a flashlight; he wasn't scared of the dark.

He found her lying down, curled up by the water fountain. He bent and noticed that she had been crying. He tapped her on the shoulder, and she opened her eyes.

"Let's go home," he said, and was about to help her up.

"Did you fall in love with me after you kidnapped me, or is it still part of your big plan?"

He took his hand back and put them both in his pockets, took some steps back, and sat on the other side of the water fountain so he could properly stare at the moon. The primary thought on his mind was how best to keep his promise to Denise.

21

WHAT IS JUSTICE?

She had been crying, and he'd kept silent the whole time. Now she stood in front of him, asking for the third time. "What kind of monster are you?"

He stared at her, but she could sense that he was distant. "The kind that puts others first," he said coarsely.

"How do you even justify what you did? How could you sleep with me after all you've done? How is that putting me first?"

"I didn't know you then," he simply said.

Someone who didn't know him would say he wasn't taking her seriously.

"That's your excuse? You kidnapped me! You kidnapped me! Do you know that's a capital offence? You know how long your jail sentence would be?" She put her hands to her face and continued to cry.

There was something about the whole thing that made him want to smile. He tried hard to keep a straight face. Something must be seriously wrong with him. It was not like he didn't understand how she felt; it was just that he couldn't bring himself to the empathic place she was in.

"I'm sorry you feel that way. But if I go to prison for that, which won't happen, there will be no hard feelings. I would not feel terrible about it."

"You're not even capable of remorse," she said in disbelief.

"I am," he said, angrily. "I do feel remorse, but I do not regret my actions, and those are two different things. I know the consequences of my actions, but I won't carry the guilt. I bury and forget. It was war; all of it was fair. Pardon me, but you were supposed to be a minor casualty until love happened. You say you know what I am. Are you only now surprised at how I am what I am? Concerning remorse, why should I bother showing any? How will a sorry expression change what you already think of me? Would it not even serve to help you acknowledge that I might be faking all that I express?"

"Are you just using me?"

"I am not. Not anymore; you're mine now. But that had to happen, Nadia. I had to be the one kidnap you. I couldn't risk your safety in the hands of someone else, and even then, I didn't know you."

"Is that supposed to comfort me? You planned the whole thing… it was so perfect; I should have known."

He grinned smugly. "Thank you for noticing. I told the engineer that…"

"I'm not praising you. I'm angry! I'm upset, Elzaiya! You violated my privacy. All those nights you watched me. It's one thing to kidnap me, but another to spy on me. You're sick and evil! You're a psychopath!"

She sobbed. "How could I not see that? You hid it behind so much innocent brilliance but…"

"And so what?" He sprang from where he sat.

She stepped back, afraid. "Yes, I am. But so what? Your father tried to kill my brothers. Two innocent men, for the sake of power. I could not sit idly by and watch them die. I would not watch my family burn. Not when I am alive. So who's the real monster? Your father is a cold blooded murderer. I'm not even close to what he is, and you dare judge me because he's lied to you your whole life and you found out just one crime I perpetrated? Everyone knows my face. Unlike him, I don't hide behind a mask. I am not a good person. I only try my best to work within the confines of morality. I don't care what you think about me; I'm doing the right thing. And yes, I might have crossed a few lines, but so have your father, your uncle, and his daughter. These people's evils have masquerades lurking in the background. So don't come judging me like I am the most be-devilled of them all."

"You are their brother? A Quinn? They have a stepbrother?" She stared at him in disbelief.

"I am their brother, by birth and by blood. I am not a halfling."

"So, all this while…" She gasped and covered her shock by putting her hand to her mouth.

"I'm sorry, but I did what I had to do."

She slapped him across the face.

"Are you mad?" He yelled at her.

"You don't have the right to tell me you're sorry as if you are giving food to peasants." She raised her hand to slap him again.

He held it. "All the things they said about your father are true. But you're different. The children are not their parents." He let her hand drop, and raised a hand to clean her tears.

She stepped away. "How do you know that?"

"Because I've watched you."

"You've seen me naked," she corrected.

"I always turned it off."

"You did?"

"What kind of man do you think I am?" He came closer.

"I was raised in a world of political lies. I'm not surprised at all by this. I'm just upset that I heard it from your ex-girlfriend's foul mouth. You should have been brave enough to tell me yourself."

"I would have," he stared at her eyes and noticed that they were not red for someone who had been crying for so long.

"Did you sleep with her?"

"Yes," he said.

She exclaimed in Arabic, and he laughed.

"We slept together, but I did not have sex with her. You are my first."

She sighed. "Okay, then I will keep all of your secrets."

"I know that."

"But what will you give me in return? And no, you can keep your black heart to yourself."

"What do you want?" He took both her hands in his and laid them on his shoulders.

"I want you. I want to have your child. And I don't want any more lies. And…"

"You still want my…"

"Yes," she knelt on the grass and pulled him down. The ground was soft, and the grass cushioned it.

She kissed him. "Something makes me feel that our love will not last for long."

"You should erase those thoughts," he said.

"It wasn't the fire or the bullet, it was you. You did things to me that I couldn't understand. Most nights I would stay awake having fantasies about…"

"About right now."

And I'd have trouble sleeping, so I'd just fantasise and feel embarrassed because I didn't know if you were already with someone else, but it felt right. It just felt right to miss you and want you. Even though I barely knew you, I started to love you incognito."

"Is it alright to say something stupid?"

"It will always be alright," she said.

"I…" he seemed unable to breathe.

"I love you too," she said. "You might eventually get used to it."

When they woke up, it was 6 a.m. The morning birds were chirping, but the insects were not awake. They came out when the sun was yellow and on weekends. They ran to the apartment and bathed.

The family meeting was at 9 a.m., and missing it wasn't among Elzaiya's options. She told him she would be going over to the palace to get some things. He told her that he didn't think it was a good idea because of the publicity. But she told him she had to, sooner or later. He kissed her goodbye and left.

When he went into the meeting, it was 8:58 a.m. It was the first time he was breaking his habit of being there at least twenty minutes before.

"I'm sorry about the…"

"You're right on time," Quinn said.

He would not be surprised if his father were an oracle.

Machiavelli winked, and Merceides shook his head at them.

"What do we do about Harlequin?" Quinn started the meeting.

"We let him finish his tenure, and if he's lucky, we let him run for another," Merceides said.

"Just like that?"

"Merceides is right," Elzaiya said. "We have tried by showing him the right way and the best things for the people. If he has decided to venture out on a different path, then all the punishment we can give is to watch how it plays out."

"But if we don't help him…"

"Emerson will. Let him learn his lesson," Merceides said. "He didn't flinch when he subtly accused me on national television. It didn't bother him that his brothers nearly died. The only thing he sees is the power he can gain, blind to everything else. If he can let us down, so can we, but that's not what I'm saying. I'm saying that we should let him progress on his own."

"And you, Machiavelli, what do you think?"

"I agree, sir," Machiavelli said. "Harlequin and Emerson are in the same bed, and he's like a child that you're trying to warn but who doesn't understand the danger unless you let him learn by experience."

They deliberated on the matter for a while before shifting on to other family business. Quinn told them that he was thinking about retiring and wanted his sons ready to take over the business, and that included Machiavelli, who beamed from ear to ear until Elzaiya told him to cut it.

After all matters were settled, Merceides left. Denise had told him that she was going out and would be back before 1 p.m., and it was past 12 p.m. Machiavelli, as usual, was eager to get back to Cairo. Quinn asked Elzaiya to wait.

He shut the door and waited. The study was more familiar to him than it was to all others in the house.

"I didn't do anything bad, did I, Daddy?"

"No, you haven't. Have a seat."

He sat as his father brought a bottle of wine and two glasses.

"Am I old enough to drink?" He teased.

"Don't condescend to me, boy." Quinn poured the wine, smiled to himself, and nudged a glass toward his son.

Elzaiya picked it up and waited for his father to start talking.

"I'm happy with the way you've bonded with your brother after the incident with Denise."

"Was this about what happened in the kitchen yesterday?"

"What happened there?"

"Don't condescend to me, Father; I know you're always watching."

Quinn smiled. "Whatever it is that exists between you two, remember that she is going to be your brother's wife."

"I have a feeling that's not going to happen," he said as he sipped his wine.

"Why?"

"It's just a feeling."

"Then let it happen naturally and not by your hand."

Elzaiya knew what a warning was. He wasn't scared of his father. But he knew enough to know who could outwit him in a game of power.

Not yet, anyway. He admired the way his father belied his capabilities in the country.

"Okay, Father."

"So, what about Nadia? I see you've taken a liking to her."

"Yes, I have," he looked to see if he could read his father. No luck! The man was better than him.

Quinn looked at his glass for a while and wondered if he should tell his son what bothered him. He changed his mind. "Take care of her, she seems like a nice girl."

"Is it still the age thing, Father?" Elzaiya laughed, dropped the empty glass, and stood to leave.

"I'm proud of what you've accomplished," his father said. "I couldn't ask for anyone better. But more than that, I want you to take care of your brothers. They might be older, but that doesn't matter, okay?"

"I will, Father." Elzaiya nodded and left with a courteous bow.

***

Denise was with her father, who had told her that he wanted another father-daughter moment. This time, they went to the beach to enjoy the crashing sound of the waves. They had come to be more honest and trusting with each other.

Their conversation finally settled on the Quinns, and Denise had asked a question about Aaira.

Emerson figured honesty would score him some points here. He looked at the sand like one who was embarrassed. "I still am."

He allowed his mind to flashback to their last meeting. He couldn't erase the moment of bliss that they had shared. Only two people knew the truth about Aaira's flaw as a sapiosexual nymphomaniac. One, which he started to think she had transferred to her children. After all, his daughter was intelligent. Research wasn't a bad thing.

"After all these years?" Denise looked at him with surprise. The man was a Pandora's box.

"It's love by default, you can't help it," he said, almost with guilt.

"So how do you live with the feeling of knowing that she doesn't love you as much?"

Emerson smiled. She loved him as much. She always would. Arden Quinn was just in the way. "Hope."

"Hope?" She drew circles in the sand.

"It's what keeps us humans alive. Sometimes we need it more than we realise. It gets to us, even when we don't know or think we have or want it."

She shook her head and dug her toes deeper into the sand.

He knew she had something on her mind. "You're still in love with him, that boy you told me about?"

"I've tried to let it go, but it's as if he's mocking me. I can still feel that he loves me too in a way, but…"

"But he chose someone else, just like Aaira. And you can't deal with it."

"Yes." And on a lighter note, she said, "Maybe it rubbed off on him because they live in the same estate."

"He lives with the Quinns?"

"Yes. Almost like a part of the family. He and his friend."

"Who?"

"Machiavelli."

Emerson heard a whistle blow in his head. "Elzaiya?" He asked to be sure. "Elzaiya and Machiavelli?"

"You know them?" She asked nonchalantly. "Of course, you do; they have been to the palace before."

Emerson didn't mention that he and Elzaiya were more like buddies.

"Of course. I know them, and I like Elzaiya a lot. He's…"

"Almost like a son to you, too?"

The phrase made Emerson freeze. If Elzaiya was with the Quinns, it meant he had been friends with the enemy. He had been blindsided the whole time.

"What does he do for the Quinns?"

"He works in IT," she said.

"That's just a cover," he said with a laugh that would make you sound stupid if you believed that.

"To be honest, I think so too."

"You do?" He asked with the charm of an innocent child.

"I'm not sure how this would sound, but I think he was the one who single-handedly orchestrated Nadia's kidnapping."

"How could you say such a thing?" Emerson decided to play good cop. "Kidnap her to save her? What would he gain?"

Denise told him to wave it away, that it was just her suspicion. Emerson agreed and went on to ask if the girl he went for was Nadia. They went on talking while the whole thing kept twisting in his mind. Somehow, he didn't feel anything else but pride. The boy had exceeded his expectations. If only he were his son... He steered the conversation back to Elzaiya, and Denise reluctantly talked.

"How old did you say he was?" He asked.

"23 or thereabouts."

Emerson recalled being told that his sperm donation had been anonymously bought. That had been more than 20 years ago. If calculated properly, it was almost 23 years ago. His heart was pounding. But Aaira had never gotten pregnant. She had been unable to have another child. But Elzaiya, his eyes... the boy had his eyes and his face. If he were his son...

"If you want something, you should take it," he said comfortingly. "Life won't hand anything to you."

She looked at him as one waiting for counsel. The better part of him told him to let the matter go, and he agreed.

"Could you do us a mutually beneficial favour?" He asked.

***

The press swarmed the front of the palace. Luckily, Nadia knew more than one way in. She slid in like a passerby and took the turn that led to the back. It was fenced, but there was a small gate that the gardeners used sometimes; it was always open. She sneaked through and then passed behind the mosque into the house.

She was climbing the stairs when she saw her uncle driving out of the main gate through the stream of reporters. She shook her head and headed for her room.

She had no opinions about Emerson. She looked up to see her father waiting for her with folded hands at the top of the stairs. She grinned childishly and paused where she was.

"Nadia, ki zo nan," he called.

"Baba, Inawuni," she said, climbing up to meet him. She passed by him and stood backing the door to her room.

"Kalou. Where have you been?"

"My friend was sick, I was taking care of ..." She didn't know if it was best to say it was a he.

"Boyfriend, you mean?"

She looked up at him. He didn't seem upset.

"Yes, Maryam told me everything. I am not angry; you're old enough to know the right thing to do. Just be careful about it." It occurred to him that, just like his brother, he too was clueless about raising children.

"Thank you, Father," she said and then stared at him in silence. He looked worried. She didn't want to ask if what they said on the news was true; Elzaiya had told her everything, and she believed him.

He was about to say something when a servant boy came running up the stairs. He bowed to her and the Sultan and then whispered something to her father, who quickly rushed away with him.

She wanted to get to her room, but she was curious, so she followed close behind them.

They stopped at the lab, where they met Dr Sani on a bed. He looked pale and was sweating. Her father sat on the bed and held his hand. The doctor was trying to tell him something. She moved closer so she could catch it too.

He gave Sarki an envelope and a key.

"Who did this to you?" Sarki asked with furious compassion.

She had the feeling that her father felt vulnerable.

"I don't know." The doctor looked at Sarki. Even at death, he was playing advisor. "I don't think it's your brother. There is someone else far more dangerous involved in…" He started to cough. A dry cough that scared Nadia.

"Let's take you to the hospital and…"

"There is no cure," he rasped. "The effects cannot be reversed. I have only taken something that will slow the process," he clutched Sarki tighter. "Be careful; trust nobody."

Nadia had not seen anyone die before. She watched, partly out of horrific curiosity and then out of dread, as he passed slowly and painlessly into the afterlife. She watched as her father closed the dead man's eyes and sent the servant away. She said nothing to comfort him.

When they were alone, Sarki tore the paper open and read through the contents. There were a lot of things that would have infuriated him, but the part that enraged him was the possibility, as the paper said, that Emerson had a son who should, by now, be in his early twenties.

He tore the paper to shreds and escorted his daughter out of the lab without a word.

22

THE USUAL SUSPECTS

Harlequin stumbled into Navina in the echoing halls of the presidential building. Passageways that she had once described as human holes. She had left him in Taraba to resume her stately duties, promising that she would see him on weekends. The next thing she knew, he was on the news, and she was almost as disappointed as Quinn. She had been avoiding him since, but now he stood in her path.

She walked up to him and was about to voice her disapproval when he silenced her and motioned to his office.

The corridors were busy today; everyone was trying to keep up appearances. She followed him, holding her files like she held all her cards—close to her chest. He opened the door and waited for her to get in. She entered the newly decorated office and faced him.

"You went against your family's wishes."

He smiled. "I know, I have plans of my own."

"It doesn't matter. You didn't even tell me what your plans were. And I thought you trusted me."

"I trust you. But those were dangerous waters. I didn't want you dipping your toes in such places."

She hissed. "You told me that whatever we do, we do together, and you can't even tell me your plans? By the way, how did you pull it off, Harlequin? Who helped you out?"

He walked past her. "I have friends in high places."

"And those friends freely gave you all that you needed? All that information? Come on, Harlequin; this is politics. We are in Nigeria, and things might have changed, but you can't sell me that crap."

"Okay!" He was tired. "I stole it," he said as he sat on the edge of the glass-topped table.

She gave him a long look before dropping the files on the table and flipping her neck so her hair could fall down the side of her neck. "I know you're offended…"

"Offended?" She gave a small laugh. It sounded like an American high class, haha. "Why should I be? You tell me only what you feel I need to know. You never share what bothers you, even now that you've turned too shady to be trusted."

She stood squarely in front of him. "It's fine if you're seeing another woman. What we had was, in any case, a fleeting dream on my part. I should have known you were not the type to stay. So, if you expect me to be offended, no, I'm not. It's fine; I understand."

"What?" He laughed before taking her hands in his. "I'm not seeing another woman. Of that, you can be sure. But okay, to remedy it all, I'll tell you everything."

"Now?" She asked. More like insisted.

"It's a long story, so…"

"We have time."

"You look sexy when you're pissed."

"Start talking." She pulled her hands away and went to sit in his chair, crossing her legs.

He proceeded to tell her about the day Emerson had met him in the club and how he had used her as leverage. Then he told her about how Machiavelli had gathered all the information through infiltration. He went on to connect the dots to the parts of the Quinns' plan and family that she didn't already know, ending with his brothers and how the youngest was the one who handled all the plans and safeguarded most of these documents, so he knew where to steal them from.

"So Elzaiya and Machiavelli are your brothers?" She was taken aback.

"No, Elzaiya is my brother by blood. Machiavelli is adopted. More like my brother's brother."

"I've been living with you under a veil of secrets all this time," she said, realising herself. The Quinns never ceased to surprise the world.

"You should see your face right now." He went to where she sat and stood before her.

"Are you back in the game?"

"Yes. I was sent the link as soon as I finished addressing the reporters."

"You're some lucky fellow." She stood up to leave and started to gather her files, but he pulled her close.

"I thought you said you had time?"

"To listen to what you had to say," she pushed him away and continued. "By the way, what would happen to the terrorists now that you have their location?"

"I would deploy a strike force. The coordinates have been forwarded to the army and air force. At least putting an end to them would be a move big enough to land me back in power next term."

"And the Sultan?" She asked. "This is the first time an issue like this has come up. Would our judicial system want to handle it, given that we are prosecuting the leader of a religious group? Aren't we indirectly sowing the seeds of another war?"

"I know that our judicial system is not equipped to handle the case, and luckily, it is beyond us. It is now an international matter, what with the clause "crimes against humanity." Therefore, the Sultan would be summoned by the ICJ soon enough."

"And your brothers would be cleared."

"Not really. Merceides will eventually be cleared because he is innocent. But most importantly, he has our brother on his side. Anything is possible when he is on your side. I would have loved to get back into the family's good graces, but I can't perjure myself."

"Hmm!" She sighed. "A political fight among brothers. Don't be frightened; you have me."

He laughed. "I am not frightened. I have you."

"Now, if you will excuse me, I have to submit these files, and then I'll be right back. Don't change that mood."

She left him, smiled and took a deep breath after closing the door. It had been a wonderful idea to have pinned the recorder in her hair at the last minute. He would have detected it had she hidden it in her ear.

She submitted the files to the lady in charge of the file room.

The woman was so frail that Nadia always felt hungry whenever she left her presence. She changed directions and headed to the toilet. There was no one else in the stalls.

Finally, she was alone. She removed her hair clip and pulled out the small jewel-like device, then flashed it in front of her phone. The NFC detected it instantly, the same way she had put it on, by flinging her hair backwards.

She played the recording first to make sure the file format was right. Without wasting any more time, she forwarded it to her benefactor. She had done her last favour, and she hoped they were even now.

***

When Emerson returned, Sarki was waiting. When Nadia saw him leave, he had stopped to get a briefcase and had driven out immediately. Now the house was in a solemn mood. But he was in high spirits, and the atmosphere didn't seem to bother him. He whistled his way around and was headed for his room when Sarki stood in his way.

Nadia was in her room, peeping through the keyhole.

Sarki didn't bother to speak. He flung Emerson against the wall and held him there with his arm around his throat. Emerson wasn't as muscular as his brother, but he was as fit as any athlete could hope to be.

"You killed our father…"

Nadia couldn't catch the words properly. She was tempted to open the door a crack, but that would be stupid.

"And if that wasn't enough, you killed Dr Sani too? Whatever did he do to deserve it?"

Emerson had had enough of struggling. He raised both feet and, pinning them to the wall, propelled himself forward, pushing Sarki to the other side of the wall. If not for his brother's big frame, Sarki would have landed on the floor.

Sarki threw a punch and Emerson ducked. Emerson caught the second punch in his stomach, and his anger flared. When Sarki threw the third punch, Emerson blocked it and, using his hand as a club, hit his brother on the collarbone. The force of the blow made Sarki reel, and Emerson held himself back.

They stood on both sides of the wall, glaring at each other.

"I didn't kill the doctor, I liked him too," Emerson said.

In his way, he respected the man. In better situations, they should have been good friends.

"And I don't know why you think I killed our father. I would never do something like that."

Sarki had been too angry to remember what Dr Sani had told him about his brother. If his personalities were split, with his kind of intelligence, there was a chance he didn't even know what the other was doing.

"Omar, you pile of horse crap..."

"Don't call me that, you hypocritical backstabbing piece of shit!" Emerson lashed out.

Sarki stared. He wondered if he should use the gun in his robe.

"I'm sorry, I shouldn't have said that. But I did not kill the doctor or our father," Emerson said, adjusting his suit.

"Then find out who did, and I will forgive your crimes. Let's talk about them when you return," Sarki said.

But that was diplomacy. The only talk they would have would be the one before he put a bullet in his brother's head. He couldn't handle his headache anymore.

"When did he die?" Emerson asked.

"About 35 minutes ago," Sarki said. "Why?"

"Nothing. But whoever did it wanted to make it look like I was the killer. Because before then, I was driving out..." He paused. "Just like I do every other day. May I see the body?"

"You'd better hurry," Sarki said. The ambulance was already announcing its arrival with the blaring of sirens.

Nadia watched Emerson leave.

She wanted to avert her eyes when she noticed her father fondling his robes. She knew she should look away, but she had always been curious. He brought out a pistol and turned on the safety, then put it back in his robes.

Emerson got to the body in time. "I'm a doctor," he told the men there and flashed his ID. It was fake, but it always worked. He had paid well, and it had served him well.

He examined the body for puncture wounds with his knowledge of anatomy and observed that there were none. The good doctor had died peacefully. He was about to leave when the man's hands caught his attention.

The doctor's palms were black as if blood had coagulated in them. He checked the feet and observed the same thing. He thanked the medical team and watched them carry the body away. He had seen this kind of poison before. But why pin the murder on him?

***

When the president was sworn into office and his officials with him, Sarki had taken his time to study those surrounding him. If the tower could not be brought down by force, the other option was to remove the blocks one at a time.

He had scouted for weeks until he decided to create some luck. In a hit-and-run, Harlequin had lost his secretary.

The position had been filled by a very grateful and promising Muslim girl from a devout family, whose parents were both in debt. All she had to do was make sure she did her work well enough not to be replaced. And Navina had not disappointed.

In no time, her family had been lifted from the middle class to the rich and bossy crème of society, and all she had done was anonymously share an occasional draft, memo, and agenda. It was only recently that she traced it all to the Sultan. But it was too late to back out. She wondered where it had gone wrong, unwillingly selling her integrity for her family's sake or falling in love with the enemy?

Sarki watched Emerson drive away after the ambulance. He decided it was time to listen to the recording Navina had sent. The girl had been resourceful. And Harlequin was in love with her. How foolish even the wisest of men could be when they fell in love.

He listened to the recording in his room, satisfied with what he heard. The coordinates and locations she had sent proved that it was a bluff. Those were just hideouts. He would not take any chances, though; he would make plans to move the terrorists, and when that was settled, he would address the public, telling them that their president was nothing but an optimistic liar.

Just then, he heard something that set his heart ablaze.

"Butan Shayi!" He exclaimed.

He rewound it, increased the volume, and listened intently. His eyes seemed to have been covered with a velvet cloth. The anger he felt was more than the adrenaline his body could produce. He swung his hand and smashed the lamp at the head of his bed.

How could he have been so stupid? Elzaiya, one of the Quinns' sons? How many more secrets would that family hide? The boy had kidnapped his daughter, and he had allowed him into his home. He had let him eat his food and drink his wine. He had even bought him a new phone and bought his friend a damned car. He had literally paid them for kidnapping his daughter. God knows he might even be sleeping with her. What sort of witchcraft had they used to blind him to all of these? Even Emerson, as wise as he was, had been played. For the first time in his life, he felt like a complete fool, and that feeling was intolerable.

He was about to make a call when his eyes brightened. A son!

You didn't need to stand close to see. He had been fooled once, but he wouldn't be fooled again. Emerson had a son, and he had said in his own words that Elzaiya was like a son to him.

According to Doctor Sani's findings, he was in the age range. That boy was dead. Emerson's or Quinn's, it didn't matter. He would rain hell on all his enemies.

When he came out of his room, he went to knock on Nadia's door, but Maryam told him that she had just left.

***

Before Denise got to the house, she concluded, although it wasn't logically correct, because she wasn't thinking from a straight place, that if Elzaiya was Emerson's son, ergo her brother, she didn't have to be told that he was going to be heir to all her father's wealth, but that was not just it. She was more concerned about the fact that they had already bonded together as friends.

She had learned what she wanted, going through the pictures on her father's phone. How much more damage would be done when

Emerson learnt that he was his son? With the way he had sent her to fetch him some proof, she knew he would toss her aside and focus on him. Everybody chose him; they all preferred him, but she, she would not share her father's love.

***

Machiavelli and Cairo were in the room on the third floor of the Quinns' family house. The room where the boys had grown up. Cairo seemed to be more interested in their origin today. They had resorted to scrolling through all his pictures while he told her the story behind what was what.

She sat up to see who had come in through the gate; it was Denise. She noticed that she didn't drive in. She walked in and took the left to Elzaiya's place.

She shook her head. Denise was a different kind of nutjob. Thank God Machiavelli was smart. She looked at him and smiled, and then a picture caught her attention.

"Scroll back to the right, to the picture before this one."

Machiavelli scrolled to the right, and she took the phone. It was a picture of the boys and Emerson. Elzaiya had taken the picture when they went to get Machiavelli's car.

"I know this man," she said.

"He's famous. He…"

"He's the doctor who came to our house to find out if I was the Sultan's daughter."

"Emerson?"

"He's the killer. He's tied to what you guys are into, isn't he?" She jumped and stood on the bed.

Machiavelli was still trying to feign surprise. "Are you sure? He…"

"Oh boohoo! Don't pull that stunt on me. You know he's dangerous. What ties do you have with him?"

"He's Denise's father… we just met him…"

Cairo knew that Emerson was Denise's father, but she was not one to be interested in a family tree that she was trying to escape, so she had never bothered tying a face to the name.

She jumped off the bed and ran to the door. Machiavelli pursued her down the stairs.

"Where are you running to?"

"Elzaiya! I'd rather ask him about it. At least he can lie to my face without me finding out."

***

People were drowning, but that wasn't his concern. He couldn't save everyone; it was their screams that just wouldn't go away. He couldn't save everyone. The water was red and thick with blood, and more were dying.

"You can't save them all," he kept saying.

And then there was Nadia. "Please... please don't," she looked at him, speechless. He could see the disappointment in her eyes. He had failed her.

He ran, but it appeared that the ground moved instead. He couldn't reach her, so he jumped in again to save her. He couldn't care who else died, as long as he could save her. His shadow watched him try, and just when he got to the edge of the river, he slit her throat.

He screamed in anguish and finally came awake with a deep breath, the sunlight hitting his eyes. Instantly, he noticed that he was not alone. Whoever the other person was, their energy wasn't positive. He felt the immediate need to protect himself.

Denise was staring at him from the foot of the bed. She had her hands behind her back, and whatever she was holding wasn't going to work in his favour.

The afternoon was strangely cool. That alone was a bad omen. It was the spirit of death.

"What are you doing here?" He asked, trying to move.

"Where is your newfound love?" She wore a black gown that seemed to go with the mood.

He felt dizzy. He tried to stand, but instead fell from the bed.

"Damn you!" He cursed.

If only he had not fallen asleep. He should have known better than to fall asleep in the afternoons.

"You are heavily drugged," she said. "Soon, you will be unable to move at all, and you'll be at my mercy. Did Nadia tell you that I told her everything?"

"You have a sad soul crouching behind the exotic dresses you put on," he said. "I recommend some parental love. Oh! Sorry, must be the drugs. Papa doesn't love you any more than Mama did before she left.

Her hands emerged from her back, and she raised them for him to see. The knife reflected the sun's rays, and she turned it so it gleamed in his face.

"A pound of flesh?" He mocked.

He couldn't fight, not under the influence of the drug. But he could muster all his energy for one move, and that was what mattered. The human body was a kinetic chain. If he made the wrong move, he would be screwed. What would it be?

"You know what I'm going for," she said. "But before I do, I came to steal something of yours. Emerson seems to think that by some magical means of conception, you are his son. Yes, I know that all things are possible, but I don't want to leave it to chance."

"He must be deluded too," he said.

He was trying to move his legs, but they were stiff, although the muscles in his hands could flex.

"We know he would find the proof himself."

Elzaiya laughed. "You are the perfect child for a man like him. Just as unstable as he is. Do you know he was in love with my mother, and it wrecked the hell out of him? It seems to run in the family. Look at the mess you've become. Looking for an excuse to blame it on me."

"I don't have time for this," she said as she walked to where he lay and looked down at him.

His heart was pounding. He knew that look; she was going to kill him. He had threatened her, and now she had the upper hand. She would not leave him alive to see his words through.

"For a human," she said, "you are somewhat unreal."

"I…"

She raised the knife with both hands and brought it down. This was it. He moved up so the knife tore through his skin, inches above his upper ribs, directly under his heart. It didn't go deep and missed any vitals. Then, with all the strength he could gather, he maintained that position and screamed. Pain pumped in adrenaline, and that was what you needed to undo a paralytic. She tried to pull it out, but he wouldn't fall back.

She thought about pressing on him with all her weight, but he was a sly one. If he got his hands on the knife, she was dead. The sight of his blood dripping also made her giddy. She kept staring at him.

He remembered Nadia telling him to pray. Maybe this was the right time for the manifestation of faith. So, he did what anyone who was being killed would do. He prayed and screamed.

Denise knew that the screams wouldn't be heard at the main residence, but she wasn't willing to take the risk. She would leave him here to die. She had not left her prints anywhere. The Quinns had enemies, so no one would suspect her. At least she hoped so. Her mind was not working properly anymore. She left the room, looking back one last time to make sure he was giving up.

***

Machiavelli was still running after Cairo when he heard the car drive away. Cairo had taken the long route to the apartment, hoping that he would not catch up with her. He increased his pace and took the other route that Denise had just left so that he would cut her off before she got to the door. But it wasn't just that; it was as if he had heard his name. It was almost as if someone had screamed his name, and the wind was carrying it. He must be imagining things.

Cairo got to the house first. She found the door locked and waited outside after knocking. There was no response. Some minutes later, Machiavelli caught up to her. He smiled and turned the handle, but it was locked from the outside.

If Elzaiya wasn't around, he would have let him know. He always told him about his plans. He reached for his keys, opened the door and found Elzaiya on the floor, soaked in blood with a knife by his side. He closed his eyes when he saw Machiavelli rushing to his side.

***

Emerson met his daughter at the beach. He was always right on time. He was still pondering about Dr Sani's death, and it took a while for him to realise that she was not quite herself.

"What's wrong?" He asked.

It was after some coaxing and reassurance that he finally got her to speak. She told him that Elzaiya was out and that it was the only place she could get something they could use to get his DNA, because he would notice if she went to the other house where he stayed with Nadia.

Unlike what she expected, Emerson did not appear disappointed. He told her it was fine and that whatever was on her mind was not something she should take to heart. He then made her feel better by telling her that he had wanted to be sure because he didn't want to complicate things between his children in the long run.

After all, even if he was his son, the Quinns would do all they could to keep him from Elzaiya, so there was no point trying to get him back as a son when he wasn't even father material.

"You are my daughter, and I will always love you," he said, taking her hands.

She told him that she wanted to move away from the Quinns' residence for some time, and he said it was fine. He persuaded her to allow him to drive to get some snacks, to which she agreed. So, he drove her across town in her car to get some shawarma. After that, he drove back to the beach and told her to use his car to get what she needed and then meet him back here. She was exhilarated.

When she got to the house, she noticed that everything was as she had left it. She thought about going to check if her work had been successful, but the condition of the house proved that it had. No one had found Elzaiya out, because the environment appeared calm.

She would be gone, and then she would say he had threatened to kill her for telling Nadia the truth, so she had run away. She met Merceides in the room, worried sick. She had left her phone on silent and had forgotten it in her car. She didn't want to appear suspicious, so she told him she was going to meet her dad and she was in a hurry; she had just come back for her credit card. He said it was fine and escorted her to the gate.

He noticed a black Jeep parked at a corner of the street. Undoubtedly, it belonged to Sarki. He had trailed it before and could see through the intention of the tinted glass.

She entered her car and started the engine. He waved her goodbye, and she blew a kiss. He was still watching as she drove away.

She had driven past the black Jeep and was about to take the corner when the car exploded into smithereens and fiery bits of molten metal. All that remained was the frame of Emerson's car and the smoking sacrifice of what Denise used to be.

23

A VERY LONG DAY

3:00 p.m.

"It's done." Sarki ended the call and tried Nadia's line again. After two more tries, she picked up. The place was noisy.

"Nadia, ina ki ke?"

"Baba, ina cikin kasuwa. Zan buga wayan ka Anjuma."

He wanted to say something, but decided otherwise.

"Ba lefi."

He ended the call and dropped the phone in his pocket. He would plan for her safety. Today was going to be Bloody Friday.

3:17 p.m.

Aaira didn't know which would have been better. Living with the guilt or telling her husband, knowing the pain it would cause him. They had been here before.

"I'm sorry," she said again.

She was sobbing, and his back was turned to her. The first time, he had understood. But now he wondered if she was not only using it as an excuse to indulge. He said nothing while the anger in him burned.

"I love you," she said. Knowing what those words meant to them.

"You damn well love him too, don't you?"

She kept silent. Unwilling to make it worse.

He turned. "Christ, Ira!"

"I chose you. I chose you over him," she said.

"And that is what? My consolation? You cannot erase these things with words. I chose you, too; I always have. Have I given you a reason to doubt that? Why do you have to be the letdown?"

She said nothing and looked at the floor with tear-filled eyes.

"No more!"

He left the room before she could say anything else.

6:58 p.m.

When the car exploded, Merceides lost it. For a minute, the world was silent. A shrill, smoky silence followed by the sound of his heart pounding so loud he felt blood would pump out of his ears.

It was when the Jeep steered away that he collected himself and ran toward the burning car. But he did not believe in miracles.

Denise was gone, the same way she had come: suddenly.

He couldn't stop his legs from moving, nor could he control his breathing. He could feel his hands sweating, and all through, he felt numb.

He knelt close to the car, watching the flames go sky-high, trying to catch up to the smoke. He could see her ghost, a fiery lady going up with the flames. The sparks of fire that flew with the smoke tried to cling to her, to chain her down to him. But she would not be tethered. She would find peace where she was going.

When he couldn't hold it in any longer, the pain ruptured, and from deep within, it started to flow. Tears, in force with the fire, tried their best to quench the part of his soul that was burning away with her.

7:02 p.m.

Sarki was facing a glass of wine in the study when he received another call. He was not a man to betray his emotions, be it joy or sadness.

He told the messenger to close the door while he continued his visceral meditation. It had begun!

Aaira had fallen asleep in tears on the floor. The big bang was what woke her. She ran to the window and saw the smoke rising, close to the east gate.

When she ran downstairs to find out what had happened, the security guard told her that it wasn't safe. After persisting, he had told her that

Merceides was outside and that a security team had gone out to investigate the cause. He didn't want to break the news to her himself, but he couldn't risk letting her out either. It was protocol.

She waited for about twenty minutes, after which the team returned, escorting Merceides, who was broken down.

She ran to hug him before asking what happened.

"Denise." That was all he said.

They wept together, and that was when she seemed to have been released from a trance. She ran into the house to the study to meet her husband. She found him waiting for her beside the window. She rushed toward him, slapping and clawing, hysterical, blaming him for Denise's death. She knew he was ruthless, but what was this? She accused him of killing the daughter of his enemy out of spite.

Quinn said nothing and, with the gentleness that he had taken years to master, held his wife down. He could feel her pain, even his son's pain, but it had happened, and the future was all that mattered. The dead would bury their dead.

16 Hours Later

Merceides was grieving, with vengeance on his mind. The Sultan would pay, one way or another. Aaira was asleep in her husband's bed. Dr Kendrick had helped sedate her. Quinn said he didn't need her for what came next. Harlequin saw it on the news and saw a tear slip out of Navina's eyes. He understood; she had come to accept the family as her own. Pack mentality; something he admired about her. He felt sad, but the tears didn't come, not until he called home and was told that he was disconnected. He called Elzaiya. Whatever their differences, Elzaiya would still be rational in his decisions. But there was no reply. Not even from Machiavelli. What had he done? Could it be that all this could have been avoided if he had acted according to plan? He suddenly felt guilty and cold. Had he exposed his family to vulnerabilities? He had paid a seemingly cheap price for the power he had gotten. But was this the accrued cost?

Machiavelli had not left Elzaiya's side. Dr Kendrick had thought it best not to tell their parents about it until it was all under control. Fortunately, there was enough blood for a transfusion, and the knife had not damaged any vital organs.

The doctor had stitched the wound and had said the pain would make him very sore, but he would be fine. He had been unconscious through the process because of the drug in his system, which might have killed him if the doctor had not run a test first to make sure he had passed out from blood loss alone.

He started to regain consciousness by the time the stitch was ending and was fully awake minutes later.

Cairo had been distressed throughout the whole process and was only relieved when the doctor told her that he would live.

The explosion was not heard in the hospital. It had been a faint thud that had faded away. It was when Dr Kendrick received the call from Quinn to sedate Aaira that he learned what had happened. When he came back in, he called Machiavelli aside and whispered to him what he had been told.

Quinn had asked for Elzaiya, but he told Quinn that Elzaiya had just called about something they had to check out. Machiavelli nodded, and the doctor left them for the house.

"It's not good news, is it?" Elzaiya asked Cairo as the doctor closed the door.

"You should rest," she said.

"What was all that knocking on my door for? You could have shown some respect; a man was dying in there."

"That knocking gave you hope," she said.

She seemed shaken by the fact that someone like him could be vulnerable. How much more, her Avelli?

"Stop, you two." Machiavelli joined them.

"What did the doctor say?" Elzaiya asked.

"He thinks you should rest before someone tries to kill you again."

"That's helpful. But seriously, what did he say?"

Machiavelli sat down and looked at Cairo.

"I don't think she's going anywhere," Elzaiya said.

"You see why I like him?" Cairo said. "He gets me."

"He gets everybody, and that getting could get him killed soon," Machiavelli said. He looked at his friend. "Before that, I'd better tell you why we were at your door," he preferred to stall.

"Cairo wanted to know what we have with Emerson. He's the one who killed the Sultan's other children."

"What?" Elziya tried to sit up.

"Emerson was the doctor who killed the Sultan's children. I don't think he wants the Sultan to have any heirs."

Elzaiya paused in his sit-up. "And I don't think he wants to be the Sultan either. That makes the situation worse."

"Worse?" Cairo asked.

"If he doesn't want power, then he wants something else. And if in totality, you're only safe because he thinks you're dead. He won't stop until…" His eyes widened. "Someone, please get me my phone."

Machiavelli knew his mind. "I've tried her line; I've been trying it for about two hours now. It isn't going through."

Elzaiya tried to stand, but that would require some getting used to. He managed to sit at the edge of the bed. *The nightmare! Please don't let it happen.*

"What did the doctor tell you?" He asked again.

Machiavelli looked at Cairo. Elzaiya was beginning to lose his patience.

"Avelli, what did Dr Kendrick say?"

"Denise is dead."

7:13 p.m.

Emerson had waited; he couldn't wait any longer. Getting stood up by his daughter was way above his level. He decided to use her car to drive to the Quinns' residence to check up on her. He didn't know why he had switched cars with her in the first place. He couldn't even remember why he had switched the briefcases in the cars. If the one here held his documents, why had he gone back for the other? He was still thinking when he passed by a burnt car that was being towed away, followed by the police. The Quinns' street was sure busy today.

When he got to the gate, he blew the horn, and a security guard came out to meet him. It was a young lad who seemed to have no respect for, nor the aptitude to recognise, famous people.

"Who be you?" The chap asked.

"I am Denise's father," he replied. Trying his best to resist the impulse of tying the guy to the front of the car and smashing him repeatedly into the gate.

"Who be Denise?" The lad seemed to be new, naïve and intolerably stupid. Emerson found that it now strangely amused him. A contrast to the irritation he had felt seconds ago.

"The fair girl in a black gown that entered with a Mercedes-Benz 20…"

"Oh… Ehya!" The chap exclaimed. "You know am?"

"Yes, I'm her father." He had said 'father' twice in the same conversation. If this lad were his son, he would be too ashamed to want to send him to school in the first place.

"Walahi, I am sorry, but I cannot let you in. Kagani ko?"

"I don't want to go in. I just want to tell her to hurry up. She forgot her phone, and she took my car."

"Allah mai girma!" The chap exclaimed. He looked undecided.

"Mei ne a massalan ka?" Emerson exploded into Hausa.

The boy seemed to want to tell him something, but couldn't find the right way to put it. "Ka yi hankuri mallam, ina zuwa."

Mallam? This brat had no future. Emerson hurled curses at him in his mind while the guy ran in and, after a while, returned with someone who appeared to be his superior. By the look of it, this one was supposed to be sophisticated.

The runt employed as security made you question the intelligence behind the picking of brawn. He waited till they finally got to the car.

"Good evening, sir. I hear you're Denise's father?" The man squinted and looked at him.

That was the reaction Emerson was used to.

"You're that famous man, aren't you? Mr Emerson, the Sultan's brother?" This man just spoiled a good ovation. Just when he was starting to like him. How he hated being behind his brother. As if his fame were attached to his brother's title.

He grinned nonetheless. "Yes, I am."

"I'm so pleased to meet you, sir." The man said. Emerson nodded. He would have given this man some money, but unfortunately, he didn't walk around with cash for the same reason.

"I am sorry, sir, but Denise isn't available."

"But I thought she came to the house?" He wasn't surprised. The girl had lied about a lot of things today.

"Yes, she did. But I don't think you'll be seeing her again for a very long time."

"Is she in trouble?" He asked.

"No, she's not." The man seemed uneasy. If he had a sense of feeling, he could have felt it faster.

"Can I come back later?"

"No, sir, I don't think you'll ever see her again." The man said, wondering how Emerson was so dumb for a genius.

Emerson finally understood. "What happened?"

"Her car exploded. Just at the corner of the street. She didn't make it; she didn't even get the chance."

He appeared confused. He looked down at the street where the car had been and then at the gates of the estate. With a coarse voice, he managed to say, "Thank you. Tell the Quinns that I will be coming over tomorrow."

The man nodded and watched the car speed away. It must have been the sun, but he could swear he saw the man's beard turn blue.

11:02 a.m.

18 Hours Later

It was his voice that woke her up. Aaira washed her face and ran downstairs to see Emerson pointing and yelling vehemently at her husband. He was seething with rage, and she understood why. But she couldn't afford a war; these two must not fight.

Merceides stood beside his father, more like an advocate than a soldier. He was dishevelled.

"I didn't kill your daughter," Quinn said point-blank. The man could go string himself up for all he cared.

"What have you got to lose by admitting it? You killed her because you were jealous and angry, and I get that. But your son was in love with her for God's sake," he said, almost with disbelief. "She was my only child."

Who's this one selling this crap to? Quinn thought to himself. He had better things to do than play with this madman. "You should go ask your brother. Most probably he's the one who…" He wanted to say 'smoked', but he needed his son on his side. "killed her. After all, I know what you do in the dark, Omar. All your evil ploys and desires. I know them all."

Emerson jumped at Quinn, but Aaira stepped in.

"He didn't kill her, Emerson, please listen to me," Aaira said. "He did not kill Denise."

Emerson pointed at Merceides while he looked at Aaira. "An eye for an eye, love," he said. "I shall have the blood of a child by sundown if I don't have my justice. And I won't care which child it is, or whose."

He adjusted his suit and left the house in sparkling blue.

11:43 a.m.

Emerson had not returned to the palace since yesterday. When he drove in, Sarki was ready for all hell to break loose. He went to meet Emerson outside, but before he could speak, Emerson turned on him, partly out of grief but mostly out of anger.

"Don't condescend to me, you low-life scumbag. I know of the wickedness of your heart. You quote all manner of good to those who are misguided enough to believe you good, but I know you. I can see through your miasma. I can taste your deceit. You accused me of killing your friend and our father and set me on the path to find the killer so I would be caught unawares while you plotted to have my child killed right before my eyes."

"I did not do that," Sarki defended himself.

"Then tell me who did!" Emerson yelled.

Sarki was silent.

"In that case, I will give you the same option you gave to me: find out who killed my daughter so I can have my justice. And you yours, for your friend; so you will be redeemed. I am bloodthirsty and on edge. I am pained beyond what I can comprehend. Because, unlike you, I haven't had a child to love all my life, and just now, just when I have admitted that she was my child, you stole her away from me. I will have my satisfaction in due time. If you're not the one who did it, then you have a day to redeem yourself, brother."

He walked past him into the house, and Sarki followed close behind, the pistol still in his pocket.

Emerson went up to his room and started to gather his things. Sarki waited outside the door. The man was in mourning; let him mourn his daughter first.

Some 20 minutes later, Emerson was done, and Sarki watched him leave. He would hunt him down later.

Nadia was still not answering her phone, and Elzaiya could now walk. He was off the drip, and even though his chest was beyond sore, he knew he had to do something. Everything was happening too fast.

Machiavelli had told him to wait, but he had insisted he would go find Nadia. So, Cairo and Machiavelli had said they would come along, but he had prevented them.

When Machiavelli asked if he had a plan, he told him to follow his trail to make sure no one was after him.

Dr Kendrick should have been back by now, but he returned late sometimes. He'd given Elzaiya some pain relief and left, as he did every Saturday night, for a doctor's programme hosted by his wife. Elzaiya couldn't wait for him to get back. He sneaked out through the tunnels since the house was locked down.

The truth was that Elzaiya had received a text from Emerson telling him to come alone if he wanted to meet Nadia. Elzaiya knew it was better to play it safe than be stupid. He knew Emerson would not hurt him, and he was willing to be reckless when it came to Nadia.

His nightmare flashed before his eyes, blurring his path. He had just passed Quinn Street when a car pulled up around the corner. Something told him to run, but he knew he wouldn't go far.

He increased his pace, but his chest was killing him. He was trying to catch his breath, wondering if he should fight, when he felt a zap in his back. The shock brought him crashing to the ground. Whoever said electricity ran the human body had not experienced a taser firsthand.

"Bundle him into the car; I'll take it from there," he recognised the voice; it was Sarki.

Two men carried him to the back of the van and were about to close it when he heard a gunshot and then another. He saw Sarki raise his hands, and then a man approached, pointing a gun at him.

Sarki was too focused on the first man to notice the other shadow that snuck up and, with a deft move, covered his nose with a cloth. Seriously, what was up with this trend of abductions that he had started?

The gunman approached Elzaiya, and he was about to sit up when he was zapped with another dose of electricity that left him curled up at the back. He couldn't see beyond the black mask on the man's face. The mask came closer and tore his shirt open; that was when he passed out.

When he awoke, he was gagged and strapped to a chair. The place was dim, but he could make out some figures. When his eyes cleared, he saw a long bar in front of him, high enough to tie someone so that their feet or toes only touched the floor. There were moving bodies tied to it, and the sound of chains clanking. The gag in his mouth did not help his situation. Someone had taken their time to bandage him up again.

He was trying to get the bodies right when the lights brightened and the place lit up. They were in a chamber of sorts, a sacrificial or experimental chamber.

There were three people tied to the bar: Dr Kendrick, Sarki, and Nadia.

"Nadia."

The muffled sound came out wrong. He tried to stand, but his neck, both hands and feet were tightly strapped.

A door opened behind the hanging bodies, and Emerson walked in. For someone whose only daughter had died violently, he was in high spirits, and Elzaiya knew that didn't bode well for any of them.

24

NOW, THE ENDGAME

Machiavelli heard the gunshots, but he was too late. All he found was Elzaiya's phone on the ground. He told the Quinns what had happened, and Quinn didn't take it lightly. Arden couldn't believe that of all his sons, he was going to lose the most precious.

"There was 24-hour surveillance. The house was locked down, and there was to be no movement in or out. Why did you allow him to leave?"

"I fear Emerson had leverage, sir," Machiavelli said calmly.

"Leverage?"

"I think he has Nadia."

There was silence. Machiavelli did not tell them about the gunshot. He didn't want anyone biting his head off. Elzaiya had taught him that when you did the telling, you only shared half of what you knew.

"What about Kendrick?" Aaira asked. "Is he back?"

"He isn't answering his calls either."

Quinn steered the topic back to things he could control. It had taken him years to learn how not to lose his nerve.

"I haven't seen you boys in a while. What new developments came up?"

His people were in harm's way, and Quinn wanted to know all about his enemy's doings. Machiavelli still had a lot to learn. He looked blankly at Merceides, who stared back at him wide-eyed and shrugged.

"Denise tried to kill Elzaiya," Machiavelli said.

"What?" Merceides and Aaira burst out. "She would never do something like that." Merceides went on. "She…"

"Shhh…" Quinn hushed his son. He wasn't surprised. Machiavelli wondered if the doctor had told him.

"What? How? Why?" Merceides ranted.

Machiavelli understood that he needed closure.

"She stabbed him with a knife," Machiavelli continued. "Missing his heart by a few inches. Dr Kendrick thought it best not to bring it up since it wasn't the right moment. Not when you were saddled with other issues. As to the why…" He looked at Quinn and decided to keep what he knew to himself. It was a smart move. One that he could see

Quinn respected. "I don't know why, and he didn't say. We know they had their disagreements."

Quinn nodded; he understood. Aaira seemed not to. She wanted to ask something, but Quinn countered her with a question. "Did you tell him?"

The answer could go both ways. There was Elzaiya, and there was Emerson. She shook her head in the negative.

"Tell who what?" Merceides asked.

"It's something we found out about Emerson. It's not going to help matters." Quinn lied.

"Could it have something to do with my fiancée's death?"

"Denise sealed her fate the moment she entangled herself with that accursed man," Quinn said coldly. He was frustrated at his wife's actions, and now his son angling on like a sissy. For god's sake, the only reasonable person he had left was Machiavelli.

Merceides didn't take the statement lightly. He turned on his father with shimmering eyes, but Quinn was full square waiting for him.

Machiavelli stood between them. "The police are searching for them. I've told my sources to exhaust all resources in finding them."

"If you don't mind," Machiavelli turned to Merceides. "I would be on my way to see what I can do," he said, leaving them in the study.

He would have preferred to go search for his friend, but Elzaiya had asked him to do something else. He was to call a certain line if anything were to happen to him. He called the line and waited.

***

Synai and Vivian had just returned to Nigeria, where it all began. This place brought with it disconcerting memories. His welcome had been a heavy downpour to remind him that it was the season when the earth was moulded into sandcastles and everyone sat outside, catching fireflies and bullfrogs. But that was in the 2000s, when children knew how to play. When they understood the value of family and communal living. Now they have Xbox.

There were five contestants left in the game, and the rules dictated that they all be in the country. When they got down to three, they were to be in the same state.

He had not been to Taraba before, but that was where his flight was headed. The state looked beautiful from above. But looks in Nigeria could be four-one-nineny.

They landed and lodged at Savannah Getaway. Elzaiya had told him that once he was in the country, they were to cease direct contact. He had contacted the chef, the friend of a baker, who had contacted his baker friend, who had then contacted Machiavelli to tell him that the noodles were ready.

It was night when Machiavelli got to the suite. Elzaiya had taught him, no matter what, to always put the plan before the person. That was what he was going to do now. And for some strange reason, he was cool-headed about it. It did not seem to bother him that his friend was missing. It was Nadia he was worried about. Elzaiya was too much of an asset for anyone to kill, except if Sarki had him.

Machiavelli had not met Synai before. His expression was caught unawares when he opened the door and met a big man in his mid-forties hanging his suit in the wardrobe. He closed the door and waited. He had learnt by experience to let the other person speak first. The man gave a heartfelt smile and stretched out his hand. Machiavelli took it and smiled back.

"I presume you don't open up easily, Avelli?" The man sure seemed to know him well enough to call him that.

"It's been a rough three days," he said gruffly.

Synai went into the other room and returned with a book. Machiavelli recognised it as Elzaiya's journal. He gave it to Machiavelli, who opened it to make sure.

"He hides this in his place. Only he and I have the keys."

"He has three keys, one of which he gave to me. You were too busy to watch the house. It was broken into while you were attending to other stuff. They didn't take anything, so it seems they were not out to steal."

"They meant to kill him."

"I know. They were Sarki's men. Luckily, he was at home with you."

"Where he was stabbed and later snatched."

Synai was taken aback, and so Machiavelli filled him in on the details, concluding with the fact that it had to be Emerson who had done the abducting.

"When he came to me, he was anticipating something out of his control." Synai said, "That was when he gave me the key. As you know, this journal contains all his speculations and deductions. I can only say that we should continue right from where he stopped, instead of waiting for the police to do something we know they can't."

Machiavelli opened the book, and they started perusing through a maze of locations, dates, names, codes, and passwords.

They discovered that there had been two sets of coordinates to the terrorist's hideout. One of them, the one stolen by Harlequin, which had been lying around in Elzaiya's cabinet, was a camp that contained hostages. The other in the journal was the location of the real camp base. If Harlequin were to order a military strike based on the coordinates he had, hostages would die.

In the journal, there was a section of secrets that he kept from everyone. This included his knowledge of Navina working for the Sultan. Which was why only one location had to be made available to Harlequin when he stole the files. The Sultan had to be deceived. He hadn't told anyone about Navina because he believed it was a circumstantial decision, and she had come to love his brother. He would not allow his knowledge to ruin his brothers' happiness. They both deserved to be happy.

He had also found that Sarki had called an asylum on several occasions. He had been curious as to what Sarki had to do with an asylum. So he had gone to the asylum under the guise of the Sultan's agent and had learnt that the Sultan had requested that a special place be set aside for his brother. He had donated a fund to that effect for as long as his brother was alive. Out of curiosity, he had asked to see the files to prevent errors in the paperwork and to make sure the institution was equipped for someone as reputed as Emerson. He had gone through the files and learnt about Emerson's mental state. So, he had gone back to the drawing board to put things together. He had traced calls and intercepted messages. Learning that Emerson was the one who had blown up his oil wells. It could easily have been blamed on the Sultan, who had every reason to, as Emerson did. But it was the message's content that gave it away, and it was a very simple mistake. In all the Sultan's messages, he never adhered to punctuation. But that single message had a full stop. He knew Emerson was looking to pick a fight. He was setting the scene for war.

He had tried to discover what made Emerson the way he was. But he couldn't get any information. He had ended that trace with a question mark. He also had the date when Emerson had met with his mother. They had lasted almost three hours in the church, after which they had gone their separate ways—Aaira first and Emerson later. He had told his father, but Quinn had told him to drop the lead. The journal told them that he was troubled because he couldn't conclude who had murdered the woman and who had tried to kill him and Merceides with the explosion. Despite overwhelming evidence, it was not the Sultan, and it was certainly not Emerson. It looked as if it had been arranged by one person or staged by two. Whoever planted the bomb was the same person who had drugged him. They knew he would figure out that a warm handle meant danger. They needed him out of the way without harming him; the others, they believed, they could take care of.

There was another concern that he overlooked. He remembered flashes of the night before he had fallen ill. When those men held him, he heard something insignificant, but it mattered. It was the sound of clicking heels. But he couldn't remember where he had heard them before. They could almost paint a picture, but he still had no face to it. His enemy wasn't Harlequin, Sarki, or Emerson. The answer was in the heels. But that was a hunch; he let it go.

They spent another hour sifting through. When it was 10 p.m., Synai told Machiavelli that he had better leave and take the journal with him. Machiavelli said it was best for Synai to keep it. There was too much information in it, which, in the wrong hands, could affect the Quinns.

Synai agreed, and Machiavelli left. He took the road that led into town. Elzaiya's phone recorder had been turned on when he picked up the phone, and he had murmured something before he was carried away.

***

The light hurt his eyes. He wondered how long he had been out.

Emerson walked to where the others were tied up and stood beside the bar. He was like a judge, and they were on trial. Were they?

"You all are here to stand trial," Emerson said.

So, they were on trial. He wondered what sort of twisted thinking puzzled its way through Emerson's mind. His voice was low and calm. The control he possessed seemed to be that of one who had done this before. A monster was hiding inside the man, one which he now wanted to feed. He couldn't seem to help it. Elzaiya understood.

The voices in his head drove him mad sometimes. Half his life he had spent silencing them. As the Joker said. All it took was just a bad day to snap. How loud were the man's devils? He wondered. Who was the loudest?

In his thinking, he had not paid attention to all that Emerson had said, but this part he heard. "At the end, you all will be liberated."

He did not find comfort in those words. He knew that Emerson was a rational man. But not when his other personality suffered a stifling messiah complex.

He was removing the gag from Dr Kendrick's mouth. The doctor looked tired. He was in his late fifties and had been with the family before the children were born.

"Dr Kendrick, you are on trial because you aided the Quinn family in keeping an essential truth, not just from me but from others to whom it was essential."

Dr Kendrick looked at Elzaiya. For a while, he was silent before asking what truth that was.

"You did not tell Elzaiya here who one of his fathers is."

Nadia stared at Elzaiya. Even he wasn't sure he had heard it right. It was understandable if Emerson thought he was his son. But he had used *fathers*. Emerson was too big for errors.

"His mother did not think he was ready for it."

"Of course, Aaira," Emerson said fondly. He brought out his phone and scrolled through some pictures.

Elzaiya knew from the doctor's reaction that it was a threat to the man's family. "So, will you tell us the whole story?"

Elzaiya nodded to the doctor, who sighed and began. He talked about Aaira not being able to conceive anymore after the twins. About how she had suggested an experiment without telling her husband. She had brought a sperm sample, and he had not known it belonged to Emerson.

He had grown the foetus in the lab, and then he transferred it to a lady Aaira had brought. For some strange reason, Aaira had insisted that he mix not one but two different sperm samples.

"After the first insemination, the lady appeared to be carrying triplets, and Aaira was overjoyed, until the lady had a miscarriage. They thought they had lost the babies, but one survived. It turned out, it had absorbed the DNA of the others to survive. The lady later gave birth, and that was when Quinn learned about the child's origin. He was furious, but he accepted the child and was the one who named him Elzaiya. The lady took care of the child for a year. But when Aaira noticed that she was becoming too attached, she termed her unstable and sent her away, allowing her visits for two more years only.

The child, as we observed, did not mind. He didn't even cry most of the time. We all felt that something was wrong. As he grew, we learned that his mental aptitude was extremely sharp. While we were happy, Quinn saw it as a red flag and started to do what he could to make sure the child did not end up like him or Emerson. The child also did not have the family blood type. His genetics were mostly linked to Emerson's. As it turned out, the part of him that was Quinn was family loyalty; no one taught him that," he wanted to say more, but Emerson gagged him.

"Thank you, doctor," he clapped and bowed.

"You people deem me unstable, but you should see Aaira at her worst. She is like a bird of paradise on the loose. But that's not something I should share with you lot. It wouldn't stop you from judging me."

He remembered something and ungagged the doctor. "Doctor, if you don't mind me asking. Do you know anything about the poison called Kandle? After all, you invented it and are the only one who has it. My brother seems to think I used it to kill his doctor friend."

Dr Kendrick squinted. "I haven't shared the prescription with anyone. But the bottle was stolen from my collection recently."

"How many drops does it take to cure an infected wound?"

"Two drops."

"And how many kill a victim without any visible signs?" Dr Kendrick was silent for a while before he reluctantly replied. "Three."

"How many people know the exact dosage and where it's kept?"

"My assistant and I, and…" the doctor spoke as if from an epiphany.

"Thank you, doctor. I take it you know who killed Dr Sani?"

Dr Kendrick kept silent. Emerson smiled and gagged him up again.

He walked over to Sarki and whispered something in the man's ear. Sarki kept staring at Elzaiya like a bloodhound. Elzaiya was grateful the man was in chains.

"Dr Kendrick, you are an honest man whose only fault is truth and loyalty. You are therefore liberated."

Emerson injected something into the man's neck, and in a minute, Dr Kendrick was out and stopped breathing. Emerson untied the body and wheeled him out in a wheelchair.

He came back and injected the Sultan. And while he drowsed to sleep, he ungagged Nadia, leaving them alone, taking the Sultan with him.

"You are full of complications," Nadia said. Her voice was calm for a girl who had just been abducted a second time. Somehow, she found a way to smile through everything.

He wanted to talk, but it was useless with the gag in his mouth. So, he listened.

"If I don't get out of this, know that I will always love you," she began.

***

The game was down to three, and Harlequin was feeling jittery. He had made the wrong move, and it told on him. For the first time in his life, he felt alone.

Two days from now, Synai will have to travel down to Lagos. The three contestants had to be in the same vicinity. They would meet in a place where they would engage in the final test, whatever it would be. He looked at Vivian, who was asleep, and wished his world were as simple as hers. But that was wishful thinking. Everyone had their cross to bear.

***

Merceides was sitting with Machiavelli under the almond tree in the garden, and Cairo was in the house. Machiavelli had told her not to come out, except if the room ran out of air.

"The prophecy was right," Merceides suddenly said, cutting into the silence.

Machiavelli had refused to tell him why Denise attacked his brother. "What?"

"The prophecy was right," he repeated. "The whole of it. Elzaiya had dismissed it as alcohol-ridden talk, and Harlequin didn't even listen to it. I, for my part, was mistaken about the interpretation. We all got it wrong,"

Machiavelli was willing to listen to anything at this point. Hell, he had lots of time to spare. "Please explain," he said with witty carelessness.

Merceides started to recount the prophecy in the bits it had come in. "I told her I had come to ask about my future, and she asked what was wrong with my brother. I told her I didn't understand, and then she said, "*You* have no future without him. She said, 'his shadows are your saviours, and yet, he is everyone's darkness. He is the greatest of you all. Yet, surely, unfailingly, he will fall by the hand of God.

"I still don't get how…"

"Don't you see?" Machiavelli was used to Merceides getting excited over meaningless things.

"See what?" Merceides realised that he was not the only one who had been oblivious to it all along.

He explained to Machiavelli how it made sense to him. They had found Elzaiya on the ground, dying from a wound caused by Denise. He had not died in the sense of 'fall' that they thought the prophecy meant. He had literally fallen to the ground, just like Denise's initials were on every custom thing she wore and signed. Denise Emerson Omar: *Deo!*

Machiavelli got it at once.

They were so excited with this insight that they proceeded to interpret the other parts of the prophecy. He was the greatest of them all, in that he was the one who held the ladder they had all used to climb. In a way, they owed him for what they had become, even though they seemed to be more accomplished than he. The truth remained that kingmakers were great. And how true was the last part of the prophecy? Now that he wasn't here, their world seemed unable to move.

The hardest part for Merceides to grasp was who Elzaiya's shadows were. But Machiavelli already knew that. Synai was where he was supposed to be, and only Elzaiya and he knew the plans they had together, which correlated with having a shadow. Being one with something without being it. Just like Emerson was another of Elzaiya's shadows. He had been a saviour when Harlequin needed someone to give him what he wanted.

But were there just two?

Machiavelli's eyes brightened. Elzaiya didn't write random words. His journal had a single page with the phrase 'in the beginning,' after which it skipped to the next page.

What had happened in the beginning? And which of the beginnings?

The license plate number he had run in town had belonged to Sarki, but the police had still found nothing.

Who was... Emerson! Emerson was everyone's darkness. The prophecy wasn't organised. There was the problem of separating the individual from plurality, among other issues, but it was accurate. So the question was, who could be linked to Emerson and still be their saviour? Who was light and who was darkness?

It wasn't Denise, for sure. It wasn't Merceides, not Quinn, not Cairo, not him, not Dr Kendrick... It was the question Elzaiya was trying to figure out. The answer was in the heels.

"Sometimes I wonder how you appear as if you're not a genius," Machiavelli tapped Merceides, who laughed. They had never really bonded, not until now.

25

EMERSON'S CHECKMATE

It had been 48 hours of silence. The police, as always, were not reliable. Harlequin called again; this time, his father picked up. Quinn, unable to mask the disappointment he felt toward his eldest son, could not bring himself to speak. Aaira was the one who told him that other important issues had come up. She told him she would explain better when they met, and that she would be in Lagos soon.

Quinn had wanted her to stay, but Aaira wasn't one to be told what to do. Dressed in a flamboyant red gown that floated with the wind, and a scarf that pointed North. She left for Lagos, saying she needed to get away from everything. She kissed her husband goodbye and told him that she hoped he could bring himself to forgive her. He hugged her and bade her farewell.

Machiavelli passed by her as she walked down the dining hall to the car. He greeted her and wished her a safe journey, all in passing, from the other side of the hall. He was about to head upstairs when he was entranced by the clicking of her heels. He did not turn to look, but closed his eyes and listened to the sound die away.

There was something about those heels. Aaira's shoes were custom-made.

He brought out his phone to look up the company. It was hers alright. But her shoes, unlike the rest, were produced by a biotech engineer. Underneath, they were steel-plated with some kind of technology he didn't have the time to understand. Her shoes essentially had retractable heels and a technology that balanced the person to the shoe, which eliminated the problem of breaking heels or twisting ankles. You could run a marathon in those heels without breaking a leg. How anticlimactic.

However, this technology was peculiar, in that, it made a different sound on every surface she stepped on. Never making the same sound twice, even on the same surface. She was the one!

Machiavelli scratched his face. He couldn't believe it. She had been the one. She knew their plans. She knew they had a great chance at winning. Harlequin would have been put out of the way, too, if not for Emerson. Elzaiya's shadow had been Harlequin's saviour. He wondered what to do with this new knowledge.

***

Synai was already in Lagos. The city was amazing. He had wanted to bring Vivian along, but she had insisted on waiting for him. She didn't want him to start bothering about her. Regardless, he was becoming distracted, and he could not afford that now. He had received a text telling him where to wait. His hands were sweaty, and his heart was pounding. The text had told him to wait… to sit and wait, and so he did.

***

Machiavelli found himself perplexed as to what move to make. If his guess was correct, Aaira's plan was a power move. She was aiming for the presidency. It was no wonder she'd never taken the meetings seriously after Harlequin had been installed. She'd pretended to be anti-political to deceive them. In that way, she exceeded her famed reputation. He wondered if Cairo was the same.

"Why are you looking at me like that?"

He shook his head and schlepped to the window. There was something he had been thinking about since Elzaiya's disappearance. It was stupid, crazy. But it was the only thing that could prevent the nation from degenerating into chaos. He had seen it happen numerous times. When there was no shepherd, the flock scattered.

"Have you thought about the possibility that you are the only heir left to the title of Sultan after Nadia?"

She shifted on the bed and dropped her phone. The matter disturbed her. "I have thought about it. Do you not think Nadia will be alright?"

"I don't know," he didn't look at her. "But I want to know what you have to say about it."

She took a deep breath and stood. She held him from behind as he looked down the estate through the carvings on the window.

"I am not inclined to power," she whispered in his ear.

His tone was cold as he replied. "You should think about it."

He faced her. She was beautiful. He hoped her soul was just as pure. He hated himself for doubting her, but he now understood what Elzaiya meant when he said to use life as it came. It never came the same way.

"You don't trust me to make the right decision?" She asked, letting go of him.

"A lot of things have happened."

"So, compartmentalise and deal with it. Don't generalise problems; it's not right."

"I'm..."

"But don't apologise when you do."

He smiled and kissed her on the head. "You're not the only one who learns things fast," she said.

"You will make a great leader," he pushed.

"It is almost unattainable," she said.

He shook his head. He'd seen too much to agree with the concept of impossibility.

When Sarki came awake, Emerson was staring him in the face.

"How the mighty have fallen," Emerson laughed.

Sarki stared at the ceiling. He knew where they were. This was the place he used to bring Emerson. The place Nadia had been kept when that bastard kidnapped her.

"This is where it all started. Do you still remember?" Emerson asked.

"As much as I wish to forget," Sarki spoke with the same authority he used to address his servants. Wasn't it Nietzsche who said it was best to die proudly when living proudly was impossible?

"Back then, when we used to come here to drink and smoke. We were truly free. We had no responsibilities, no power to lust after. We could have been anything we wanted to be. We were happy until you screwed me up."

"Omar," Sarki said coolly. "You were always more screwed up. I had no hand in twisting your mind."

Emerson laughed. "But you did."

He stood from the chair to look around the room. This chamber led to the torture room under the palace, opposite the library.

"You were the only one who knew how I loved dancing. I told you that I wanted to do ballet. I never mentioned it to anyone else, not even Aaira. And then, on that night, I was settling in, and you were lying in bed, pretending to be asleep. You turned to smile when I was taken from the room. Sarki, it's been years, but Kani, I remember. Father brought me to the torture chamber blindfolded, so I never found the way in until my last visit. From that night on, the only comfort I've had was in planning my vengeance. So I could pay you back measure for measure until I found my peace."

Sarki laughed the last sentence away. "I must confess, I told father everything. But that wasn't why he did what he did. You see, you never got the complete picture. I was proud of you, my genius brother, and so was Father. Until you started to dance, putting me to shame. People knew about your passion for dancing. I paid them to be silent because I couldn't bear the humiliation. I was teased about my handsome brother, who wanted to become a professional dancer. When I couldn't take it anymore, I told Quinn about it. He told me to tell Father what you were up to, that he might talk you out of it. He told me he would keep an eye on you and get me proof when Father asked for some. So, when you snuck out that night. He took some photos of you and added them to some photos of you drinking beer. I wasn't happy to sell you out; I didn't know the extent of what you would suffer. I gave Father proof, and he did what he did. So you see, I am not your sole enemy."

Emerson was silent for a while before speaking. "Aaira was the one who killed Dr Sani. Elzaiya had been digging into his past, and she didn't want him to get any information from the doctor. Do you see why she is the bone of my bones? Quinn never deserved her, but his time will come. Our father and his doctor, I killed them both out of spite. And today, I would liberate the world of our cursed bloodline."

Sarki laughed again. "I want to be free," he said. "If you let me be, I will be disgraced. I will face the chair or be hanged. It would be a mercy to die at your hands in secret. An honour in fact," he changed his tone. "I just wish I could have treated you better when I had the chance. You didn't deserve to be reborn in a swirling case of blood, shit and flies."

Emerson felt his skin crawl. He was repelled from the core of his being.

He walked to the end of the room, where it was dark and returned pushing a trolley. On it was Dr Kendrick's dead body. He smiled and pulled a knife from the foot of Sarki's table. He pulled it out of the sheath and slid his finger across the blade.

"It's custom-made," he said. "A knife fit for a king. I had the maker carve your initials on it," he bent and wiped Sarki's brow with his handkerchief.

"How thoughtful of you," Sarki jested.

Emerson whispered something that made Sarki start to swear.

He turned away and started to laugh. He laughed so hard that he nearly lost his balance while Sarki cursed. He was still laughing when he turned and, without warning, slid the knife across Sarki's throat. He kept on laughing as he watched him choke on his blood.

***

Machiavelli tried to recall the contents of the journal. 'In the beginning,' but it was a loop. Which beginning? He was sitting on the stairs when Merceides met him. If Merceides had gotten the prophecy aligned, who was to say he wouldn't be the one to help solve this mystery?

"They'll be fine." Merceides sat down as if to comfort him.

Machiavelli knew he was looking for a distraction from himself. To an extent, he was as insensitive as Elzaiya. The difference was that Elzaiya had terrible timing.

"You don't seem as shaken about Denise's death as you were earlier," he said.

Merceides frowned and stared at his feet.

"I'm sorry, I didn't mean to…"

"It's fine. I'm still grieving. I just want to get my brother back first."

"This would be a one-time thing; you calling him your brother."

Merceides laughed. "We used to be close. We fought a lot, but we were close. That was before you came. I guess he never told you about our pact?"

"No, he never did."

Merceides went on to tell him about the accident and how he had nearly killed Elzaiya, then his pledge to protect him. He never really kept his end of the bargain, as it was Elzaiya who had done much of the looking after.

"It's almost compulsive," Merceides explained. "It's his nature to put family first, just like Father."

"I wish we could go back to when this all began."

"Back to when the Sultan wasn't our enemy?" Machiavelli sighed.

"No, I mean, back to when times were simpler. When we didn't have to kidnap innocent people, manipulate information, spy, and watch out for our lives."

"It would eventually have come to this." Machiavelli paused. There it was! Of course, that was the beginning. The kidnapping! The idea had started with Elzaiya and Machiavelli stumbling onto the underground passageways.

Machiavelli recalled that one of those passageways ran directly beneath the Sultan's palace, implying that, just as the location where they hid Nadia was not on any map, so were many other locations. Merceides had done it again. This guy just passed off information without any idea of what he was doing.

"Do you want to go for a walk?" Machiavelli said, standing up.

"You might need to get a gun."

When Aaira got to the mall, she asked for directions and found where she was to wait. A man was already inside waiting. So this was her opponent. He looked somewhat impatient.

When she entered, he looked at her almost as if he knew her. He smiled and approached her, and they shook hands. She had seen him before, too. He had been among those who fought during the Second War.

They were getting to know themselves when Harlequin walked in.

Synai was relieved they'd never met before. The president did not look as confident as advertised. He understood why. Seeing his mother as an opponent must come as a shock. The family is betrayed by the son, and the son is betrayed by his mother. He realised now who the traitor was.

The way they shunned him proved that Elzaiya hadn't mentioned him to anyone else in the family. Just like Elzaiya, he didn't use his birth name. He had changed it sometime before the war, and his fame after had kept it that way.

They were to stay in the room for eight hours without food or drink. And so there they stayed. It was clear that they were anxious, and each of them suspicious of the other. Only two people would leave this room happy. And only one would have the honour of being president.

Machiavelli and Merceides entered the tunnels carrying five guns, two knives, and torchlights. Going in with a team would attract unwanted attention.

They found the closest passageway right behind the south gate of the Sultan's palace. The entrance was camouflaged, and a vehicle was parked there. Machiavelli raised the cover to be certain. He was right. It was the van, with the same license plates. He nodded to Merceides, and they went in, stepping gently. They would have told Quinn where they were headed, but no one had seen him since Aaira travelled.

***

It was almost 3 a.m. when their phones vibrated. They all checked. Each of them with the same gaze. That of hopeful uncertainty. Aaira had a green line on hers; she was good for the next round. Synai looked at Harlequin to be certain. It was when Harlequin hugged his mother that Synai checked his. There was a yellow line on his; it made no sense. It was absurd. The lines were either green or red.

He and Aaira left the room and walked out of the mall, each taking a separate route.

Harlequin felt lost; all his efforts had been for nothing.

Aaira smiled as she left. Everything had almost worked out fine until her son interfered. He should have stayed out of the way. But she knew Emerson would not hurt the boy. No one would willingly hurt him. Elzaiya would be safe with his father.

***

The board was silent as they ran through each participant's files. If any of these board members were to reveal themselves to their family or anyone, the sentence was death.

"Are you sure?" The board secretary asked Chairperson 31, the head of the board.

"The woman Aaira isn't ready to handle that kind of power." He was hidden behind the opaque blue screen, just like the rest of the board members. His say was final.

The silence lingered until the buzzer sounded to signify that he was out of the building. They came in at separate times and left at separate times. Everyone left today, knowing that justice had been served.

***

Nadia spent her time talking to Elzaiya. Emerson had not taken off his gag, and he knew it was intentional. The man was clearly angry that he had deceived him. What did he expect? Wasn't that what people like him do?

Nadia, beautiful even in this dungeon, gave him hope.

Now that he had stayed a while and observed his surroundings, he recalled that he knew this place. He had strayed here during their first adventure. Machiavelli had said it was a bad idea, but he had considered it a beautiful one. Who would see the speck when it was in their eye?

Emerson came in, interrupting the ambience that was Nadia's sweet voice.

"Ironic, isn't it? Ending it where it all began."

Elzaiya wanted to correct him that it had been underwater, but that would be hubris. He had thought about it too, 'In the beginning.' He had wanted to detail it, but thought otherwise. It wasn't wise to condense information. Fragments were better. The truth had to be in fragments. People couldn't handle too much.

He didn't know how he felt, now that he knew he was Emerson's son. Nadia had not made a fuss; she had not talked about it. She was truly the girl of his dreams. If only those were not nightmares.

Emerson did not find the silence interesting anymore. He was about to remove Elzaiya's gag when he changed his mind.

"That thing that Dr Kendrick said about Denise. You know she was your sister? It's funny how circumstances let that part handle itself. Your mother was bothered about your and Nadia's relationship. She didn't tell me why. I, in turn, didn't tell her the truth, that the Sultan isn't her father; how amazing is that?"

Elzaiya's face betrayed no expression, so he turned to Nadia and was pleased with hers. "It's like you two were destined to be together," he laughed. "Just like Aaira and I. Her father and Dr Sani knew. But, what hypocrites! They wanted her to remain the heiress and have a son who would fill in the blanks."

Nadia looked at him. She had thought about telling him what she was thinking. She felt she was with child. It was more than a conviction, but it was too early to say.

"Your mother and I are connected, just like you and Nadia. Her heart speaks to me. I know she doesn't want me to kill you, and why would I? You're my son, and I'm so proud of you. You are everything I dreamed you would be. Brilliant, wise in a maturing way; you will be wiser still. Unaffected by emotion, too. Unlike your mother and brothers, we share more things in common. You are my family, and you have something the Quinns can never give to you, which is why they need you. You have the potential to become whatever it is you wish to be. So today, I will make you my son in blood and destiny, and you will forever be grateful."

Elzaiya shook his head and kept on shaking it. Hitting it on the chair until Emerson undid his gag.

"You are a very respectable man," he began. He was surprised by how stable his voice was. "And we could have made great friends. I know I crossed you in a lot of ways, but I was doing it for my family, and I know that, as much as I was doing it to save them, I was mostly motivated more by the fact that I enjoyed it. I can indeed separate myself from my emotions, as you have well noticed, and I may be a product of you three, but I am nowhere like you." He chose to bluff here.

"I know what your father did to you, and I know you seek to liberate men from their weaknesses. I know you see yourself as a god. But people need to make mistakes. They need not be liberated because they would always strive in their own way to liberate themselves. How else would you find the world interesting if everyone were as perfect as you? People don't need help; that's the beauty of it. You may not have figured it out like this, but people need their suffering, their sorrow, their shame, and all that comes with pain. They need something to fight for. If not, there's nothing worth living for; nothing worth dying for, even. Don't take the other side of hope away from them."

Emerson got the drift. He knew this was a plea.

"You might be my father, and I might be like you. But Quinn taught me to find myself when you were not there for me, and I don't blame you; you didn't know I existed. But I don't want to be made, not in his image or yours. I want to find myself outside of you both. And I'm grateful that I have the genes of someone like you. In a way, I'm glad I'm your son, and I..."

"Tut tut tut!" Emerson sighed and pulled at his beard. Quinn has burdened you with too many unnecessary virtues for you to see things as they are. You have been taught to rein in your true self."

He put the gag back in his mouth and left the room.

There was no negotiating with this lunatic. Elzaiya thought.

Nadia was about to say something when Emerson returned with a bag of medical tools. He laid it on the floor and smiled, then selected a sharp steel needle. It was thick, long, and thin, about the size of a small nail, but with the mouth of a syringe and was about 26 inches long.

"Nadia, do you have any last words?" He pulled at the needle.

Elzaiya felt a chill in his heart and he keep on hitting his head but Emerson paid him no mind, and then it felt like his heart stopped beating altogether.

Nadia looked at him, and he saw that she was not afraid. She had accepted her fate. Somehow, she had felt it would always end this way. Worse than that, she had feared he would be the one to die in her arms. Allah ya kawo! One day, they would all die. If this were her fate, she would not cling to life in the face of the inevitable.

He wanted to move, but he was paralysed; he was breaking. That was what he felt like. Like his mind was glass cracking at different speeds under the force of heavy impact. He didn't understand why tears wouldn't come to his eyes.

"It is not your fault that you can't control everything yet," she said. "But someday, I know you'll become a very powerful man who will do great things. And till then, I want you to know that I will always be close to your heart. In all that you do, remember, you're strong, you're free, you're brave, and you are not alone. Always do good and never become what took me away from you. I will always love you."

Emerson smiled and, with admirable gentleness, placed his hand on her back. Then, with precision, he placed the needle under her breast, directly under her heart and slowly pushed. She started to scream.

Elzaiya found that he was gripping the arms of the chair, pulling them from underneath. The straps were cutting into his skin, and he could feel his tissues tear. His bones were about to shatter, and he felt like his neck would break. But he couldn't stop himself.

The more she screamed, the more he felt himself trying to break free to save her, and yet he felt he was not the one. He wasn't trying. His real self was paralysed. The blood dripped to the ground and formed a pool.

Emerson pulled out the needle and waited a bit, enjoying the silence. She had stopped screaming. He waited for a while before letting her down, then he brought her body to Elzaiya's feet, and then, slowly, unstrapped him.

Elzaiya knelt beside her; she was dead. He looked at her beautiful face. Her eyes were closed. She looked peaceful. He instinctively turned to Emerson and dove toward him.

Emerson was ready; he skidded out of reach. When Elzaiya attacked him again, he defended himself and swung a blow that caught him in the ribs. He didn't want to break the boy's body, but if that had to be done... He was unprepared for the blow that landed on the side of his neck. Elzaiya sprang swiftly to the table and reached for the needle Emerson had used on Nadia, turned and struck as hard as he could.

When the pin tore into his shoulder, Emerson fell to his knees, and Elzaiya started to hit him. Emerson tried to fight back, but the boy was ferocious. All he felt was rage. That was what he wanted him to feel. He heard a bone break as the boy landed blow after blow. Emerson knew it wasn't his bones that were breaking.

Elzaiya continued to hit him, using his arm as a club. Even as his bones broke, he didn't stop. Nothing would satisfy him; Emerson knew that. Not even his death. He had made him in his image, and he was proud. In one moment, he had stolen all that Arden had used a lifetime to build. Now he had a son in the truest sense of it. Now he was liberated; he was free.

***

When they found the place, they could smell chemicals and blood. Fresh blood like in an abattoir.

Machiavelli opened the door to find Sarki and Dr Kendrick's dead bodies on two separate tables. Merceides called him to the other room in a panic. They found Emerson tied to a chair, bleeding profusely; someone had taken their time beating him up before deciding he wasn't worth the kill.

There was no evidence of Elzaiya and Nadia. They were glad to have found something, but not all they hoped for.

They left, calling the police and an ambulance. Quinn tried searching further, but Elzaiya was nowhere to be found. They feared for the worst, but no one was bold enough to say it out loud.

26

ALL'S WELL. RIGHT?

Two weeks had passed, and Elzaiya had not been found. No one dared say anything. Emerson had been jailed until the asylum where Sarki had registered him came to claim him. He had raved and cursed, but the deed was done. Aaira returned home certain that she would win, and Harlequin knew it was time to get his office in order. He couldn't believe that his mother had been involved in everything the whole time. This February had been the most Aquarius of its kind. Aaira was aiming to seize the title of the first female president. She was damned well going to make it a real federation.

Dr Kendrick's death had hit Quinn badly. He mourned in his room and seldom came out. He didn't want to see anyone, including his wife. Machiavelli caught Cairo crying once. He didn't know who she missed the most, Elzaiya or her sister. He had hugged her in silence, steeling himself to the fact that Elzaiya might never return.

During those two weeks, Machiavelli had gone to the asylum. Sideline Creek, they called it. The gates reminded you of the castle in Disney's *'Beauty and the Beast.'* Going in made you wonder if people ever got out.

He had been allowed to see Emerson, who seemed to be doing well. He was even allowed to teach aspiring medical students, under watchful surveillance. Machiavelli had waited until he was done before he went in. Emerson seemed glad to meet him.

"My very good lad." He wore a victorious smile.

Machiavelli wished he had a gun. He proceeded to ask the question on his mind.

Emerson helped him out. "If you're asking about why I …"

"Elzaiya first," Machiavelli said.

Emerson betrayed his surprise. "What?"

"What did you do with him?"

"I didn't do anything with him; I freed him."

"So where did you keep him?" Emerson seemed the more surprised.

"Don't play dumb with me," Machiavelli threatened. "Where did you keep him?"

"I let him go." Emerson studied his reaction. "I figure, by the look of things, he never came back home?"

Machiavelli kept silent.

"You shouldn't be concerned," Emerson said with a smile. "He's finally a free spirit."

"Was he the one who did that to you?" Machiavelli looked at the stitches and bruises that covered several parts of Emerson's body.

"Yes, but you already know that, don't you? You've seen the violence in him and wondered where he got it from, as neither of his parents is as barbaric. You've seen how he's not afraid to draw blood, and it scares you. You should have seen the transformation. I could never have been prouder. When I killed Nadia in front of him, he ceased being human. He transcended. And when I unleashed him, the way he fought, he was like a demon. I could hear his bones breaking. First, it was his fingers, then his wrist. The impact of his force on my body was breaking and killing him. Osteogenesis, right? But he was too possessed to stop. For a while, I thought he would kill me. Now I'm glad that he didn't. It means he'll be back. That anger would stay with him forever, haunting him until he becomes me."

Machiavelli sighed.

"I guess you did not find Nadia's body either. He took her with him, raising her on broken shoulders. Do you know he tied me down with his teeth? He couldn't use one of his hands, so he pulled the rope with his teeth. He isn't an ordinary creature anymore. I've sharpened his instincts. You should be afraid if he does return. He would not be himself anymore. He can never be."

"There is something you've forgotten, doctor," Machiavelli said calmly.

"Yeah, and what's that?"

"He is human, and humans have something that most other animals don't. Now I don't know the thoughts that pigeons have, but if elephants mourn their dead, I think other animals feel the same. We, those animals in that class, share something in common: hope. He might be lost, maybe even to himself. But he would always find a way to heal and be better than he was. And even if he doesn't come home to us, he will not forsake us for you. He might be your son in more ways than one. But he's better than you could have made him. And now that you've exposed yourself to him. He knows who you are, and he'll do all he can never to be like you. In wanting to make him you, you've only pushed him to wanting to be himself: what his father had always wanted for him. It's got to hurt, knowing that you were the final lesson in Quinn's prep session."

Emerson liked how the chap reminded him of Elzaiya. "You've learnt a lot by observing him."

"He was always a better man than you all were. And yes, I learnt a lot. He was the one who made me. In that way, I too am better than the lot of you."

Emerson shrugged. "You should come see me sometime. I like the way you think."

Machiavelli smiled and shook his head. "I'll try coming around if I have the time." He was about to leave when Emerson called him back.

"I didn't intend to kill Denise. I regretted it ever since I've been here. I've had time to reflect on my actions, and that was among the things I wish I had done differently. The bomb wasn't for her; I didn't know when I switched briefcases. And you will agree that my brother had to die. Because if he were alive, he would try to kill my son."

He paused, then went on, "If you go to Denise's car, the one your police friends have seized as evidence, there's a briefcase in it that holds a copy of my will. I have willed all that I have to Elzaiya. And as much as this part makes me want to kill him, too, he is the only man alive entitled to the Sultan's throne. He has the potential to bring about unprecedented change in the Muslim world."

Machiavelli wanted to talk but held his tongue. "Under different circumstances, you would have been a better man." He nodded to the attendant who led him out, securing the door behind him.

He left Sideline Creek with the knowledge that Nadia was dead and he might never get to see Elzaiya again. It suddenly felt very cold, and it was not until he entered his car that he began to cry.

***

So, today, the people would know who their new president was. Harlequin had a week left in office. He had thought about carrying out Operation Bee Sting! That was what they called the force that was to wipe out the terrorist camp. But he had stalled, hoping to make it his first act in the second term. Now it was too late. He would leave for home as soon as the handover was complete.

He opened his drawer and looked at the case inside. He had bought it yesterday. When all of this was over, he would ask Navina to marry him.

***

Synai had returned to Taraba and had shown Vivian the yellow slip. She said maybe it meant that his matter was being deliberated on.

"But for what? There had never been a yellow slip in the history of the games."

"And military personnel have ever run for the presidency," she said. "It makes sense if you are under the microscope."

"I hope they find gems on me," he said.

She squinted for a moment and started laughing when she got it.

"It would be alright," she said.

He hoped so. Machiavelli had told him everything. Elzaiya was still missing, and he had not contacted him either, not that he expected it. Machiavelli had tried to track him down by payment history, but there had been no trail of transactions; nothing at all. He was a ghost.

Etim Ekpo Local Government

Akwa Ibom, Nigeria.

It was past 7:00 p.m., and Aretta was returning from her therapy session. She lived in the second flat, the smaller one that backed up to the duplex in front. She was trying to handle her issues as best she could. Today, her therapist told her to continue reassuring herself: she should smile and say that all would be well.

"All will be well," she said again and smiled.

It didn't make any difference, but it was just the 14th day. Just! She was tired. She had kissed her therapist today, and he had reciprocated. But it didn't make any difference. To who? It didn't matter that he had lusted after her since the first time he saw her and had used his knowledge of her diagnosis to manipulate her. She knew what he was doing. She just…

She alighted from the cab and saw that the lights in the duplex were on. Did she have new neighbours? She hated all the past tenants. They'd been naive fraudsters who spent their nights listening to music and their afternoons smoking or sleeping. They were like bats in this peaceful neighbourhood. And then she had hated the next family that moved in because their father was a drunk who would come back singing and pissing on the walls of her house and then pass out there sometimes with his trousers hanging down. Seriously, what was up with her and bad neighbours? She had hated the next, and the next, and the next, because their kid was fat and looked like Santa Claus, and then because the other one kept asking her if she had matches, and then the other one tried to sleep with her.

"I will pay upfront for a year," the new tenant was saying.

She stood in front of her house. She could hear them, though not clearly. The house was hollow, so it echoed. They were in the store room.

He coughed.

"Nna ndo," her landlord said with his thick Igbo accent.

"Thank you, sir," the new person said.

He had a slight accent, as if he had grown up in the Great North. Right! Now she was going to be neighbours with a herdsman.

"See my number here, for this line. My name na Mr. Felix ehn! If you need anything, just call me. I dey fix sink, and roof. I get shop where I dey sell zinc. My wife dey sell building materials too, anything ooo."

The guy laughed.

The sound of his laughter was distressing. He had come to inconvenience her, and he was laughing about it. She didn't want stress or noise; she just wanted serene silence. That was why she had chosen this place. The closest house to theirs was three roads and several bushes away. She couldn't calculate it in miles; maths wasn't her thing.

She had a cab man who came to pick her up according to schedule, and she had him on SOS in case she was stuck in the rain. He had been faithful so far; better than most relationships she'd had.

"I don't need anything now," the guy was saying.

"You fit fetch water from well, shey? The tap no dey always run. No be every day water dey come."

"I'll manage."

"So Nna, when you go carry your load enter?"

"I will buy what I need. I didn't come with anything."

"Oya na. I no know," the landlord said. "Buy my own join ehn. You fit come my shop too oh! I get sister wey dey sell clothe. You fit buy the whole boutique as you dey like this." They laughed about it.

The landlord left the house, and she greeted him. He replied cheerfully after looking her over. Really? He too still?

He rode away in his small Honda Accord. He must have received extra for him to be so caring.

She heard the door slam, and she was disappointed. With all her cursing, she had been eager to see who it was. The tap was on. She heard him walking around in the house; he was going to bathe. He went into the bathroom and closed the door. She knew she shouldn't, but she couldn't stop herself. She went to the back window, stood on her toes and peered through the window. The net would not allow him to see her, since it was dark outside. His back was turned to her. Lucky for him, the shower was working.

There was a scar on his back, a welt. She should go now, she told herself, but she wanted to see more of him, his face at least, not just his fine body. She caught herself.

He turned on the shower and raised his hand to rub some soap on his head. His hand was bruised; he could not even raise the other.

As the water poured, one of his wounds started to bleed. It seemed he had come from far; he was very dirty. But it wasn't just dirt. The water was too red, and it wasn't just one wound. He was bleeding from his left arm and his chest. But he didn't seem to mind.

He kept on washing himself and sobbed occasionally. Cursing something or someone. Sniffing sometimes to hold back his pain.

She felt sorry for him. She knew he was the type who wouldn't cry if he knew he wasn't alone.

When he was done, he pulled the towel from where he had hung it and cleaned himself up, then left the bathroom for the bedroom. The curtains were drawn, so she could not see anymore.

All this while, he had not turned fully, almost as if he knew she was there. She left and went into her room, kicked off her shoes, and turned on the TV so she would not miss today's news.

Aretta was not the only one who had turned her TV on. The whole country was watching, as was Elzaiya, from his phone.

Aaira wasn't bothered; her opponent wasn't worthy enough. She knew she would win; tonight was her ovation. The day she had schemed and planned for. After today, all will be well and everything would be forgiven.

The women of this country would remember her as the one who had set the pace, the one who had shown them the way. She was enjoying the cold drink in her hand. The occasion demanded something better, but she didn't feel fulfilled—not with the way Quinn had shut himself off. She felt guilty about lying to him. But he always forgave her; he always found a way to.

Machiavelli had had a very busy day. He had scanned Emerson's will, which granted Elzaiya total control of his assets and made him heir to all that Emerson owned, which was a whole bloody lot.

He forwarded the will to Elzaiya's email and waited. There was nothing else to do. He passed by the Sultan's palace and saw the people organising a ceremony for their dead leader. He recognised the old man, the librarian, the one who chose the person who filled the Sultan's seat. The man looked like he was retiring; the empire would fall without an heir, and chaos might reign.

Machiavelli waited for them to bury the body before he left the car. His first choice was the librarian, but as he approached, he was accosted by a doctor, whose face was familiar. The young assistant had risen to fill Dr Sani's shoes.

"Abdulrazak?" Oh damn! He knew him.

"Mach?"

"It's me," he said, looking at the guy in his suit with a stethoscope around his neck. He had grown; it had been years. They had been great pals in school.

"What are you doing here?"

"Hmm…" Machiavelli touched his chin. "I came to solve your problems."

Abdulrazak laughed. "Yeah, right, which one?"

Machiavelli took him aside, and they chatted for a while about everything. Not honestly, as Machiavelli didn't tell him that he played a major part in the fiasco. Abdulrazak, on his part, shared his main concern of being unimportant and unemployed now that there was no heir. The bloodline had been wiped out, and that meant the complete dynasty. If it were to survive for the sake of the Muslim world, it would have to be shifted to another family, and that was unprecedented.

"How would you know if the person is of the bloodline?" Machiavelli asked.

The doctor coughed. "It's a secret, not that I'm sure it matters now. But aside from DNA testing, there's a record book of names with all the women the sultan has ever had relations with. In that book are the names of all the children they bore him, alive and dead. Everyone who is part of the dynasty is in that book, pictures included. But they're all dead."

"Not all of them," Machiavelli said, and told him about Cairo.

"Her name was crossed off." The doctor said. "She died in an accident."

"She was never found; she had always been with me," he brought out his phone and showed the doctor a recent picture. He could see that the doctor didn't know how to feel.

"We would have to perform a test to be certain," he said, hope lighting up his eyes. "But then, a woman has never assumed the role."

"Times are changing, my friend," Machiavelli encouraged him to push the matter to the Muslim leaders. The doctor said he would, and Machiavelli bade him farewell.

He headed for the house to watch the news like everyone else. He anticipated a certain turn of events.

Quinn watched the news in his room. Machiavelli watched Cairo, while Mercedes sat on his bed, staring blankly at the TV, just waiting for the name. Harlequin was with Navina in the office as a result of the happiness that lovemaking could bring.

"And that brings us to the end of today's news." The reporter said, "Here we finally announce the newly elected president of the Federal Republic of Nigeria. This is an event that has never happened in the history of the country. A renowned person with distinct leadership skills who has, in the game, proven to be honourable and true and has managed all obstacles that have come up along the way. Let us all rise as we celebrate President Synai Michaels."

Aaira dropped her glass as her smile changed to a frown. How was that even possible? He had been given a yellow slip. She had been the obvious choice.

In the room, Machiavelli found himself ecstatic. The plan had worked. They had done it, and Elzaiya would be so proud.

Harlequin was surprised, but it was unlikely that a woman would have the seat. No woman had ever been president, even though he knew that his mother was capable. He was about to turn off the TV when the reporter went on.

"And this is also a new and rare event. This set of officials has qualities and traits that cannot be overlooked by the board or the system. And as the games ended with just one vote above the other, it has been decided that for the first time in history, the country should have its first female vice president. So, let us now rise to honour our newly elected vice president, Mrs Aaira Ivery Quinn."

Surprise ran through the whole country and everyone, except Quinn. You could hear the cheers from afar as women started to scream with joy. Aaira had wanted more, but that was what she had wanted: to show them what they could do. She found that she was sad. She would have felt better if she hadn't received the news alone. She went to her husband's room and knocked on the door. There was no reply.

"Let me in," she said.

He did not reply.

She knew that he was listening. "Please let me in, please…" She started to cry, banging on the door. She wanted to apologise.

She sat on the ground in front of the door and cried. That was where she fell asleep, even though the tiles were ice cold. When she awoke in the morning, she was still on the tiles, but she had been covered with his blanket. It meant he'd understood, and he had forgiven her.

***

Harlequin and Navina would be returning today. He wanted to reconcile with his family before he told them the good news.

His mother had told him that they would be glad to have him back. She had sounded optimistic until he had asked about his brothers. She had told him that he should return first.

***

When Synai went back to the hotel, he saw a card on the table. Vivian said she had met it there and had not touched it. He opened it and smiled. It had within it two tickets to a dance he had wanted to take Vivian to when they were younger.

Vivian asked what he was smiling about. He asked her if she would like to go to a dance. She jumped on his body and told him to go dress up; they had a long-awaited ball to attend.

***

The matter had gone further than Dr Abdulrazak thought it would, but finally, all the leaders saw reason. Cairo was the only heir left. So, finally, they had convened, and she had been summoned.

When all the votes were unanimous, she was given the title Queen Sultana, the first female sultan to wiggle into the seat of the caliphate. She had carved out her piece of history, and she was to rule until she had a son who was of age. And if she ruled wisely, she would set a precedent for other Sultanas who were fit for the title. It had looked impossible, but it had happened.

***

When they got back from the coronation ceremony, they found a canary, caged in the middle of the room with a small case tied to its feet.

After some deliberation, in which Cairo had to prevent Machiavelli from killing the bird, he picked it up and untied the case tied to its feet.

Inside were two gold rings with embedded diamonds, and their names carved into them. Underneath was the single number 7. Machiavelli smiled and did what he knew had to be done. It was time to settle down.

Merceides had not left his room in four days. He had spent the time sleeping and then crying himself to sleep. Machiavelli came to check up on him sometimes, but he always lied, saying he was fine.

He'd just finished a long-overdue bath when he noticed a large, brown envelope on his bed. He opened it and poured the contents on the bed. What it contained made him sit down.

There were printed photos of Denise dating back to when she was a child and up until the day she died. There was also her phone, which he thought had blown up in the car with her. He knew she had a fingerprint password. He turned the phone on, and it came alive, open, and unlocked. He scrolled through the phone and saw all the pictures they had taken. The memories that had been forcefully taken away from him. All the things he needed to find closure.

There was something else in the envelope. He shook it, and a bracelet fell out. It was made of half the beads on the one he had given his brother. He smiled and lay down on the bed, clinging to her pictures. He felt heartbroken and happy all at once.

***

Quinn was staring at a letter that he had found pasted outside his windowsill. Whoever kept it there sure had some guts to climb that high. Whatever prank they were trying to play, he would deal with them once he found them out. But the letter changed his mind.

'...shouldn't be mad at Mother, not for long anyway. Forgive Harlequin; he was misled by Emerson, and I know the truth about all that I am, but you're still the only one I'll call my dad. I hope you find peace knowing that I'm alive. I will always live in your hearts, but I can't come back home because a part of me has died. I will be fine; I just need to be away from the family. I need to forge my path and find out who I am. A lot of things have happened. A lot, for the first time, and I am glad but also disheartened. I know you understand. Trust Machiavelli; he has made me proud. I see things have turned out better than we planned; it will get better for everyone along the line.'

Quinn closed the envelope and smiled.

***

When Aretta woke up, she saw him trying to fetch water from the well. He had his right hand in a sling underneath his coat and was using his left hand and knee to fetch the water. He would dip the fetcher in the well and pull with his left hand, then hold the rope to the edge of the well with his knee. Surprisingly, he made a lot of progress.

So, her new neighbour was a disabled herdsman.

The fetcher had gotten to the mouth of the well when he bent to take it, but it slipped, crashing back into the well.

"Damn it!" He exclaimed and cursed, unaware that she was watching.

When the fetcher crashed back a second time, he shouted and kicked the well and then reeled in pain. She found him amusing, even though his beard needed a shave and his body was a wreck.

She approached the well with her bucket. He looked at her and then shyly turned away. He was about to lift his bucket with the little water in it when she got to the well.

"Let me help you," she said.

He smiled and looked at his feet. "Thank you, but I can handle it."

She observed, just by looking at him, that he had never drawn water from a well before. He might look unkempt, but he was from a rich background. Thank God he had good manners.

"You were doing just fine before I came. Have your way," she said.

He nodded and threw the fetcher back into the well. It was half-filled when he started pulling at it. This time, he held the rope between his teeth. She could not help but watch, amazed. It was crazy what people could do in desperation or with a disability. The human body was indeed designed to adapt for survival. He pulled it out and poured the water into the bucket. She threw her fetcher in.

"Where are you from?" She asked.

He had thrown his fetcher back in. Now, he put the rope in his mouth and started to draw. He didn't want to answer. When he brought it out, she waited for a reply.

He said nothing.

This one wasn't a talker; the most reasonable neighbour she'd had.

He pulled the fetcher out and poured the water into the second bucket. There were three others beside it. He was going to fill them all, slowly, deliberately, and painstakingly, even if it took him all day.

"Let me guess. You're from a rich family, but you ran away from home and got into an accident on the way? Or, you got robbed on the way here. Or maybe you're looking for work just to prove to your family that you can live without their help. Or is it the quiet, and you want to figure things out before moving somewhere else?"

He pulled out the fetcher and poured the water into the bucket. He threw it back in and looked at her. His face was strange. That was the only way to describe it. He was handsome in a fearful and childish way. His eyes were striking, and as he turned, half his face seemed to flash a blue hue. The vein on his neck was thick; it seemed he had been using it to pull things heavier than water. She suddenly felt guilty about peeking at him the previous night. This was no ordinary human being.

He looked at her. She was beautiful, but that wasn't all there was to her. He didn't know why it seemed like he could see the world much clearly now.

He wanted to talk, but then he heard Nadia's voice in the wind. He could see her face in the water. It called out to him. It moved around him, enveloping all that he did. Her ghost followed him everywhere, just as she had promised. She would be with him forever. He felt it welling up again, that thing that he had felt during her death. A feeling he couldn't name. He took a deep breath and turned it off.

He looked at the lady on the other side of the well and smiled.

"Neither."